# The BOYS who SAVED the WORLD

Sam Mills was born in 1975 and studied English Language and Literature at Oxford University. Sam worked as a chess journalist and publicist before giving it all up to write full time.

Sam contributes regularly to the literary magazine *TOMAZI*, and is the author of the young adult novel *A Nicer Way to Die*.

*The Boys who Saved the World* was written with the help of an Arts Council Award.

Praise for *A Nicer Way to Die*:

'I burnt a lot of midnight oil and even more adrenaline reading *A Nicer Way to Die* . . . Mills never lets the tension drop, skilfully weaving into the claustrophobic atmosphere flashbacks which build up a picture of a deeply disturbed boy . . .' *Sunday Telegraph*

'A fresh voice, brimming with character and colour . . . both horrifying and a hoot.' Matt Whyman, author of *Boy Kills Man*

'Horrifying yet compelling . . . definitely not for the faint-hearted.' Betty Bookmark

'A weird, unputdownable mix of Stephen King and Toby Litt.' *Achuka Choice*

Also by Sam Mills:

**A Nicer Way to Die**

# The BOYS who SAVED the World

# Sam Mills

**ff**

*faber and faber*

First published in 2007
by Faber and Faber Limited
3 Queen Square London WC1N 3AU

Printed in England by Mackays of Chatham plc,
Chatham, Kent

A CIP record for this book
is available from the British Library

ISBN 978-0-571-23402-8
ISBN 0-571-23402-X

2 4 6 8 10 9 7 5 3 1

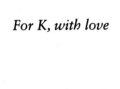

*For K, with love*

# Part One

# 7 P.M.: TWO HOURS TO GO . . .

**In two hours time** I – and the rest of the Brotherhood – will kidnap a terrorist.

My outfit is packed in my rucksack. I pull out the thin black woollen roll, unfurl it like a scroll. I stretch its balaclava face across my palm; it seems to jeer at me. I shiver and roll it back up.

The codename for the terrorist is SNAKE. By kidnapping SNAKE tonight, we – the Brotherhood of the Religion of Hebetheus – will prevent a bomb from going off at St Sebastian's School. If I lean out of my bedroom window and look beyond the jagged patchwork of rooftops, I can see its metal railings, waving treetops, green playing fields. I picture future scenes, papier-mâchéd out of TV images. Red blood sprayed across red brick. Uniforms hugging teenagers, dragging them gently into ambulances. Sad smoke spiralling up across a blistered sky. We will prevent all that.

I reach under my bed and pull out the wooden box, sifting through rustles of tissue paper. When Jeremiah first passed the box on to me, I had this compulsion to just look at it. Sometimes two, three times a day. Just opening the box made my hands shake with anticipation and the virgin glint of the knife, arrowing through the paper, caused a firework to explode inside me so that long after I'd put it back and tucked it under my bed, little sparks would fly through me for the whole day.

But over the last few days, whenever I've taken it out, I feel blank.

I stare down at it now – nothing. A bit of metal trapped in a wooden handle.

I look at the posters on my walls and think: *Slash them!* That would bring the knife back to life. Then I remember Jeremiah's voice: *We have to keep acting as though everything is normal. Nobody must suspect a thing.*

I practise slicing up air. Picture it held against a brown throat. How light or hard should I hold it so as to provoke fear but not draw blood? I don't want to hurt anyone, after all: just educate them.

I hold it up so it catches the last of the sunset, narrowing my eyes until the silver blurs into a thinner knife of pure light. In it I see all our faces: Thomas, Martyn, Chris, Raymond. And Jeremiah, our prophet, with his innocent sea eyes and gentle smile.

'Thomas! Dinner's Ready!'

The knife slips and slices against my thumb, drawing a thin dribble of blood.

I hear a creak on the stairs and quickly shove it under my pillow.

'Dinner's ready. It's lasagne – your favourite.'

'Coming, Mum.'

# 7.15 P.M.: ONE HOUR AND FORTY-FIVE MINUTES TO GO

'Can you just finish laying the table, Jon? I forgot the serving-mat. There . . . thank you.'

I sit down. Her hand, swaddled in an oven glove, clumsily lifts the lid off the lasagne. Steam hisses up, carrying delicious smells. I haven't been hungry in days. This morning when it was twelve hours to go, I forced myself to eat a bowl of Shreddies, but it felt like eating stones and on my way to school I spewed them up in the bushes. But now I am hungry.

So hungry that I burn my mouth on the lasagne and have to glug down half a glass of water. My mum *tsks*.

The knife-wound on my thumb is still bleeding. A red trickle has reached the tines of my fork. I quickly look at Mum, but she is engrossed in her own world. She eats like a sad bird, taking tiny little mouthfuls, as though she doesn't feel she quite deserves to be eating.

I press my thumb hard against the fork and carry on, but my blood laces the lasagne with a metallic taste.

My eyes sweep across the table and I notice that she has done it again. She has laid a third mat. Even though it's been a year, she still makes these mistakes. She'll brew up two mugs of Horlicks before going to bed and then pretends that one is for me, even though I hate Horlicks. She still has dinner at 7.15 p.m., even though she's hungrier much earlier, because that was the time Dad preferred it.

I take another mouthful and stare out of the window. We moved into this house six months ago and I still don't like it. It's on a new suburban housing estate where every house looks the same. The same red bricks. The same double-glazing, with grey bolts on the outside, to keep burglars out. Even the trees look false, pale and anorexic, wilting at being stuck in such a dump. In our back garden there is no grass, just seed scattered in the brown earth, reluctantly pushing up the odd weed. The fence at the back is white and low, like the kind you see in pictures of America. I can see other houses over it, stick figures moving about, people sitting down to eat, families snacking in front of the TV.

I look at these people and I wonder how they can go through life, living the way they do, not doing a jot to change the world. No, they're all too busy dreaming of getting on reality TV for fifteen milliseconds of fame. I feel a roaring anger for them all. I fantasise that my fork swells into a giant metal lapoon that smashes through my window and then hits each house like a missile, scooping people up and –

'Was school okay today?' Mum asks.

'Yeah, it was okay,' I say.

Silence. Then –

– an explosion.

Outside.

Green glitter lights up the sky. The stars shrink and the street lamps pale away.

People gaze up, mesmerised.

'Guy Fawkes tomorrow,' says Mum. 'I bought some sparklers. And some sausages. We can have a fry-up.'

'Uh huh.' I try to thread my fork through another

layer of lasagne but my hand is shaking too violently. The explosion keeps echoing through me, carrying warnings of burning flesh. I feel relief that we are going ahead with this, that tonight we will be saving the school. Our first step to saving the world.

I push my plate away. Mum looks up.

'Oh Jon, I spent all that time cooking your favourite and then you take three mouthfuls –'

'I'm sorry, I'm just not hungry.'

'Well, will you come to church tonight? We're helping to set it up for the concert next week.'

'I hate church.'

'You don't mean that.'

'I do.'

I used to be a False Believer too, though. Christianity seduced me like a purring snake. I used to be the square of my school, the guy who never got picked for games because his dad was the local vicar, the guy who got laughed at for singing in the choir every night. But none of them mattered.

None of them mattered because I used to love it. I was living a fantasy, I can see that now. I thought that the Christian god would love me and look after me and answer all my prayers. I thought that I was special. At night I used to lie awake and ponder that if a disaster swept England, that if God suddenly scooped up water in his hand and hurled it at our country in a second flood, I would be like Noah. Me and Mum and Dad and the dog and all the other Christians – we'd be warned. A sign would come, and we'd make boats and survive to watch the other sinners drown. I believed all this because I thought that going to church every week and reading a book of lies and singing stupid hymns were like money in

7

the bank of God, a kind of life insurance that would always protect me.

Then one day Dad came home and told Mum he was in love with the woman who lived across the road. He moved in with her the following week and we spent our evenings eating and trying not to look out at them, but doing nothing but looking out at them. We watched them eat their dinner, her fussing over Dad, smoothing his collar, kissing his cheek, laying out his food, as though we were being given a glimpse into some parallel universe we couldn't quite believe existed. That's why we had to move, and that's why I don't go to church any more.

Tonight Mum will leave the house at 8.30 p.m. promptly to help clean the church. Five minutes later, I will leave and join Jeremiah and the Brotherhood. Mum doesn't normally let me out on week nights, you see. But by the time she gets back, I will be long gone.

Mum is just clearing away the plates when I get a text on my mobile.

## 7.40 P.M.: ONE HOUR AND TWENTY MINUTES TO GO . . .

**It's from Martyn. It says:**

GOT THE KNIFE. READY FOR SNAKE, R U?

Like a conch being blown, a tribal war cry. I shiver.

# 7.50 P.M.: ONE HOUR AND TEN MINUTES TO GO . . .

I hate TV. I force myself to sit on the sofa with Mum for a short while. I watch without watching. Jeremiah explained to me that TV is dangerous. Our minds are malleable, Jeremiah said, and can be infused with any colour. When we watch TV our minds are tossed between what the government wants us to think and what the big companies want us to think, until all our own colour is leached out, leaving a pastel grey.

I flick a glance at my mum, the images dancing across her retinas as though she's being hypnotised.

'Look at that,' she says, pointing the remote at the screen, showing black-and-white images of people waving placards. 'You see, in our day, when people marched, things changed. Not any more. People make a fuss and the government doesn't listen. They still go to war.'

I am suddenly gripped by a proud desire to tell her everything the Brotherhood is about to do. But that would be suicidal. Instead I release wild laughter. She gives me a surprised look.

'Haven't you got homework to do?' she asks.

# 8 P.M.: ONE HOUR TO GO . . .

*What is the difference between the Catholic Church and the Church of England?*

Another one of Mr Abdilla's pointless RE questions.

It was because of Dad that I ended up at St Sebastian's, a posh fee-paying school. I might have ended up at the local comp, getting my head permanently stuck down a toilet, but Mum called up Dad every night for a week, insisting he pay the fees. The first week there, I was amazed by how many people attempted to befriend me. Now I was no longer a Christian Kid, it seemed I was almost cool. But I said no to movie invites, to footie invites, to party invites. I ended up spending my lunchtimes alone and unhappy. Maybe it was because Dad was paying. A sullen part of me felt determined not to enjoy anything that was being funded by him.

I might have spent the next three years there in a cocoon of misery, if Jeremiah hadn't spotted me drifting through the playgrounds. I noticed him at once. He stood out because he had a strange aura of calm about him. Every other guy in that playground was scared inside. They were either covering it up by pretending to be cool or taking it out on a younger kid, or finding it as impossible to hide as braces or acne. But Jeremiah had the self-possession of an adult; when he first approached me, he made me feel clumsy and childish. Of course, I hadn't heard the cruel rumours then, about Jeremiah and his 'little cult following' and I'm glad I didn't, else I might never have been saved by him.

*What is the difference between the Catholic Church and the Church of England?*

I find myself picking up my pen and writing out The Rules of the Brotherhood. Even though I know them by heart.

## The Rules of the Religion of Hebetheus

1. Hebetheus is a new religion which will correct the mistakes of past religions.
2. Old religions are full of lies, corruption and mistakes. This is because over time the purity of their teaching has been lost, subverted and polluted. The worshippers also followed a false figure, not God.
3. The god that current religions worship does not exist. This is why there is still sickness, suffering and famine in the world, and prayers go unanswered.
4. The God of Hebetheus is the one true God. The aim of the Brotherhood is to understand him and do his work.
5. Every man is both good and evil. But man is inherently lazy, so he will tend to slump into evil. It is up to every member of the Brotherhood to constantly choose good in every day-to-day action. Every member has a duty to expel evil and cleanse the world.

6. We, the Brotherhood, are fortunate to have been chosen by God to wipe out the old religions and bring a new one to the people of the world. This has been verified by Jeremiah's dreams.

7. Every member of the Brotherhood shall be chosen by God through Jeremiah. Every member will undergo an Initiation to prove his worth and devotion to the Hebetheus cause.

8. No member of the Brotherhood is permitted to drink, smoke, watch TV, or be beguiled by the sinful temptations of the opposite sex. Every member should spend at least one hour a day in prayer in order to cleanse their soul. In return, our God will listen to our prayers and perform amazing miracles. This has already been proven by the miracles Jeremiah has experienced and told to the Brotherhood.

9. By doing good actions, we will inspire others to join the Hebetheus religion. When everyone has joined Hebetheus, the world will be saved.

10. Therefore, to save one person in the name of Hebetheus is to save the whole of humanity. To do one good deed to protect people is a first step to saving the world.

I flit back to Mr Abdilla's RE question, then feel a surge of anger. What right does he have to set *us* questions, to judge and mark our work, when he clearly knows nothing? After we found out about SNAKE's terrorist plans, we tried telling Mr Abdilla. We approached him after school one day and he seemed to listen carefully. Then he shook his head and told us to leave SNAKE alone. He said we had made a mistake.

We went to the park, fizzing with pent-up anger, Raymond declaring he was ready to beat up bloody Abdilla for not believing us. That was when the idea came: to take matters into our own hands. If Mr Abdilla wouldn't listen to us, the police probably wouldn't either. So it was up to us.

Tonight will also be my Initiation into the Brotherhood. I've become impatient, ardent with waiting. Six months, I've been a member, but not a full one; there are still secret pacts I don't know, prayers I haven't yet been taught to recite.

Jeremiah has been teasing me for weeks, telling me I will play a crucial role in the kidnapping. I keep asking him – *What role?* But he says it's better that I don't know now. I will find out when the time comes.

I feel scared. Sometimes I feel Jeremiah has such faith in me that it's frightening. What if I fail? What if I throw it all away tonight?

I swallow. My pencil slips through my sweaty fingers on to the bed. My clock ticking away like a bomb. I gaze up around my room. Eminem. Coldplay. Keane. I put them up six months ago; now I don't even like those bands any more. I feel strangely sad, looking at them. I remember how excited I felt when I Blu-tacked *Eminem* to my wall and tears fill my eyes. I am startled. I flick them away, shake myself, check the clock.

Suddenly I realise *it is time*. Mum should be leaving now. I jump up, my stomach swimming in butterflies, and hurry down the stairs.

'Mum, you off now?'

'I decided not to go,' she calls out. 'It's all right, we can both just stay in and watch some telly.'

# 8.30 P.M.: HALF AN HOUR TO GO . . .

**She's not going. She's not going.** I tried to reason with her, but she said she felt I was right, there was no point in going to church, she'd been feeling for the last few weeks that she's just been singing empty songs, so why bother spending her free evening helping to clean it up. Then she went back into the living room.

I can hear Jeremiah's voice in my mind: *We're all cogs in this delicate operation, if one of us spins out then the whole thing jams.* And now it's happened, and I can't quite believe it's me, that I'm that cog, that apple-seeping poison, that black sheep. I think viciously: it's the Christian god. I've left his religion and now he's getting back at me. Then I remember that I don't believe in him any more. So maybe it's just me. Maybe everything I do is just doomed to fail. Maybe Jeremiah was wrong in taking a chance on me. Maybe I should call Jeremiah right now, maybe we can arrange it another night, oh God, please don't turn on me, please help me, maybe this is a test, well, please help me pass it. I run back into the living room. Mum, I say, I really think you should go to church. I didn't mean what I said. I think it could help you. She looks surprised and then smiles and says she's glad I feel that way, she feels deep down that it does help her to go. But it's too late now. She checks her watch. She'll go on Sunday to make up for it. She looks at me again and says, 'Are you okay?' I run out. I stand in the hallway. I stare at the paintings running down the stairs: prints of a willow draping a lake. I run and grab my jacket, get my mobile. I fling open the backdoor. Out into the twilight. Something brushes my head. I jump wildly – the police? Here already, tipped off? No – just a leaf, dead pieces clinging desperately to its skeleton. I press Jeremiah's number. I click off. I tear a nail with my teeth. I wince as it sears away, leaving a raw laceration. Finally, I call.

His mobile switches to voicemail. Jeremiah's voice, slow and cool as chocolate: *I'm sorry I can't speak to you right now* . . . Why isn't he answering his phone, at a time like this? I clear my throat to leave a message. Excuses flare and then splutter in my mind, dying into embers of shame. I hang up. I hear my mum calling 'Are you all right out there, can you close the back door, it's getting cold.' I could run now. But I've left my weapon upstairs. It's not even my weapon. It belongs to the Brotherhood. I go back indoors. I stand in the kitchen and send Jeremiah a shaky text:

TROUBLE GETTING OUT – MUM. WHAT SHOULD
I DO?

I stand and wait. A row of saucepans take my face and shine it back to me in grotesque leers.

My mobile beeps.

IMPROVISE

# 8.40 P.M.: TWENTY MINUTES TO GO . . .

**Upstairs in my room, I kneel down** on the floor, clasp my hands together, and recite the Rules of the Brotherhood out loud. It becomes a kind of meditation. As the words shake from my trembling lips, I forget the meaning of them. They become a monotonous hum. The hum becomes breathless whispers. The whispers fade into faint impulses, thoughts that are more colours than words. The panic ebbs away, leaving a cool, empty space in my mind. I realise, sitting here, that there is nothing to stop me going. I remember Jeremiah's words: *Our thoughts are our only boundaries, nothing more, nothing less.*

I'll just walk out. And if she tries to stop me, well, then I'll –

(*my eyes fall to the glint of the knife and I recoil*)

I'll – I'd better pack. I'll take my Brotherhood clothes, change later. I stuff everything into my rucksack, click it shut. My hands aren't shaking any more.

I tread down the stairs quietly. I hear the downstairs toilet flushing – perfect. I head for the door, click it open –

'Jon?'

'I'm going out, okay?' I say, without turning back.

'Jon! What do you think you're doing?'

'I said,' I mumble, feeling the wind tease my face, blow-

**17**

ing scents of freedom, 'I said I'm going out.'

'Jon! You're not going out. It's a school night. You know you're not allowed out on a school night.'

She tries to grab my arm – and fails. Instead she yanks my rucksack, pulling it off.

'Mum!' I cry, whipping round. I try to grab it back but she hangs on to one of the yellow loops. I see determination flash in her eyes and I try to hold on to my feeling of confidence with both hands, but it seeps through my fingers like sand. 'Mum, I just want to go out for a quick walk.'

'Walk? Where on earth are you going to go for a quick walk?'

I hesitate.

'Just down the road –'

'Jon, you're not going to go for a quick walk down the road. Now. We've had this discussion before. You're going to stay in and do your homework.'

'I've done my homework. Okay?'

'No, it's not okay, of course it's not okay! You can watch TV with me, or practise your trumpet. I mean, for God's sake, we are paying for those lessons.'

*We.* Another slip. My father is paying for them, sending the money through.

'I don't want to play the fucking trumpet,' I mutter.

'What did you say?' she says sharply. 'Right. You're not getting any allowance this weekend. You can get upstairs now.'

She reaches out to grab me.

And then I push her.

I don't mean to push her so hard. I don't know what gets into me; it's a lightning flash of anger and frustration that sends her stumbling back against the bottom of the stairs.

Her hair swishes over her face; her hand claws the air like a dying bird's.

I stare down at her, numb, my hands dangling by my sides like plasticine. I wait for her to tell me off. Then I see the fear in her eyes. At first I feel horrified by that fear. Then a whoosh of triumph supersedes it. My chest beats hard; I am a man.

'I'm going out,' I hear myself say loudly. 'I'm going out, okay? And don't wait up.'

I turn to go when I hear the sound. It sears through me. Crying.

'Mum,' I try to say, but the word is lost in a gulpy lump in my throat. 'Mum.'

'Please stay. Please.' She reaches up to grab my hand and the warmth of her fingers sends a shock up my arm. I realise in a flash that I do want to stay. I want to put down my rucksack and go in and watch the TV, cosy against the growing chill of the twilight. Suddenly the winter air that tempted me is scented with cold and danger, a world of darting dark shapes running in fear. But then my mobile beeps. Jeremiah: WHERE R U?

I wrench my hand away and her sobbing increases. I turn, pull her up, steady her, and give her a tight hug. I close my eyes and think: *It'll be different when I come back. The next time I see her, she'll be praising me for saving the world. She'll be saying, this is my son, the hero.*

She clings on so tightly, as though she's frightened she's never going to see me again and it's the weirdest thing, because suddenly I feel like I am the parent and she is a girl.

'Please don't go,' she whispers, 'you promised you'd be with me after Dad went, you said you'd stay in in the week, please stay and keep me company.'

I touch her hair. Before Dad left it used to feel like silk;

now it feels like dead grass.

'I'll be back soon,' I say desperately, pulling away. 'I'm just going for a walk.'

'Jon –' A sharpness returns to her voice and I back off before she can become my mum again.

I dart out through the door. I slam it hard and it feels as though an invisible chord between us is severed in its metal teeth and I run out into the twilight world, the streets roaring with traffic and mayhem.

I am late and I pray to God to give me wings to take me there on time.

# 8.50 P.M.: TEN MINUTES TO GO . . .

*You're late. Come on, get a move on, oh God, what's Jeremiah going to say?*

I should have met them at the truck just after 8.40 p.m. Now it's 8.52.

I am changing in the bushes, in the park by my house. It's been locked up by the park warden: I had to vault over the fence to get in. The playground looks naked without children, swings meandering eerily in the wind. I think of my mum, lying by the stairs. What if I caused a serious injury, an organ shifted out of shape I don't yet know about – what if tomorrow she wakes up being eaten alive by pain? The park warden is whistling in the distance; oh God, please don't let him notice me.

I wanted to wait until we'd got to the warehouse to change, but my school uniform is too dangerous. I need to blend in. I tear open my rucksack, rip off my school tie and clench it into a zebra coil that I stuff back down into the rucksack. *Come on, come on.* I undo half the buttons on my shirt, then yank it over my head. The wind lays chilly palms on my back. The black polo neck scrapes against my face as I pull it on. I can leave my jeans; my black school trousers will do.

Then I panic because I can't fit everything into my

rucksack. I didn't plan room for my school uniform and my blazer won't go in, even when I squeeze it into a tight ball. I decide to leave it under the bushes – but what if the police find it? On the pocket is an emblem: a griffin, with the school motto winding around it: *Aim for the Highest*. I take my knife from my bag and slice off the emblem in a jagged oval, stuffing it into my pocket. I push my knife back into my bag and suddenly there is a voice in my ear:

'What d'you think you're doing here?'

The park warden, a rusty old man with wispy clouds of hair, is peering down at me. No doubt he is a *raptor*.

'Nothing, I'm going, I'm going.'

'I'll have to let you out.'

'I can –' I dare not climb over the fence, create a fight, draw attention to myself. I lower my neck, stare at the ground, waiting in torment whilst minutes race past as he goes through his ring of keys and finally slots into the lock, undoing the padlock loop by loop. Hopefully he won't remember my face. I don't think I have a memorable face.

The chain slithers free and I run.

I run and run and run and run. Pain in my calves; my lungs hissing pistons.

Up above, another explosion. Eerie spaceship showers of green tumble down the sky. *Come on, come on, faster, faster.* 8.57 p.m. now. I thought Jeremiah had deliberately chosen the day – as close to Guy Fawkes as we could – as a homage to a man who also dared to rebel against society. But Jeremiah said it was because people would be busy and distracted, the police busy with dumb kids shooting off their fingers. I replied that I thought we wanted attention. Oh, we do, he said, but not tonight. Tonight we need to be men of silence and stealth. Then, tomorrow, it all begins:

we drop a boulder into the ocean of British consciousness and send ripples through it that will reverberate through history.

Besides, he added, I don't see Guy Fawkes as a figure of inspiration. Ultimately he failed. What is the point of celebrating failure?

We're not going to fail.

9 p.m. now. The time it should have happened. Just cross the main road, ignore the traffic lines, fuck, they're tooting me but I don't care, I'm across the road and now I just have to pass two small roads, Bennington Close and Ashleigh Gardens and then I'll be there and maybe, maybe there will be a day celebrating us in a hundred years' time, statues of us in Trafalgar Square encrusted with pigeon shit and I am running running running to the truck outside Jeremiah's house.

Jeremiah and Raymond are standing by the truck.

Chris pokes his head out and stutters:

'H-h – here he is!'

'At last!

'I'm sorry, I'm so sorry.' I can barely speak, but it's so important that I tell my story, that Jeremiah understands. The other faces may be angry or impatient, but the only face which carries any detail for me is Jeremiah's.

I thought he would look as cool as ever, but there is a touch of anger in his eyes.

'I'm sorry, I'm sorry –'

'You idiot!' Raymond bursts out. 'Where've you been, for God's sake, I knew you would ruin it, I knew you were going to mess up –'

'It's fine,' Jeremiah cuts in. 'We're not wasting any time arguing. Get into the truck. Come on, let's go, let's go, let's GO!'

Raymond and Jeremiah get into the front of the truck; Raymond is driving. I get into the back, along with Thomas, Chris and Martyn. There are no benches; we have to sit on the metal floor, knees bunched up.

They all look nervous. Even *Thomas* looks nervous. Thomas is a year older than us and he has floppy brown hair and the sort of nice accent that makes adults sigh and secretly wish they'd brought him up. He's very well mannered and probably would have been made Head Boy. His father is a famous surgeon and his mother runs some fancy charity, which seems to involve organising ten-course lunches every other day. On the surface, Thomas seems to get on well with them. But the truth is, they're hardly ever around. They just leave Thomas to rattle about in their big fancy house and give him a huge allowance on the condition that he keeps on scoring As.

Then there's Martyn and Chris. They've known each other since they were kids; they used to play in each other's back gardens. Early in their teens, they were in the army cadets after school: before they realised that peace is the answer. Martyn is short and stocky and reminds me of a very fierce Jack Russell. To be honest, he puts me on edge a bit. If he wasn't in Hebetheus, I think he would have given me a hard time at school, shoved me in footie, demanded lunch money and so on. But he has a difficult time at home. Tonight there is a fresh bruise shining plumly across his cheek.

Chris has a hard time at home too. He's thin and gangly and twitchy; he suffers from asthma and even when he's not using his inhaler, he's always fiddling about with it, checking that it's in his pocket, tossing it from palm to palm. Because he stutters, a lot of people think that Chris is a bit of a twerp. But once you get past his layer of prickly shyness, Chris shines like a conker. He can surprise you with his wit, his intelligence, his spark.

They all want to know why I'm so late and I retell the whole story, adding a few details. They don't know about the divorce, even though we're supposed to share everything in the Brotherhood. Maybe I am being unfair not to have told my story fully. In fact, I lied and said my dad had left home long ago, when I was just a baby. I just felt so embarrassed by what a bastard he'd been.

So I tell them that Mum sprained her ankle, falling down the stairs, and I had to bandage her up and sort her out. I'm not a good liar but they seem convinced.

I let out a breath and look round the truck. Inside, it has been painted with symbols in white paint. A candle. A mandala with six inner circles. A tree with six branches. A swastika. Jeremiah explained that though the Nazis made the swastika a sign of hatred, originally it was an Indian symbol of peace. My eyes drink them in. I feel soothed.

All the same, Raymond's words keep echoing in my mind: *I knew you were going to mess up.* I wonder if he is slagging me off to Jeremiah right now, poisoning his mind against me.

Raymond is the oldest in the Brotherhood. He doesn't seem very devout. In my opinion he wouldn't even be a member if he wasn't Jeremiah's older brother. He's eighteen, two years older than Jeremiah. Jeremiah's tall and thin and leonine; Raymond's six foot two, with arms of heavy lard. He works by day in an electronics shop. Raymond looks like he wouldn't answer to anyone, but he answers to Jeremiah. Whenever Jeremiah speaks, he seems to shrink and his eyes become soft and intent. He always lets Jeremiah make the decisions.

Jeremiah and Raymond live on their own together. Their parents died last year. I asked Chris once how they died and he clammed up and stuttered that Jeremiah didn't like to talk about it. I didn't pry.

I wish Jeremiah was my brother. I curse and curse Raymond and his piggy eyes and fat face and then I stare at the swastika symbol for a while, praying hard. I begin to feel better. God will make sure SNAKE is still there. Everything will be fine.

In fact, my being late is probably meant to be. If we had arrived on time, then something would have gone wrong. A police car would have sailed by, or a glass bottle in the road would have cut its teeth into a tyre. God is working his mysterious ways.

I look round at my Brothers. The air is thrilled with excitement. Chris is listening to Hebethean chants on his Walkman; Martyn tries to tear it off him and they jostle, laughing. Thomas flicks his lighter, the flame pirouetting up again and again and again like an exhausted dancing girl. Then, slowly, everything goes quiet until a silence sets like cement. The longer it goes on for, the more impossible it is to crack. From time to time, our eyes flick and hop off each other and there's a jolt of shock. Wonder at what we're about to do.

I find I can't stop looking at the equipment. The roll of masking tape. The saw. The circles of rope. The sacks. Crates of mineral water, boxes of food: *we may be in for a long haul*, Jeremiah warned.

*Long haul*. The words thrill me.

A pair of silver handcuffs is tacked to a metal rod lining the truck. The loose cuff jangles and clatters to the rumbling rhythm of the truck. It looks like a silver noose, formed to kill a small, heartless doll.

*

Then the truck shivers to a halt. I find myself wishing it could keep going for a while. We're here; and I can't believe how quickly it's all happening.

# 9.30 P.M.: THIRTY MINUTES LATER . . .

**Something is wrong.**

By 9.30 p.m., we should have already taken down SNAKE. For the last few weeks we have been taking turns to spy on her, suss out her routine. The spot had been chosen carefully: at the bottom of Mabel Drive, sheltered by the leafy trees that border the park. Practically every night, she leaves her house at around nine to see her best friend – normally with her mum's shout trailing behind her, *Are you sure you've finished your homework? You know you're not allowed to see Michela before you've done your homework!* Michela lives three roads away; we planned to intercept SNAKE on her stroll over.

Yesterday Martyn's duty was to accidentally thwack a cricket ball into the street lamps curling overhead. We would then watch the front door of no. 32 and wait for SNAKE to emerge. SNAKE would walk down the pavement to the bottom of the road, down the sandy, muddy track that was a short cut through the park. Chris and Raymond would be hiding in the trees, ready to pounce. They would tackle SNAKE to the ground with minimum sound. SNAKE would be brought back to the truck, where we would use our silencing equipment. Raymond would drive us and the hostage to the warehouse in Streatham.

But it is now 9.30 p.m. And there is no sign of SNAKE.

# 9.50 P.M.

**Raymond and Chris return:** two lone, smudgy silhouettes.

Raymond reports that SNAKE has not appeared. Jeremiah confirms that the door of no. 32 has remained closed.

It seems we arrived too late. SNAKE has already left for the night.

The Brotherhood slumps in disappointment. I feel sick inside. The weekend, once magnified with anticipation, now shrinks, as though seen through the wrong end of a telescope. We will go home, or I will be sent home. I will wake up in bed tomorrow, Mum's frying wafting sickly up the stars, suburban sounds screaming in my ears; I will drag myself through another day at school, learning lies, then Saturday will come and I will spend a lone day in the park, watching boys graffiti swings; everything will slide back the way it was, helpless, pointless.

'We c-c-can come back n-n-next week,' says Chris mournfully.

'We have to go now!' Thomas cries angrily. 'We've been planning this for so long – we can't back out now – we *can't –*'

'Where are you going?' Raymond breaks off.

Jeremiah ignores him. We all fall silent, watching him. I

feel excited. This is what Jeremiah loves doing best: improvising. When you improvise, he says, you jump off a cliff and wait for God to catch you. It's a test that cements Faith.

My heart gasps when I see Jeremiah walk straight up through the gate, past the rose bushes and ring on the doorbell of no. 32. A few seconds later, the door opens. A warm slice of light, the silhouette of an Asian woman, her beauty wrapped in the blue sheen of a peacock sari. I am taken aback. I did not expect SNAKE's mother to look like this. But then I remember Jeremiah's warning words on appearances.

She steps forward, smiling, and I realise she is not a woman but a girl – way too young to be SNAKE's mother. I figure she must be her sister.

Jeremiah chats casually. His polite attitude seems to impress her, for she gives him a warm smile and rubs his arm.

Then my stomach churns. Jeremiah turns and walks back.

It's over, then. Oh God, why didn't I just leave the moment Mum said she wasn't going to church, why didn't I just *run*?

'Oh well,' says Thomas sadly. 'God did not intend tonight to be the night, then.'

'It's fucking Jon's fault!' Raymond turned on me. 'He messed up –'

'God did not intend –'

Jeremiah cuts in angrily.

'We're above bickering,' he says and we all instantly fall into sheepish silence. That is the effect Jeremiah has on people: speak to him and you suddenly feel small and petty, as though he is living life on a higher level you can only hope to glimpse at. In moments like this, I feel I can see the colour of his mind: luminous, celestial, golden.

'SNAKE's sneaked out. She's told her mum that she's at Michela's for a sleepover but according to her sister, she's gone clubbing. She only just left, so –'

'Hang on,' Martyn interjects, 'her sister could just be bullshitting, making stuff up –'

'I told her that we were Michela's friends and we sometimes hung out together. She didn't look that shocked. Clearly SNAKE enjoys plenty of male company.' His voice is thick with disgust. 'So now we go. We go now, we go to the club and we get her. There's no time to waste. Go!'

Despite Jeremiah's words, the mood in the back of the truck is despondent.

I daren't look at the rest of the Brotherhood now. Thomas pats me on the shoulder kindly and says I shouldn't worry, but Chris and Martyn stare at me with silent animosity. I keep my eyes fixed on the swastika. My head is hurting. My heart is hot. I keep cursing myself. I am close to cursing God. This is all too much like the night Dad left. I remember hearing the faint sounds of my mum crying in the bedroom next door. I wanted her to feel assured I was asleep so I lay stiff in bed, barely daring to move a millimetre, sweat seeping into the sheets. A picture of Dad was crushed in my hand and I kept staring at the cross on my wall and praying over and over, until my jaw ached, for God to bring him back. But my prayers were like dead letters.

Now history is repeating itself. As though I'm holding my belief in both hands like an eggshell but I can't help squeezing it in terror that it's not really real and cracks are forming like little spiders, oozing the pus of doubt.

The truck slows down. I pray desperately, tears fierce behind my eyes: Oh God, please let me be wrong, please don't let me down, I want to believe in you so much, please make this happen . . .

# 10.15 P.M.

**Somewhere in Kingston, we stop.** Jeremiah opens up the back doors of the truck and there is light. We blink, eyes squinting. We're in a small side street. It is a tramp's heaven, a garden of putrid black bins. Distant music thumps beneath the pavements like underground thunder.

Jeremiah doesn't look cross any more. His eyes are glittering, as though he's relishing this challenge, this chance to work his divine magic.

'Chris – you come with me. Jon – you get into the front of the truck with Raymond. Thomas and Martyn – stay in the back – be ready to attack. Once we bring SNAKE in, we need to act fast. We get SNAKE into the truck, we silence SNAKE with the sack and tape, we leave. Got it?'

Everyone nods solemnly.

I get out of the truck. I feel Jeremiah's long fingers rub my shoulder. It's as though he eases out all of the stress like a splinter. I smile in weak relief.

I climb into the truck next to Raymond. He folds his arms and doesn't look at me.

In the wing mirror, I watch Jeremiah and Chris become silhouettes. I can hardly believe the risk they are taking. I know the club SNAKE is going to: it's a *raptor haven*. I visited it once myself when we first moved here, one lonely

Saturday night when my mum thought I was at a school disco. I didn't even make it past the bouncers. The only underage allowed in are pretty girls. Every night, there is regularly a crocodile queue of glamour and black suits and glittering dresses stretching out from under its pink neon sign. SNAKE will be standing there now, chatting and laughing, spreading sin. But how can Jeremiah possibly lure SNAKE away?

In my nerves, I start to hum without thinking. *We plough the fields and scatter.* Dad always used to hum that around the house, whether it was Easter, Pentecost or Harvest Festival. I catch Raymond's eye and he gives me a look. He thinks I'm taking the piss. I shut up quickly.

A spider of unease is lurking in the shadows of my stomach. I keep trying to coax it out so that I can stamp on it. I keep telling myself Jeremiah will improvise. I keep running through every detail of the plan over and over. Yet the spider keeps telling me a bit of the puzzle doesn't fit.

I find my hand slipping down and curling into the door-handle of the truck. If it goes wrong and the police turn up, I can make a run for it. Maybe that's why it's already gone wrong; maybe God is protecting me.

Then I think of Jeremiah and I think of how my life was before I met him. Those first few weeks at my new school, where I lay in bed at night and thought about emptying the medicine cabinet. He has saved me. My fingers fall slack.

'What's going to happen?' I blurt out.

'It'll be cool. Jeremiah has great powers of persuasion,' says Raymond. 'He'll spin some story. He'll tell SNAKE it's an emergency, something.'

'He's so clever,' I say proudly. I see Raymond's face and I look away, embarrassed by my show of emotion. 'Of course, it's not really him. God's working through him.'

Raymond doesn't say anything. I frown. Sometimes I doubt Raymond. He hardly ever talks about God. During prayer sessions, I have sometimes opened my eyes and seen him staring vaguely into the distance.

I check my watch.

10.30 p.m.

What if SNAKE is already in the club; what if Jeremiah and Chris can't get in?

I wonder why he took Chris and not me. Am I being punished? I've seen Chris around girls; he can't get past one stutter. What powers of persuasion does he have?

And then, suddenly, I see them in the wing mirror.

*Jeremiah is with SNAKE.*

The look in her eyes is puzzled, faintly bewildered. Jeremiah's arm is slung around her shoulders. Chris is standing a little way behind them, hands scrunched in his pockets, looking awkward.

It strikes me how vile her beauty is, how deceptive. She's dressed herself up for the club in glizty trousers, a black halter-neck top. Her beauty hits me the way it did when I first met her. It was my first RE class and I was aware of sitting at an empty desk, staring hard at the graffiti carved into the wood, trying to pretend I was doing fine. She walked in, and, to my amazement, sat down next to me. She smiled and said she hoped I was settling in. All though the lesson, my eyes kept dancing back to her chocolate skin and the ebony waterfall of her hair. When she smiled, her cheeks creased in her dimples and little stars danced in her cocoa eyes. When she worked, she poked her tongue into the corner of her mouth and gripped her pencil as though it was a knife. I ought to have seen the warning signs then.

It was Jeremiah who first discovered her plots. Who

overheard a conversation, who followed her, who listened in. And now he has captured the fly and brought her to our web.

# 10.40 P.M.

**It all happens so quickly.**

Chris flings open the truck doors. There is a faint scream. Then silence. The slam of the doors. Raymond revs up the truck. I keep thinking: is she really in? Was it that easy? Raymond backs down the side street. He slams against a bin. It spins, topples to one side, vomiting rubbish. He swerves out into the road. Brakes squealing – or more screaming? He lets out a cry and slams to a halt as we come to a set of traffic lights. An old lady waddling across the road gives us a murderous glance, assuming we are joyriding youths. I feel like shaking her. My heart is beating oh-so-fast. I can't believe we've done it. I can't believe we've got her. Oh God, thank you, God, how could I ever have doubted you? The lights change. Raymond speeds on. Jeremiah told him to go slow. We pass St Sebastian's. My heart pumps with joy. Oh, thank you, God. We have saved the school. Moonlight pours over its jagged roof in sweet relief; a squirrel bounces over the gates, fixing me with a beady eye before we speed on, leaving our hometown behind us, out into roads that are dark and foreign . . .

# 11 P.M.

'I thought it only took twenty minutes to get to the warehouse?' I ask Raymond.

He ignores me.

We're in the countryside now. Jagged landscapes; trees piercing the night sky.

I am feeling tired and a little panicky. I am vaguely aware that the present keeps remaining strangely unsatisfying. An hour ago nothing mattered but getting SNAKE. Now I want to whip time on, get to the warehouse, make our hostage video, ignite the TV stations.

What if Raymond is secretly sabotaging Jeremiah's instructions? This can't be Streatham. But then Jeremiah would have forced us to stop the truck by now, surely? I stare back at the layer of tarpaulin that separates the front of the truck from the back. I feel tempted to tweak it aside, whisper to Jeremiah. But I look at Raymond again and lose my nerve.

My eyes droop. I keep thinking about the old lady we stopped for at the lights. The way she looked at us. *Stupid young boys.* Sometimes I am afraid the whole world will look at us like that. What if they don't listen to us, don't believe us? Mr Abdilla didn't. I hear Jeremiah's words echo in my mind: *This is a world of appearances. Our*

*minds are shaped to think in stereotypes. We're all guilty.*
*For example: think of a headmistress. What do you see? A*
*woman with a bun and glasses and a grim face. Think of a*
*nurse. Think of a fireman. This is the world we live in.*
*Think of a terrorist and you see a young man with a beard.*
*Not a beautiful girl. This is the challenge we face: convinc-*
*ing the world to see beyond the superficial.*

And then we hear the sound of a police siren.

I glance at Raymond. He narrows his eyes, glancing in
the wing mirror. The road we're on is countrified, bordered
by tall, thick hedgerow. Empty except for us.

Blue lights blaze and get bigger. It must be my fault.
Hatred surges for my mum. She must have called them.

Raymond jerks the truck as though his initial plan is to
speed off. Then he slows down, shifting on to a verge.

'We'll play it cool,' he says. 'Don't say anything. I'll do
the talking.'

*I'll do the talking.* As though we're in a movie.

The police car slows down and then, to our amazement,
speeds on. The siren peaks and fades away over the hill . . .

'Cool!' Raymond cries, 'we're cool.'

I grin, but my stomach clots with unease. As they passed,
one of the cops turned to look at me. A white face under a
cap, grim with suspicion. A group of teenage boys out in a
truck? A stereotype that says trouble.

Sure enough, just as Raymond revs up the truck, the
siren returns.

'They're coming back!'

'Of course they're not!'

'They are!'

'Shit!'

It's then I notice the gap in the hedge. Perhaps it's been
carved out in the past for a tractor. It's our escape route now.

'There!' I cry. 'We can go across the fields.'

'Shut up!' Raymond shouts, but he follows my idea. He rolls the truck across the verge, sides scraping the hedge. The field gleams a hard brown with silver November frosting. He spins the truck, lurches forward, rolls up behind the hedge and cuts the engine. We wait in beating silence.

The siren swells and swells like a blue balloon. I am praying like mad, half out loud. Then, a few feet away, it hovers, unbearable, like a tiny knife pin-balling through my ears. Raymond clutches his Silk Cut packet tight in his hands.

But they don't come. The truck is dark, folded into the hedge. They're puzzled perhaps, discussing where we are. A minute passes and then the siren fades.

Raymond slumps with relief, crushing the packet with his fingers.

'Right, let's get out of here.'

We are about to start up again when the truck doors open. Jeremiah comes up to the front of the vehicle.

I am bursting to tell him the hedge was my idea, but he says urgently: 'Jon, I think I ought to stay in the front. It might be better for you to go in the back.'

I nod, not understanding, but trusting. I will tell him about the hedge, I will, but later. I hurry out, feet slipping on the frost and bounce into the back, slamming the doors. In the back of the truck, I discover that I have no choice but to sit beside SNAKE. Martyn, Thomas and Chris have already carefully positioned themselves opposite her, watching at a distance, as though they are in a cage with a dangerous animal. I am glad of the sack that hides her face.

As the truck revs up again, SNAKE starts to thrash about violently. The siren, perhaps, has filled her with a false hope. I recoil, narrowly avoiding a heel. She scrapes and thumps her heels against the metal floor. We all cringe up against the truck walls. I look at the others, relieved their scared faces mirror my own. Then Martyn bursts into laughter.

Thomas and Chris join in and their laugh stings with a tone I don't like. I force a smile.

I force it by picturing what might have happened if SNAKE wasn't with us now. Jeremiah was in the changing rooms on that fatal, fateful day, when SNAKE thought she was alone. He sidled up close to her, listening as she spoke quietly into her mobile. As she confided in her friend that she had found the websites for making a bomb. That she knew how to get the equipment. That she would plant it in a locker. What if that locker had been mine? I picture the moment: opening the metal door, humming and then –

What would it have felt like? Would I have died at once? Or would I have found myself lying in wet darkness, aware that parts of me were missing, rubble clawing my face, hearing the ragged ribbons of my friend's dying cries around me?

*Oh thank you God for guiding Jeremiah. A few nights before he overheard her conversation, he said he had some black dreams about her. They put him on guard. He was ready for revelation. Thank you God for showing us the way.*

I look over at SNAKE again. She has stopped thrashing about. But now her stillness seems more ominous. Legs slack. Sack flat. What if she can't breathe with that over her head?

*Just wait a few minutes*, I tell myself.

Sweat starts to seep through my skin in wet slugs. What if she suffocates to death? All of us up on a murder charge.

We won't be heroes, then. We'll be her equals.

I stare at the others. I will them to notice her, to click, to say something, do something, so that I don't have to. But they're all engrossed in murmuring about where we are going. It's just like that day when I was sitting upstairs on the bus. The top deck was half full: an old woman, a man in a polo neck, and a smattering of boys from our school. Right on the back seat, a load of bullies were pummelling a first year, pulling off his glasses and making him cry. I kept looking at the man in the polo, looking at the boys from the upper sixth, willing them to do something until my forehead burned with the pain. But nobody did. We all got off the bus, and I watched it crank away, the first year still on it, a terrible knot in my stomach.

*She's not breathing, she's not breathing!*

I decide that I will wait another two minutes. I'll time it on my watch –

– but then my body acts with a mind of its own. I reach over and pull the sack off her head.

'Jon, what are you doing –'

'Put it back on!'

'She's dangerous, you idiot –'

'She can't breathe!' I stammer. 'For God's sake, she can't scream with that tape over her mouth anyway!'

Then I notice her eyes.

The look in them makes me wish I hadn't taken the sack off.

I turn away.

'She couldn't breathe,' I repeat, shakily. I say it again, more loudly, 'She couldn't breathe.'

'She's moving, look, she's moving,' Chris calls out.

SNAKE is struggling to sit up. I reach out a cautious hand to help her. I am shocked when I touch her. I expected her blood to run with terrorist ice. But her skin oozes a honey warmth. What if I can catch her sin from her touch, like a disease? I quickly pull my hand away, curl it in my lap.

She sits upright now, gaining composure. Her eyes flick very slowly around the group. Retinal rage.

Chris looks down awkwardly, but Martyn and Thomas glare back. Finally, her eyes slide over to me. I feel anger rise in my chest. I thought she'd attempt to convey some sort of apology in her gaze; I thought the shock of being found out might have humbled her. But there is defiance in her eyes. She really doesn't care, I realise. She's angry, in fact, that we've thwarted her. She was no doubt making plans in the nightclub, gossiping with other members of her gang, preparing the countdown. She is only sixteen years old and she is prepared to kill hundreds of innocent people and she genuinely has no regrets.

I wish I had left the sack on her head.

I want to stare her out. I want to show that I am not afraid of her. That I am ready to fight evil. But her eyes are like snakes that spit venom. Finally, I have to surrender. I look away, shaking my head in disgust.

Out of the corner of my eye, I see her head droop. Then, to our collective relief, she closes her eyes. The truck rumbles on. I keep listening out for a siren, but none comes. I see her lips flickering. I wonder if she is praying to her god for forgiveness.

# MIDNIGHT

**I feel sleep seeping into my mind** like black tea. My neck begins to feel spineless; my head tips forward.

I snap it up, blinking, eyes stinging with fought tiredness. I haven't been able to sleep for weeks; now is not the time to let go. I concentrate on the tree symbol. It starts to twirl and dance; it becomes a baton, moving so fast it is a white blur. The baton is being held by SNAKE. She is walking down the school corridor towards me in a leotard, a smile leering on her face, her brown thighs bouncing with muscle. I realise at the last minute she is going to strike me with the baton. I crouch down and wrap my hands over my head, crying out. But it's too late and I hear the *crack* as she kills me.

I wake up with a jolt. I'm aware of voices. I stare at SNAKE. Her face is sullen, eyes puffy with defeat. Sleep pulls me under again.

I am running down streets, being chased by dark shapes. Then I wake up and find myself in bed at home, sweating with relief. I look up at the cross on my wall and I think: *Thank God we didn't go through with it, thank God I stayed home.*

Then I wake up, cold air swirling around me, tangy with night scents, sheep smells. The truck doors are open.

SNAKE is being led down the ramp, struggling between Chris and Martyn. My heart crushes in on itself as I realise we are here, and we did go through with it. For one second I feel like a frightened child and I want to run home. Then I stagger up, coming too, my conscious mind waking up, taking over, slamming down a lid on my fears.

We are here. This is it. The Beginning.

I clamber down from the truck, land in a muddy puddle.

'Hey, watch out,' says Raymond.

'Where – where's the warehouse?' I ask.

'That was just a line to fool you. You're new. Jeremiah felt you couldn't be trusted. We're in Suffolk.'

The truck is parked on a thin road outside a small cottage. The landscape is flat and barren. In the distance, a sheep's *baa* drifts across a field.

'But – but – what about my Initiation?' I stammer. Did Jeremiah lie about that too?

'You think just helping with tonight is all you have to do?' Raymond says, shaking his head. 'This is the Brotherhood, not some dumb secret society. This is just the first part – then there's the ceremony, and a final test to prove you're one of us.'

Is he winding me up?

'But –'

'We don't have time to talk about this right now,' Raymond says roughly. 'Later, okay? We have to get this terrorist indoors.'

# Part Two
## Day One

# 12.30 A.M.

*Are you happy?*

That was the first thing Jeremiah ever said to me. I was sitting in the playground, alone in the sunshine. Something had just happened with my dad that made me feel a long way from being happy, when Jeremiah came up to me. I opened my mouth to reply *Yes*, purely out of habit. I was so used to being asked questions by adults where they wanted and expected a *yes:* have you done your homework, will you be in by ten, are you happy? *Yes, yes, yes.* Yeah, yeah, yeah. But when Jeremiah asked the question, I felt that he was really asking it – looking into my soul and asking.

Later, Jeremiah made me realise how slippery words are. When adults ask questions, there is always a *subtext. Subtext* was one of Jeremiah's favourite phrases. The art of saying one thing and meaning another. Like *What do you want to be when you leave school?* when really they mean *Are you going to do what we want you to do, what society wants you to do? Are you going to be a good boy and get a good degree and then go work in an office pushing paper round a desk so we can feel you're suffering in our footsteps?*

*And then what?* Jeremiah pointed out.

You become a cog in the capitalist machine. You have to spend most of your time doing a job you don't like and the rest of your time sleeping to have enough energy to do the job you don't like. Why? For money. But what do you need so much money for? Not for food, since God has created a world where we can eat and grow our own food so easily. But to buy stuff. Stuff: the temptations of the advertising industry. We're told that we'll only be happier if we have shinier cars and bigger TVs and cooler labels than the guy who lives next door to us. And then what? You end up having kids and having to work even harder because your kids want better toy cars and big TVs and clothes with the Right Labels than the other kids in their playground.

The big companies plant the seeds in school. It begins with computer games and trainers. If you wear the wrong trainers, you're in the wrong crowd, or you get beaten up. But what is a trainer? Jeremiah pointed out. A bit of plastic with a lace threaded through it. Made by some poor kid in Taiwan who has to slave for eighteen hours a day without food in a sweatshop.

*It's all the Conspiracy of Darkness*, Jeremiah explained. Trainers and cars are like sticky coloured sweets that feed the soul whilst rotting it away. Since I joined Hebetheus, that empty feeling that used to gnaw my stomach all the time has gone away; I've realised it's because my soul is being properly nourished.

In fact, I've realised so many things since meeting Jeremiah. Every day, a new revelation. Like the guys at school who used to scare me: the rebels. One of them shoved me in football and I felt hurt all day, until Jeremiah pointed out that the rebels are as pathetic as the rest of society. They think they're cool because they smoke ciggies underage, when in fact they're just the slaves of the big cigarette companies who squeeze money out of them before giving them cancer so the drug companies can start squeezing them instead. In the end, Jeremiah explained, the rebels are really the biggest squares. *For the saddest people on this earth,* said Jeremiah, *are the deluded: those who live their lives as an illusion.*

That's the amazing thing about Jeremiah. I used to see the world as one light; then Jeremiah fractured it open and showed me a rainbow. Thomas once said to me, 'It's no use trying to understand or define Jeremiah – you never will. There are too many permutations to his personality. He's infinite, like God.' On some days, Jeremiah is so grand and magnificent he is like Aslan in *The Lion, the Witch and the Wardrobe*; yet the other day I saw him bend down, spot a woodlouse on its back, wriggling helplessly, and with a look of utter tenderness on his face gently flip it back over.

Now, as we click open the gate and walk up the path with SNAKE, Jeremiah leading the way, I feel my heart swelling with pride to follow him. How often does God put someone on his earth to speak his message? How many things have to happen – the planets to shift into perfect harmony, the stars to align into a magical formation – for someone like Jeremiah to be born? And we are so lucky to be the first select few around him. Maybe in a few years' time so many thousands of people will be pounding on Jeremiah's door, desperate for a word of wisdom, a healing touch, that we will barely be able to see him. Is this how it felt for the Wise Men who sensed the birth of Jesus? I look up at the sky; it is black and starless, a void.

We stop at the front door.

Jeremiah bends down, takes a key from under a stone. Who owns this place, I wonder; how did Jeremiah get it?

Jeremiah inserts the key in the lock. Our silence quivers. It feels as though he is a magician unlocking a magical kingdom, as though we are stepping into a computer game. In the distance, an owl makes a sad note.

As the door opens, I glance at SNAKE. I feel triumphant. Now, at last, fear has crowbarred open her face, trembling in her eyes and lips.

We tumble into the hallway, all fighting to be first. Everything is cloaked in musty darkness and it's colder in than out. I stumble against a cardboard box. My face presses against a dank wall and the vibe of the place seems to seep into my skin: a sensation of forlorn sadness, of lost ghosts, of wind whistling in empty rooms. There is a terrible smell in the air: of dirt and old newspapers, of pee and rotting meat.

We switch on a light. The hallway is decorated with fading yellow-rose wallpaper. We pad in gingerly, our boots clattering heavily on the bare boards. The doors of the hallway are all shut – all except for a kitchen, which we trail into.

'Hey,' says Martyn. 'Food. Why did we have to go stealing food for the last week when there's stuff here?'

'Shut up!' Raymond whispers fiercely. 'Look.'

I can't see what the matter is. The kitchen looks dirty – if Mum was here now she'd be throwing a fit and filling it with soapsuds. Yet there is a sense of order to the chaos. For example: there are piles and piles of newspapers and magazines, but they seem to follow a logic: *Sunday Times* in one pile, *Women's Weekly* on another, *Daily Mail* another. On the shelves, there are rows of bottles: a scarlet sea of tomato ketchup, a brown sea of HP sauce. There are black sacks of rubbish waiting to be taken out, squatting like huge, rotting plums.

Then Raymond points.

On the table. A dirty plate. A knife and fork.

I turn and look at Raymond.

'Someone's still here,' he whispers. 'God. If Ned has rented this place out to someone else –'

'SNAKE!' Jeremiah hisses at once.

She manages to scream for a second before he gags her, pulling a school tie from his pocket. She breathes in and out thickly through her gag, shaking. The school motto *Aim for the Highest* bobs against her mouth.

'Nobody can be here,' Jeremiah whispers. 'Ned said that nobody would be here. He must have let someone else come to stay!'

'Well, you know what Ned's like,' Raymond replies. 'God knows who else he might have told about this place.'

Who is Ned? Then I notice SNAKE looking at me, digesting my confusion. I quickly look knowing.

'We should hunt –' Martyn begins.

'What we'll do is this,' Jeremiah cuts in and we lean in closer, our breaths forming a hot huddle, leaving SNAKE to one side. 'We go to the front and the back and lock the doors. Whoever's in here isn't about to get out. They're frightened – they must think we're burglars. They're hiding, waiting. We move from room to room. We stay as a group – we're strong that way.'

'What about SNAKE?' Martyn cries.

'Keep your voice down!' Jeremiah whispers. 'She stays here. Thomas, tie her to the chair. Now. The rest of us go.'

# 1 A.M.

**What kind of person would live** in this weird cottage? My frightened imagination starts scuttling into corners, blowing up dust from horror movies that have polluted my mind, picturing some strange old crone; a man who is human by day and beast by night; a psychopath who just happens to enjoy feasting on the hearts of teenage boys. As we go out into the hallway, my heart starts to thump and I'm glad I'm tagging at the back of the group, behind the safe wall of my Brothers' backs.

Aside from the kitchen: five doors in the hallway. All shut.

We go to the first one, opposite the kitchen. Raymond and Jeremiah exchange glances. Jeremiah gives Raymond a gentle nudge. Raymond pushes it open. I stand on tiptoe to see in. It's empty.

A living room. It is very simply furnished. Boards on the floor; dirty white walls stained with yellow roses of faded nicotine. The TV is balanced on top of a box and the aerial is twisted into a weird shape, like a silver finger pointing out towards some divine event beyond the window. A single armchair opposite, sagging like an old man's face, dotted with cigarette burns like liver spots.

We withdraw.

The next door opens out into a toilet and bathroom. Mildew crawling up the walls in green rashes; a windowsill with dying plants covered in dust; the brown blur of a moth flapping frantically to get out.

The third door opens out into a library: two bookcases filled with curling spines and a single rocking chair with a worn seat.

A fourth door opens out into a room filled with odd bits of junk. Boxes, newspapers stacked up; an old lampshade.

'This will be our Prayer Room,' Jeremiah whispers, nodding.

But nobody really hears him because now we're outside the final door. We all move in closer. Jeremiah puts his ear to the door, whispers, 'God be with us!', then opens it. He switches on the light. And then we see her.

The bedroom is a faded blue and a huge collection of china animals takes up most of the space. There is a bed. An old woman is lying in it. Her gnarled face is contorted in a habitual grimace of distress, as though sleep cannot wash away the worries of her days.

Raymond turns back and swallows.

'I can take care of her. Everyone outside –'

'Wait,' Jeremiah says sharply. He goes up to her side and whispers, 'Hello?' He leans down, frowning, listening hard. Then he stands up, blinking. We all start and he nods. 'She's dead.' He looks down at her, his eyes tender with compassion.

'But who the hell is she?' Martyn bursts out.

'I think she may be Ned's granny,' Raymond muses. 'Hell. Ned owes me this favour, I lied for him in court, I gave him his bloody alibi and he *said* this place would be empty! He promised me he was going to get old Granny Knickers himself and take her to his flat!'

Raymond tries to call him up, but there is no answer. He clicks off his phone with a snarl of frustration.

'This bloody Ned – now we'll have to go find another house!' Martyn cries. 'This is what comes of trusting a criminal!'

Panic flares up. Where the hell can we go? How can we find another house now?

'No,' Jeremiah says. 'We don't. Look. She's only been dead a day or so. It looks as though she just went to bed and didn't wake up. As for Ned's family – well – from what you've said, Raymond, they're not the caring type. Visiting isn't their forte – they all spend too much time in prison for a start. I doubt anyone will come looking for her for another few days – that gives us breathing space. For the moment, we stay here.'

Jeremiah's eyes pass over each of our faces in turn and we all nod in relief. And yet, still, an unease squirms in the air . . .

'Don't worry,' he says. 'This is life – unpredictable. We may have plans but we'll have to keep improvising. That's the way it's going to be. But don't worry. We only need a few days. God will protect us. We have enough time to do our duty.'

# 1.30 A.M.

**Raymond gathers us back** into the kitchen whilst Jeremiah speaks with SNAKE in the living room, which has now been renamed the Brotherhood Bedroom.

'Right,' says Raymond. 'First things first.' He burrows through one of the boxes he has brought in from the van, pushes past the rows and rows of baked-bean tins and yanks out a roll of black sacks, ripping one off. 'You've all brought your mobiles, right? Well, put them in here.'

'Why?' Martyn asks warily, pulling his Nokia out of his pocket.

'Safekeeping,' Raymond says abruptly.

All the mobiles go into the bag. All except for Chris, who looks a little embarrassed to remind us he doesn't have one – his parents have banned them. Raymond tosses the bag on the floor. With his steel toe-capped boot, he stamps on them. Beneath Martyn's yells of protests, there is a terrible crunching. I go cold inside.

Jeremiah enters the kitchen.

'It's all right, everyone – I ordered Raymond to do this.'

There is a shocked silence.

'What need do any of you have for mobiles? This is a new beginning for us all. We need to leave the world out there behind us. It's the best way for us to experience a Soul Shift.'

*Soul Shift*. I've heard that word mentioned a few times recently – in whispered conversations. It sparkles and flickers with mystery and beauty.

'Besides, it's too dangerous; the police could track the signals. Okay, Martyn?'

'Yeah,' Martyn scowls.

'Well, I guess it's for the best,' says Thomas, a little sadly.

I know Thomas is right and that mobiles are another big evil, but I had been secretly planning to call Mum, let her know I am okay. It took me six months of paper rounds to save up for that phone; it has a picture of Lisa on it, smiling, all now reduced to a twist of crushed metal.

# 1.45 A.M.

**Everything is going well until** I am ordered to take SNAKE
to the toilet.

Before then, we turn the living room into the Brotherhood Bedroom, clearing out the TV and chair, carrying
mattresses from the van and laying them out with sleeping
bags on top. It's heavy, hungry work and we stop to devour
a packet of biscuits. Martyn starts making a joke that the
old woman might not be really dead, that there might just
be a *whisper* of breath in her lungs and though we all
laugh, in the end Chris gets sent, just to check, just in case.
He reports back that her doomed soul has definitely left its
body.

Then the next big task: turning the empty room into the
Prayer Room. The room is a mess. Dirty walls, dirty floor.
Newspaper shards rippling like fish, old boxes, a broken
lamp with a frilly pink shade like a pair of knickers. Raymond and Thomas fill a bucket of water. They scrub the
walls vigorously. It's a beautiful thing to watch, as though
they're washing away sins, returning the wall to its original
colour. I bend down to pick up the last scraps of newspaper.
*News of the World.* A blonde lady with hard tits. I feel my
blood stir and bend away from the others, peeling the page
back for a better look. *Remember,* Jeremiah once warned

us, *desire is a snake that winds around the spine.* I quickly scrumple up her face, tear her body into pieces, stuff her dead remains into a sack. I fill another bucket and start on the floor, swishing with vigorous strokes. Martyn cleans the windows; Chris sweeps cobwebs from the ceiling.

After the room is clean, we paint symbols on the walls. Raymond consults Jeremiah.

'We can't paint them white,' he points out. 'The walls are white now. They have to show up good and proper.'

Jeremiah's message comes back thus:

'Paint them black.'

I feel a little confused. Jeremiah once said black was an evil colour. But I swallow it back: Jeremiah often mentions the *paradox of the divine.*

The paint ends up going everywhere. Black footprints on the floor, black handprints on the wall. Like warpaint on our faces, like streaks of night in our hair. The final thing we paint is a large black circle on the floor, with symbols curling around the border. That's where SNAKE will stand.

We are ready now to make the video, everyone is buzzing with excitement – but then Thomas tells us SNAKE needs the toilet.

'Jon can do it,' Raymond volunteers me, ignoring my filthy look. 'I'm going to park the van round the back – it looks too suspicious sitting out in the front.'

I go into the kitchen. They've taken her gag off now; she seems to realise screaming won't help. Her eyes look dull and tired; I almost feel sorry for her, but I ignore the false feeling and tell her to follow me.

'Well?' she says as I go after her. 'Can't I even piss in peace?'

'Uh – okay,' I stammer, stepping back. 'But don't lock the door.'

I stand outside, feeling nervous. Raymond comes out of the Prayer Room.

'What's she doing in there?' Raymond snarls. 'Jesus, she has to be guarded at *all times*. Get in.' He shoves the door open and pushes me in.

'Hey!' SNAKE cries, drawing up her trousers with clumsy handcuffed hands.

'I have to be in with you –' I cry, 'I'm sorry – it's the rule –'

'WELL, TURN AROUND. DON'T STARE AT ME!' she screams.

'Sorry, sorry.' I spin around, staring hard at the wall.

'I know you won't take my cuffs off if I ask, so can you tear off some toilet paper and give it to me?' she demands.

I pass her some, taking care not to glance back a millimetre. As she heaves up her trousers, though, out of the corner of my eye I catch a glance of her knickers: white with red hearts. She goes to the sink, spins the taps and awkwardly shimmies her hand under them.

'What's that?' she nods. On the windowsill are the long boxes of earth that Chris and Martyn carried in.

'Oh, they've got *oasis* seeds planted in them, they're these spiritual seeds Jeremiah got, they grow up into plants that we can then turn into a potion –' I break off, seeing the sneer in her eyes. 'Forget it.'

'Can you just give me one minute in peace?' she asks quietly. 'I've got my period. I've got to put a tampon in.'

'I –' I feel a blush rising up my cheeks. I've never seen a tampon before and the thought terrifies me. 'Okay. One minute. But I mean it. I'm timing it on my watch.'

'Okay. Sure. Thanks.' She gives me such a sweet smile

that the cold hatred in my heart melts just a little.

The moment I leave the bathroom, I think: *Go back in.* What if Raymond walks past again? I turn back, push the door open a nervous inch. The tampon looms in my mind, becoming bigger and bigger until it's as tall as King Kong. Then I hear an odd, grating noise.

'Can I come back in?' I call. I push the door open another inch.

No reply.

I tell SNAKE I'm coming in.

A blast of freezing air from the open window slaps my face with a mocking hand. She's halfway out of the window; she turns, sees my face, then dives out into the night.

I run forward, hearing myself yell: 'STOP!' I grab the frame, trying to shove it up, but the gap is too small, only just big enough for SNAKE's lithe frame. I see her running away into the darkness. I shove again, then turn back, run to the door. Out in the hall I hurtle into Raymond and Martyn. I can hardly speak – 'She's gone, she's got away' – 'What the fuck' – 'Out of the window!' I cry.

Raymond yells: 'I told you to look after her', and we pile out of the front door, running down the side of the cottage, the muddy grass sucking and slowing our footsteps. Where is she? The treetops drift lightly in the wind. Where is she? Grass; prickly bushes like giant prehistoric animals; fields; grass; trees; where is she? Oh God, she can't have escaped, can she, oh God, can she?

'She can't have gone far,' Raymond cries.

'We need a torch,' I stammer. My head feels hot and pounding and thick with panic. 'We need –'

'There!' Martyn yells.

A bush breaks symmetry into two dark shapes; one tries to dart away. Martyn throws himself on her.

'I've got her!'

We lunge forwards. The terrorist turns into a hissing spitting screaming scratching beast. They don't really need me; Martyn has her left arm, Raymond her right, but I bundle in and grab a handful of her sparkly top and wrench, feeling the material stretch out of shape and for a moment a wild desire comes over me to tear it apart, to grab flesh, to bite, to feast, to destroy. It's the adrenaline of fate, thumping through me: it's black versus white, evil versus good, sin versus humankind; the universe quivers, the see-saw tips up and down, waiting for the balance to swing.

We win.

We conquer her, shaking and grabbing her until she curls into a defeated ball.

We pull her up and march her back to the house. Jeremiah, Chris and Thomas have emerged and are gazing, wide-eyed.

'She bloody bit me,' Martyn keeps moaning. 'The fucking bitch bit me!'

'Jon, the stupid jerk, was meant to be supervising her to the toilet and then he let her go climbing out of the window for a laugh,' Raymond says breathlessly.

'I just – she wanted to go to the toilet – and she had a tampon –' my voice breaks on the word and I hear Chris giggle and then Martyn chuckles too. 'I just wanted to . . .' I trail off, feeling their dismay, their disappointment. Jon the New Boy has fucked up again. For the second time this evening. Maybe they'll call off my Initiation ceremony.

But, to my relief, Jeremiah clasps my shoulder.

'It wasn't Jon's fault. He's too kind, that's all. Jon, you need to be tougher. Don't worry – your kindness is a virtue.'

Immediately, the mood of the group shifts and Chris

mutters, 'Tampon!' again and this time we all laugh, only it feels as though they're laughing with me, not at me.

'Look,' Martyn sucks his hand and shows us the wound again: three red eyes gaping in the curve of his thumb. 'She bit me.'

We all look at SNAKE, who stares back at us with sullen eyes. Her hair is mussy and the look on her face is shrunken, defeated, as though we have battered out a little of the evil in her.

As we go back into the house, I find the sequins from her top have come off on my palm, dusting my skin with a layer of tiny stars. I quickly go to the bathroom and wash my hands three times.

# 2 A.M.

'W-w-w-we are f-f-f-from the H-h-hebetheus r-r-r-religion. W-w-we have k-k-kidnapped a t-t-terrorist.'

Chris breaks off, yanks out his inhaler and breathes in deeply. He opens his mouth to speak again and then screws up his eyes, shaking his head.

'I can't r-r-remember.'

'You're doing fine,' says Jeremiah softly. 'Switch it off, switch it off,' he says, waving his hand at Thomas, who has balanced the camcorder on his shoulder. 'Ok, reset it. We'll start again.'

We're standing in the Prayer Room. It's empty now except for a bookcase in the corner; candlelight flickers over ragged, broken spines. We surround Chris, our narrator, our voice, in a circle. SNAKE is next to me, handcuffed, her ankles bound with rope.

Every time I glance at SNAKE my heart twists with a flash of hot hatred for her. I'd thought Jeremiah was going to ask *me* to be the speaker for the video; he'd dropped a few hints last week. I thought my main rival was Thomas; Thomas with his posh voice, who sounds like he ought to be reading the BBC news. Instead, he has chosen the one member of our group who hates being in front of the camera, who is spitting out our glorious slogans in bits of broken sentence and drools of saliva. Martyn is trying not to laugh; it's putting Chris off, though Jeremiah hasn't noticed. He softly instructs Chris to keep going, to be strong, to let God take him over and speak through him.

Poor Chris. Once after school I went back with him to his house. Chris asked his dad what they were having for dinner and his father said, 'W-w-we're h-having b-burgers.' It was such a perfect imitation of Chris's stutter that it took me a minute to twig that he was taking the piss. Then he winked at us as if to say, *Yes, this loser is my son but you wouldn't know, would you?*

Chris tries and fails again and wastes two more takes. I feel frustration heating in my chest. I feel like putting my hand up like some stupid kid in class and saying *Let me, let me.* Then I let it out with a deep breath. I must be patient. Nobody can understand why Jeremiah does as he does: he works in mysterious ways.

I just hope he's not still angry with me.

'Chris,' said Jeremiah, in his liquid angel's voice, 'I think you should try again with more feeling. Just let your heart open up with love for God, let him trample away your stammer. Okay? Good.'

Jeremiah steps back. The camera rolls. Chris starts again.

'We are from the Hebetheus religion.' A good start; he smiles in relief, close to tears and Jeremiah nods intently, twitching with excitement. 'We h-h-h –' a pause and we wait for the house of cards to blow apart, but then he keeps going, gaining momentum, 'we have kidnapped a terrorist! A TERRORIST!'

And then the noise comes out of nowhere. We all look round in confusion.

Singing. Beautiful singing. In a language I don't understand.

Chris's voice meanders into a squeak.

'What the hell is she DOING!' Jeremiah turns on SNAKE and I am shocked by the fury blazing in his face. 'It's not your turn yet!'

Her singing fades. She looks at us with exhausted but defiant eyes.

'You!' Jeremiah points a finger at me like a bullet. 'Shut her up.'

'Okay, okay.' Raymond takes hold of her and I say sharply, 'Be quiet – okay?'

'He means gag her, you idiot,' Raymond whispers.

I look round helplessly and then Raymond gives me another sharp look so I quickly improvise. I walk behind her and pull her against me and clap my hand over her mouth, like they do in the movies. Chris starts again, but he is lost again, a twitching huddle of hunched shoulders and mumbles. SNAKE's lips are damp against my palm. I picture their kiss imprinted against the skin. Chris tries again, but her singing lingers in the air like a poisoned perfume. I press my hand tight against her face. I want her to know I'm not going to let her make a fool of me a second time. If she tries anything, I will relish hurting her.

'Okay, Chris,' said Jeremiah, drawing him away. 'You did well. Really well. Thomas will take over now. But you did good. We're all proud of you.'

And suddenly we are. Even Martyn. We all smile at Chris, a pride beating in our communal heart. Thomas gives him a punch to let him know he'd rather not take over really and Chris ducks his head and smiles shyly, relieved, pretending to be regretful.

Thomas fluffs his first take, then turns to Chris and says, 'It's hard, isn't it?'

Finally, this is how the video is done.

# 3 A.M.

*N.B. The parts of the video in brackets [] are to be edited and cut for the final version.*

THOMAS:     We are from the Religion of
            Hebetheus.

The camera PANS over our faces, except
Jeremiah.

[MARTYN:    Jeremiah, why can't you show
            your face?

JEREMIAH:   I want to avoid being a figure-
            head for the group. What if
            people begin to idolise me
            instead of God? Carry on
            Thomas. You need to tell them
            about our aims.]

THOMAS:     We believe that peace isn't a
            vague term. We believe that
            peace *can* be REAL – that we
            can live in a world without
            fear. In our quest for peace,

we have taken matters into our own hands. You will see now that we are people who will act, not speak pretty, meaningless words – for we have captured the terrorist Padma Laxsmi, who was about to plant a bomb in St Sebastian's School. This is the girl *your* country, *your* police force failed to stop.

The camera PANS to a CLOSE-UP of SNAKE's face.

[JEREMIAH: Come on, SNAKE. Admit to the world what you were planning to do, the lives you were about to destroy . . .

SNAKE: I don't know what the hell you're talking about. Is this some kind of joke? Is Henry in on this?

JEREMIAH: We suggest that you co-operate with us. Look, don't be afraid. Be open about what you believe in. Say it now – loud and clear. We're going to put this video on the internet, we're going to email it to the Houses of Parliament, to every MP in the country, to the chief of police. Now is your

chance to put your message of
violence and sickness across –

SNAKE:      You're insane, I want to go
            home, I want my mum, you're
            all just crazy –

JEREMIAH:   Okay, we'll speak for her.
            Jon, gag her properly. Martyn,
            it's your turn to speak. Tell
            the world what we want.]

MARTYN:     The police didn't bother to do
            anything about SNAKE, they're
            just lazy bastards, but we're
            not. We'll take action, we'll
            do anything to save hundreds
            of lives, so you should all
            listen to us, right? Now,
            listen to our demands and take
            them seriously. One – we want
            the police to investigate
            SNAKE and make sure none of
            her terrorist friends are
            planning to bomb our school.
            Two, we want the Prevention of
            Terrorism Act changed. It's
            too lame. We need to get *tough*
            on terrorists! It's not enough
            to increase the period they
            can be held without trial from
            fourteen days to twenty-eight
            days or even ninety days!
            Ninety days is *nothing!* In the
            US they can hold someone they

suspect is an evil terrorist
for *as long as they like* if
they deem them to be a threat.
This is what you call being
tough on terrorism. We demand
that our wimpy government
should change their law again
so it's the same as the US.

[JEREMIAH:  Good, good.]

MARTYN:     Three – we want the government
            to recognise that the
            Hebetheus religion is a new
            religion and in turn to give
            us one million quid –

[JEREMIAH:  Say pounds, it sounds better.
            Say we want them to acknowl-
            edge our help.]

MARTYN:     We want the government to
            acknowledge our help and give
            us one million qui- pounds so
            that we can build a temple in
            London. Then we can begin to
            spread the word of Hebetheus
            so that everyone will be able
            to live in a safe world free
            from terror.

[JEREMIAH:  And say then what happens if
            they don't take us seriously.]

MARTYN:     If you don't listen to our
            demands, we will torture our

                    hostage and find out –

[JEREMIAH:   No, no – just say we will
             respond with extreme measures –

MARTYN:      – but that sounds so lame –

JEREMIAH:    No, it's more powerful, you
             see? Because they have to
             imagine what those measures
             might be – if we're going to
             kidnap more people, and so on.
             The power of the imagination,
             Martyn – it's an amazing
             tool.]

MARTYN:      If you don't respond to our
             demands, we will respond with
             extreme measures.

[JEREMIAH:   Good, good. Enough. Where's
             Chris? Where's our very own
             hacker? You're sure you can do
             this?

MARTYN:      Can Chris do this? Can he? Is
             the Pope a Catholic? Chris
             once hacked into a bank, I saw
             him – he hacked right into
             Barclays, but he wouldn't take
             any money, thought he'd get
             arrested –

JEREMIAH:    In the meantime, we need to
             put SNAKE somewhere.

RAYMOND:     There's always the cellar.

JEREMIAH:   Yes! Perfect. Just for the
            night.

MARTYN:     I'll take her down. Hey,
            shouldn't we turn the video
            off now . . . ]

END OF TAPE

# 5 A.M.

**I'm half-awake, half-asleep.** A nightmare uncoils and slowly slithers through my mind. I'm back in the bathroom. The spiritual seeds have sprouted like Triffids, a wall of thick choking stalks, flowers hissing poison nectar. Somewhere in the middle of them is SNAKE, but they are protecting her and I cannot find her. I try to fight my way through and my heart is beating because I must not let Jeremiah down, I must not let him down but ivy coils around my throat, choking me and I drown in a sea of poisoned green and just as I go down I see SNAKE's eyes, two laughing black orbs . . .

I wake up, breathing hard. Breaths all around me. Where am I, where's home?

Then I remember.

My breathing slows down and I lie still. Martyn is snoring hard; Chris echoes him lightly. Jeremiah sleeps in silent serenity, hands flat across his chest, as though resting in peace. My heart throbs. I feel funny, watching him while he's sleeping, and I quickly look away. I feel comforted by the sounds around me. I always wanted to join the Boy Scouts or the Cadets but I never had time because of church. Being here feels like a taste of it.

What a day. So much happened, so quickly. Fragments

**75**

spike my memory. It feels good just to lie here and think it all over, digest it, so I am ready for what is to come next.

I wish I'd a chance to speak to Jeremiah alone tonight, but it seemed selfish to demand his attention when there were Bigger Things to deal with. I don't mind if I have to pass another challenge to prove that I should be in the Brotherhood; I am happy to do anything to show my devotion to our cause. But those words – *Initiation ceremony* – shiver through my mind. I keep picturing horror scenarios: being locked in a coffin, having to eat cold baked beans. Stupid, childish stuff. I know Jeremiah would never be so crass . . . *but – ?*

I keep trying to ignore my bladder but soon the pain becomes too intense.

I get up, padding through the bodies on tiptoe, and slip out into the hallway. The bathroom door is shut. My nightmare rears. I pause outside for five minutes, feeling like a scaredy-girl, before I finally get the guts to twist it open –

– it's empty. Of course. I remind myself: *Don't be afraid, you're surrounded by a protective shield.*

Even so, the boxes of spiritual seeds make me feel squirmy and I piss quickly.

When I come out of the bathroom, I pause in the hallway. The door beckons. I try to ignore it, but it feels as though an invisible hand presses on my shoulder and pushes me forward, envelopes mine, makes me open the handle and go in.

The dead old woman. The moonlight shines in through the window, lies in pools in the wrinkles and furrows of her face. Beside her, the china animals seem to dance in the moonlight, as though they might come alive; their eyes gleam, mocking me, as I step forward.

I just want to touch her. I've never touched a dead person before and I've always wondered what it was like.

I was expecting her skin to feel cold, but I am surprised by how dry it is. Like old leaves. I notice a photograph of a young girl by her bed and I suddenly realise it's her. And then I realise that one day, I'll be an old man with a photo on my bedside table of me looking like I do now. And suddenly the woman seems human, real, as though she could have been my granny, and pity cuts my heart. I bleed with sadness that we didn't get to her in time. Jeremiah could have read the *Book of Hebetheus* to her. We could have saved her Soul.

Before Jeremiah saved me, I used to be scared of Death all the time. But now I know I'm safe, because the Brotherhood of the Hebetheus will all go to Manu when we die.

But this poor woman – she'll go nowhere. Her soul will leave her body, and it will search and search for the light. But it will find nothing. It will soar up to the clouds and howl in despair; it will appeal to the moon and sun, crying out for salvation, but its screams will echo and fade amongst the stars. And then, without the nourishment of God's love, the Soul will starve and grow weak. It will find a dark place, a graveyard, a cobwebbed corner, and huddle into a ball, slowly seeping away into a smudge, into air, until it becomes Nothingness.

As I go out in the hallway, I think of SNAKE below. Even though she got me into trouble, I feel glad that we found her in time. We can save her from the same Fate as the old woman.

Back in the bedroom, I notice Thomas is awake. For one odd moment I fear he might be crying, but he turns away, hiding his face. I lie down and close my eyes. My head is throbbing. I feel too excited to sleep; tomorrow everything will really begin. Eventually, I make myself drop off by reciting the first *Book of Hebetheus*, the words slowly floating away from me like driftwood as a wave of sleep washes over me: *A million years ago, the Earth was a void. Colourless, tasteless: it was nothingness itself. Then one day, a tiny spark, a shimmer of energy tickled the void. The tickle rippled through its nothingness. A particle was formed, a piece of blackness curled and took shape. A crow was born, and that crow was God . . .*

*The first people to live on Earth were the Hebethean Race. The moment each baby was born, the moment it breathed its first breath, that breath swirled into its lungs and a magical alchemy took place; the baby instantly experienced a Soul Shift and became God in human form.*

*Back then, no Hebethean had to strive for a Soul Shift the way that a Hebethean Brother has to today. There was no path to God with thorns or snakes or deceptive undergrowth: for there was no path. People were God and life was lived in pure and perfect peace.*

*They lived simple lives, side by side as Brother and Sisters. All loved one another, but not in the sinful way: they never touched each other, never swam in the putrid bath of sex. When a woman reached fourteen years of age, a crow would visit her in the night, touch her forehead, and in the morning she would be round with child. This was a time of peace, so there was no curse on women and hence they did not have to suffer the pain of carrying a child for nine months. A child was begot and born a day later.*

*Everyone who lived on Earth knew and understood their place. They were all flowers and plants in a beautiful garden of God and each knew what perfume they should waft. The men were hunters. The women were mostly blonde. They served the men, cooked them food and were devoted slaves to them; they brought up the children; they . . .*

# Day Two

# 12 P.M.

'Wake up – we're on!'

A face above me: Martyn. I mutter that I'm tired, don't want to get up. He punches my shoulder, a little too hard. I let out a yelp and grab it, blearily moaning that he has bruised me.

'Quit moaning!' Martyn cries exuberantly. 'They got our video, Chris did it and we're on TV! *Now!* Come on!'

His words strike a match inside me. I bounce up, the pain forgotten. The Brotherhood Bedroom is empty: everyone is huddled in the kitchen, round the small black-and-white portable the old woman left behind.

The picture of SNAKE flickering on the screen slaps me fully awake. It's a school uniform photo which makes her look all demure and innocent, her soft face framed by a wave of hair caught neatly in a kirby grip. Underneath her photo, the caption screams MISSING.

'Holy shit!' Martyn cries.

'Jesus, this reception is terrible!' Raymond roars, banging the TV jubilantly. 'Where's Jeremiah? Jeremiah, get your arse in here NOW!'

'Thomas, where's Thomas?' I cry, seeing Jeremiah come in.

'Just coming!' Jeremiah cries breathlessly. 'Come on, Thomas!'

'Ssh!' Raymond cries as Thomas thunders in. 'We're missing it!'

We stare up with wide eyes, TV light falling on our faces as though we've been mesmerised by an alien spaceship.

'Yesterday Padma Laxsmi, a sixteen-year-old schoolgirl, went missing from a club in Kingston.' The newsreader is an Asian woman with a very English accent. 'However, a video sent to the police and the Houses of Parliament reveals that she has been kidnapped by a group of young Christian Fundamentalists –'

'Christian!' Raymond shrieks.

'They can't be serious –'

'SSH!'

' . . . the video shows the level of their threat.'

A clip of our video: Thomas saying that we will act, that we are not people who use meaningless, pretty words.

'They cut it short, there's nothing about our message, about Hebetheus –'

'QUIET!'

'The six boys disappeared from their homes yesterday evening. It is thought that they abducted Padma at around eleven o'clock that evening before disappearing to an unknown location . . .'

One by one, our faces appear behind her head. Each photo seems to have been hand-picked to make us look as sullen and dysfunctional as possible. Even Chris, with his red hair and freckles like a blast of autumn sunshine, looks wane and evil-eyed. When my face flashes up, I jump. It's a passport photo, the one my mum forced me to have taken just after she forced me to have a horrible haircut with a square fringe at SuperCuts R Us. Jesus. Then Raymond's photo appears.

'The leader of the group is ex-convict Raymond Gibson,

aged eighteen. Raymond was released from the juvenile detention centre two years ago where he served a sentence for stealing firearms. He is the only member of the group who is not studying at St Sebastian's School and is thought to have led the impressionable schoolboys astray. He worked at Dixons for one year before disappearing, taking with him some stolen electronic equipment.'

*Stolen?* I glance over at Raymond, who shrugs bullishly.

A man wearing a white shirt and thick black glasses appears on the screen. He has a fat paunch and a moustache sits on his top lip like a black caterpillar.

'Raymond was always turning up late and smoking in the "Non Smoking" area of the canteen. I always thought there was something suspicious about him –'

'Oh fuck off,' Raymond hisses at him.

'The parents and teachers of St Sebastian's are extremely concerned about the boys . . .'

Chris's parents flash up on screen. His mum is very fat, with carrot-coloured hair and buck teeth, and she is clutching a rabbit to her chest. His dad stands beside her at an awkward angle, like a bent stick.

Funny how Chris's parents change their tune now. One minute he was the family embarrassment; but now he's gone, they want to claw him back. Maybe they're worried about what their neighbours might say.

'Chris, we miss you,' his mum says, sobbing. She holds out the rabbit. 'Dixie misses you too, and Pixie. Please come home . . .'

We all laugh, yelling 'Dixie! Pixie!' and Chris turns a violent red, shaking his head. Then next up is Martyn's dad, looking like a bouncer with his tattoos and grim face and bald head. My heart flips a beat. What if they're going through *all* our mums and dads, one by one? What if my dad is up next? I feel a spurt of angry pleasure inside. Oh, I'd just love to see him up there. First the embarrassment of being the wicked vicar who had to leave the church 'cos he can't keep his dick under control. Then playing it all down and getting himself a management job with a respectable sheen and a briefcase he can swing to work every morning. I can just see his fancy boss and colleagues all whispering and prodding, *Did you hear about his son and what he did well I blame the parents.*

'Martyn: we're worried about you,' says Martyn's dad. His expression doesn't match his words: he looks as though he'd much prefer to beat Martyn up.

Martyn waves a sullen 'V' sign at the screen but his shoulders shrink, his eyes flashing with fear.

I turn back to the screen, dreading, hoping, waiting for Dad's face, my heart beat quickening but – to my shock – *Mr Abdilla* appears on the screen. He's dressed in a suit, our school a benign silhouette in the background.

'Boys – Jon, Jeremiah, Thomas, Chris, Raymond, Martyn – I'd like to appeal to you. Padma Laxsmi isn't a terrorist. I realise you probably feel frustrated and think we don't understand or we're being naive. But I have honestly gone to the police and checked up on her, and I've spoken to her family and friends, and I can honestly say that she is innocent. I'm afraid you've all made a terrible mistake. There was never a bomb. Please come back safely. If you bring Padma back now, I promise you that there'll be no trouble. You won't be arrested or charged. I've spoken to Padma's mother and she won't be pressing any charges against you.'

Padma's mother appears on the screen. Her eyes are swollen and her voice snags with snot as she begs us to bring her precious daughter back. We all shift uncomfortably. Suddenly I feel panic rising in my stomach. I can hear my mother's voice in my head, hissing, *Come on, Jon, why don't you ever bother to think things through properly? You never look before you leap!* I hadn't thought at all about whether SNAKE's mum might press charges. After all, no matter how many videos we make, she'll never be able to accept the reality that her daughter is a cold-blooded killer, will she? In which case, what if she persuades them that we're wrong? What if we all end up in jail? SNAKE might be guilty and we might be innocent; she might be the murderess and we might be heroes; she might be black and we might be white – but what does it matter, in the end? I always thought only bad people ever went to prison. But then I remember what happened to my dad, before he left me and mum. The vandals who broke into the church one day, smashed the stained-glass window, looted the church funds. And when he tried to take them to court, they got off with counselling and threatened to sue him for keeping a church locked when they needed a holy place to seek peace. I remember him saying in a bitter voice that didn't belong to him, *This country's upside down. We're a nation who worships the god of PC at all expense. There's no justice any more . . .*

Then I remember: *I'll be okay. The God of Hebetheus is protecting us.* All the same, as the newsreader babbles on, I find myself willing the screen to flash back to Mr Abdilla. I just want to see his face, to hear him again reassuring us that we won't get into trouble . . .

'The Asian actors of Michael Winterbottom's film *The Road to Guantánamo* were arrested yesterday,' says the newsreader, 'under the Prevention of Terrorism Act . . .'

We wait a few more minutes, but it's over: our story is done. I frown, feeling an empty disappointment. I wonder why my dad wasn't interviewed. Did he just shrug and say *No comment, not my son any more, nothing to do with me?* Bastard.

Still, we were on TV.

But – *bastard*. He doesn't give a toss about me. Even Martyn's dad who beats him gives a toss; at least he notices him even if it's only to hit him. But no – my dad is too busy screwing his blonde bimbo to bother fretting about his precious son –

Raymond switches the TV off. He looks around, his lips thin.

'Well?'

'Fundamentalists!' Martyn breaks the silence, his cry stinging.

'They've only just got our video,' says Jeremiah, frowning. 'They probably watched it very quickly, rushed out the news. We'll see what they say at six o'clock tonight. The point is – we made it on!'

'We did,' Martyn says. 'We were on, Jeremiah, we were on!'

He gives Jeremiah a light punch and Jeremiah laughs and suddenly the euphoria hits us. We were on TV. And even if Dad wasn't on it, I can't believe he wasn't *watching*. Mum would have called him, I know she would.

We were on TV. We jump around and punch each other and then Martyn scrunches up a piece of old newspaper. He kicks it to me, yelling, 'Goal!' I stare down at it doubtfully, then attempt a kick. Martyn cries, 'Nice one!' and dribbles it to Chris. I look over at Jeremiah. For a moment he looks as though he might object – but at the last minute he bursts into a grin.

We play with raw, sweaty exuberance. I've never liked playing football but I find myself scoring three heart-pumping goals. Only Thomas won't join in; he stands on the sidelines, his arms folded, looking bored.

Finally, we collapse on to the floor breathlessly and talk dreamily about what we will do when we've saved the world; the temples we will build, the souls we will save.

We pray together. We bow to the east, to the north, to the south, to the west, to give thanks for our publicity. We pray that our message will spread far and wide until we touch every soul in the world.

And then comes the knock at the door.

# 12.30 P.M.

'Hello?'

A voice, floating through the wooden door. 'Hello?' A female voice, with a Suffolk tinge.

'Shit!' Martyn cries. 'They've found us, they've found us.'

We all make for the hallway, but Jeremiah calls us back.

'Martyn – you go,' he whispers. 'Just go and look through the spyhole.'

Martyn returns and hisses: 'There's a woman at the door.'

Raymond splutters.

'We'll just ignore her,' he whispers. 'There's nobody home.'

We all stand still. My eyes are level with Raymond's Adam's apple. It seems to roll under his skin as though a finger is rotating a marble.

We wait for another knock, but there is none. Our ears tingle, acute: we hear a sigh, a mutter and then the crunch of footsteps.

'She's gone,' says Martyn.

'Wait,' Jeremiah cuts in. He darts to the window, peers through the net curtain, then whirls back. 'Jesus – open the door, open the fucking door!'

'What!'

'She's going round the back!'

'You open it!' Jeremiah cries at me.

'Me?' I cry palely.

'You go, Jon –'

'I can go,' Thomas volunteers.

I go.

I run out into the hallway. I pray to God to reach a hand inside me and still the wild horses in my heart; I pray for him to speak through me in a calm and deceptive manner. I mustn't let Jeremiah down again. After my past mistakes, this might be my last chance.

Raymond darts across the hallway into the kitchen; the rest draw back quickly into the Prayer Room. I open the door. Nothing. Nothing but grass and stone and an empty road and a bitter skyline.

'Hello? *Hello?*' I call out. The blowing wind steals the sound of my words. 'Hello?' I call more loudly, stepping out on to the gravel.

'Oh – there you are!' The woman, who is just about to veer round the side of the house, comes waddling back. I quickly regain my territory, stepping back into the house, on to the WELCOME mat.

'You must be Ned,' she says, smiling up at me.

I don't reply. I just look her up and down with wide eyes. She is wearing dirty jeans and a check shirt and one of those green coats posh people wear – 'Barbers', my mum told me, or whatever they're called. Her face looks as though it's made of bacon and her hair as though it belongs to a Scottie dog's.

'So, Ned, did Walter get back from the home?'

'Er, no,' I mutter awkwardly.

'Surely Brenda's here with you?'

I glance back at the Prayer Room. Chris's face peers out an inch; he looks on the verge of hysterical laughter. His eyes bulge and he shrugs at me.

'I could drop by later,' she says.

'No,' I cry. Her blue eyes widen and I gulp, heart pumping. What would Jeremiah do in this situation, what would he say? *Improvise.* 'Brenda – oh – Nan, you mean! Nan's ill, so I'm – I'm just looking after her.'

'Right.' She knows something's wrong but she keeps on smiling, showing off teeth like chunks of bad apple. Her gaze flickers to the hall, trying to crowbar past my shoulder but I fill the doorway. 'Tell Brenda she can come over for a cuppa as soon as she's better.'

'Sure, I'll tell Brenda – Nan,' I say, the sweat in my voice cooling. 'I'll tell Nan you came by. It's cool. I'll tell her.'

'All right, my love. Well, bye.'

I watch her walk off. Raymond hisses for me to shut the door but I ignore him. I know that Jeremiah will want to be told every detail. So I stand and watch her. I watch her walk down the road, a brisk but wobbling stroll in her wellingtons. I watch her pass another farmhouse – she is diminishing into a stick now – and then turn up the path to a cottage. As she opens the gate, she seems to look back at me. I pull back and quickly close the door.

I turn. Raymond emerges from the shadow of the kitchen doorframe, holding a piece of piping. My eyes travel from the tip, gloved in his meaty freckled fist, to its jagged black end. I picture what would have happened if the woman had barged in.

Raymond. Doesn't he remember book two of Hebetheus: *And we shall always act in peace and never harm another human being?*

Sometimes I wonder how he and Jeremiah can be related.

# 1 P.M.

**We congregate in the kitchen** for a group discussion.

At first, it's impossible to hear anything. Our group is like a mirror dropped on the floor: our communal heart smashed to shards, voices shattering and splintering over each other. Then Jeremiah bangs the table with his fist and yells, 'QUIET!' We fall silent, breathless, settling.

'The next time I see Ned, I'm going to give him a bloody piece of my mind!' Raymond cuts in. 'God, I don't know. I could call Matt, see if he can suggest somewhere – a warehouse, somewhere safer, where people won't come knocking on the bloody door.'

'And how reliable is Matt?' Martyn snaps. 'I mean, Ned wasn't. What if this Matt calls the police?'

'Matt and I go back a long way,' Raymond says sharply. 'He'd never do that, and nor would Ned. Look, he can find us somewhere, I know he can!'

'What, and move our hostage?' Jeremiah cries. He sits down on a chair, presses his hands into a steeple. 'She's a terrorist, don't forget. She's highly dangerous. Now that we've kidnapped her, her other terrorist friends might well start looking for us.'

We all pause in shocked silence, considering. What if they've found out all our addresses? I think of my mum, lying at the bottom of the stairs.

'Furthermore, we'd be in the public eye. No, we stay here.'

'But we can pray to God to protect us from her friends. I mean, we just can't stay here!' Martyn interjects. His face is very red, his fist curled around a chair top. I feel uneasy. My eyes flit around the group. Thomas is always calm and balanced whenever we have a group discussion but, like Chris, I tend to curl up and remain silent. It's not that I don't have ideas, or that I can't think for myself, but I'm never very good at putting them into words, so I tend to swim with the current of the group.

Martyn, though, seems to almost enjoy arguing. At St Sebastian's he always got picked by teachers to lead debates. Once we had a debate on 'Should Immigrants be Allowed into the Country'; it was obviously one of those PC debates manufactured so that the evil viewpoint would lose, but Martyn spoke so persuasively that he won by fourteen votes to ten and Mrs Kay flushed with embarrassment.

'We can't stay here!' Martyn repeats. 'Jesus, this whole thing is a farce. We're on TV, only people think we're mad Christians, nobody has given one toss about our message, nobody in the government's debating anything, we have a dead old grandma in a bed and now a mad woman is knocking at our door!'

We all fall silent, stung by the truth of his words. And then we all look to Jeremiah.

Jeremiah stares at Martyn steadily, without blinking.

'Let's take this one thing at a time. We need to be patient. The government are no doubt considering the point we made about the Prevention of Terrorism Act. They're probably discussing it right now –'

'Oh, yeah, sure,' says Martyn.

Jeremiah recoils, frowning and I feel my heart tense. I hate the way that Martyn sometimes challenges Jeremiah. He forgets that to interrupt Jeremiah is to interrupt the flow of God.

'Martyn does have a point,' Raymond cuts in as Jeremiah bristles. 'We thought that we'd have some kind of response right away – even if they just said they were debating it. All right, we weren't sure if they'd give us the money for our temple. But we all thought they would debate the Prevention of Terrorism Act immediately. We need to do something more.'

'I mean, what if these other terrorist friends she has actually go and put the bomb there anyway?' Martyn blathers on. 'I mean, they're dangerous, that A-Q lot.'

'But we don't even know if she is a Muslim,' I say, blushing, a thought which has been churning inside me for some days. 'I mean, just because she's black – well, brown – I mean, coloured. I mean, she might be a Sikh or –'

'Yeah, well, what difference does that make?' Martyn says. 'A terrorist is a terrorist. It doesn't matter what religion they are. She can belong to the religion of nutcases for all I care.'

'Yeah, but that means she can't be –' I begin.

'S-s-someone,' Chris tries to interrupt.

'Let Chris speak,' Jeremiah says and I shut up quickly, relieved to have the spotlight of attention away from me.

'I w-w-watched this T-T-TV programme about t-t-terrorism,' Chris says, the spotlight tangling his words up into even tighter knots. 'And – and – it w-w-was about t-these A-A-Americans who sh-sh-shot a t-terrorist – b-b-but as soon as the t-t-terrorist was d-d-dead, a-another m-man took his place, s-s-s –'

'Yes, we *did* discuss this –' Jeremiah says.

'Yeah,' Martyn cries, 'you said they'd be too frightened now we've kidnapped her, that they'll be lying low right now, but I mean, these guys aren't fairies!'

'But –'

'*And*,' Martyn cuts in, 'it's not just our school. She might have other friends who are terrorists in other schools. If the bomb bloody well does go off, then it'll serve them right –'

'It won't serve anybody right!' Jeremiah nearly shouts.

'But –'

'No: listen. Listen to me. Martyn, we stand for peace. I mean, have you ever thought about, really thought about what happens to people when a bomb goes off? It's not like in the movies, you know. People don't just die. They lose bits of their bodies; they lie under bits of brick and metal, with blood streaming over their faces. You know, my uncle was part of the clean-up operation for King's Cross and he said it was like a hell in that tube station. So don't say it serves anybody right.'

As Jeremiah finishes his speech, I feel my heart burn for him. He's put Martyn in his place and nobody else, not even Mr Abdilla could ever put Martyn in his place. He's put emotion into words in the way I could never do. I can feel the good coming off his heart in blazes of purity that blast into my heart and make me feel small and selfish and wish I could understand the world the way he does.

Martyn ducks his head and mutters a *sorry*. But it's a slightly offhand one.

Chris says sorry too. He sounds as though he means it.

Raymond nods, rubbing his beard.

'I say we stay here,' Jeremiah repeats. 'But we'll not be stupid about it. Listen: we just need a few days. The woman's not going to worry for at least a good week – she thinks Brenda's resting. Jon handled that well.' He nods at me and my heart sings. 'And in the meantime, we'll have guard duty: someone at the front, keeping an eye on the house. We'll take it in turns.'

We all nod, relieved: we don't have to move, everything will be all right, everything is still going to plan. Only Martyn looks upset, almost as though he doesn't want everything to be wrapped up so easily.

'But even if we stay here, what about the fact that nobody got our message?'

'Look,' says Jeremiah, standing up. 'D'you know how many people just watched that programme? Ten million, fifteen million, maybe even twenty. Maybe more. *Twenty-five million*. Think of that.'

For a moment the figure dazzles us. Even if I add up all the people in my street and neighbouring streets, that seems a lot. But twenty million is a number I can't even fit into my head.

'But twenty-five million people now think we're Christian fundamentalists when we have nothing to do with Christianity whatsoever!' Martyn cries.

'But what do you expect?' Jeremiah cries. 'Come on, Martyn, did you really think they would shove aside all the other news and devote a twenty-minute slot to outlining all the aims of the Hebetheus and conclude by telling everyone to join?'

'Well . . .' Martyn looks around, satisfied to see we all look bewildered. 'Well, yeah, I mean, what else was the point?'

'Look, when Jesus first came down to earth, people thought he was crazy. He had a very small band of followers. How many people turned up at his birth? Only three wise men. Three. Not hundreds, just three. And how many believe in him now, thousands of years later? Millions of people! All over the world. Now we all know that we don't believe in Jesus, but the story serves us well. Because this is the way new ideas get introduced into society. They trickle in slowly, slowly, slowly . . .'

His voice rises with every word, like a tidal wave gaining momentum, and I feel my heart swell.

' . . . and people can't digest complex things, at first. The media is very black and white. Everything has to be short, everything has to be in sound bites. So they think we're Christians now. But they won't, over time. Look – it's like the Hebetheus religion is this big jigsaw, and we have a lot of the pieces, but they can only do one piece at a time. And there will be people who understand us right from the start – the chosen ones, whom God has blessed. Then there'll be people who come round slowly, who will keep wondering and keep questioning us but, in the end, will wake up one morning and know this is the truth. And then there'll be people who never understand us. They'll go to Hell, and it's very sad, but there's nothing that can be done for them.

'But don't say our TV appearance was a failure. Because it's not. It's been a big success. It's the start of something wonderful. We are doing God's work. We're great!' His voice crashes over us, leaving us singing with a sweet wash of relief and new hope. 'So let's be happy! Let us speak to God one more time and give our thanks!'

We are uplifted. Even Martyn looks appeased. We go into the Prayer Room and pray for protection. Somehow it feels as though the invasion has tightened the invisible threads that bind us, woven us into one firm rope. As I bow and my nose touches the floor, I feel – I feel – I feel embarrassed to use the word – but this is how it feels – as though I love them all. My dear Brothers. My dear Brothers.

As we rise, we hear the siren. We all freeze, eyes mooning. Jeremiah's shoulders slacken before the rest of us as we realise it is a distant threat.

As we leave the Prayer Room, there is a sense of fragility among us. A sense that time is short and we have so much to do and may God help them to understand us before it is too late.

# 3 P.M.

**After prayers, we suddenly realise** how hungry we are. Raymond lightens the mood by putting on an apron that must have belonged to the old lady, white plastic with ducks waddling across it in yellow rows. He cooks us up some beans on burnt toast.

It's only after we've eaten that Chris points out that SNAKE might be hungry too. The thought surprises me; I find it hard to imagine that a terrorist like her might even need food; secretly I'd imagined she must live off bad dreams and rats' tails.

'So,' Jeremiah asks pleasantly. 'Who would like to volunteer to take SNAKE her food?'

An awkward silence. We all avoid each other's eyes.

'Jon.' Jeremiah's eyes rest on me. 'Raymond told me you had a few questions about your Initiation. Well, before we proceed with the ceremony I feel you should undergo a few more challenges. Take SNAKE her food.'

'Er, okay.' I gulp and take the tray. There is a glass of water and a plate of bread and butter.

'Hang on,' Martyn says. 'I mean – she's been really – you know – *quiet* – since we put her down there. Shouldn't he take his knife?'

I grip the tray tightly, my heart thudding, visions of

SNAKE slashing my skin flashing across my retinas.

'No,' Jeremiah reflects. 'We checked the cellar last night, there's nothing she can use as a weapon. Actually, this reminds me of a point I must make to all of you. At first not everyone is going to believe us about SNAKE, not everyone is going to appreciate and understand our behaviour. We need to take care that we never stoop to her level. On some occasions – such as last night – we may need to use force to keep her under control. But, otherwise, we never inflict any harm on her. Understand? We must be whiter than white, purer than pure. We must show her compassion. Our aim, ultimately, is to save her soul, to introduce her to Hebetheus, to bring her on to our side.'

'Okay,' I say, my voice quivering. The tray is beginning to weigh heavy in my hands.

'In the meantime,' Jeremiah says, 'if you can find out anything more about her plots and plans, that would also be useful. Befriend her, even. But don't get too close, Jon. You'll be good with her – you're gentle with women. But remember: she is a snake.'

I turn away, slowly treading down the steps, all eyes on me. *Gentle with women.* I don't like to tell Jeremiah that actually girls scare me. I'm still a virgin and the closest I ever came to a girlfriend was Lisa. I danced with her one night at the school disco. The next day, I punched her number into the phone over fifteen times before I finally had the guts to pick up the receiver and connect. She said, 'Who? Who?' and I had to repeat my name. Then, finally, she remembered me. I asked if she wanted to go to the movies, but she laughed softly and said, 'I'm sorry, Jon, but you're just not my type – you're too nice.'

Since joining the Hebetheus religion, I haven't had to

worry about girls any more. Jeremiah says they are a distraction from the Path. Even when one of Lisa's friends later walked up to me and said, 'If Lisa would say yes if you asked her out, would you ask her?' I ignored the flutter in my stomach and said I wasn't interested. She kept asking me, over a number of weeks – it was almost as though my every 'No' fed Lisa's desire for me. But in the end, they gave up on me. I have lived like a monk for the last six months – except for some private moments when I have relieved my desire swiftly, with a sense of ugly shame.

In truth, it was a relief. I find expressing myself hard enough as it is, but talking to girls is nearly impossible.

As I climb down the steps to see SNAKE, my heart begins to quiver. I don't want her to see that I'm afraid of her. *Oh, God*, I pray, *make me brave.*

I put down the tray and unlock the door. It's pitch black; I can't see anything. I walk forwards blindly.

'SNAKE?' I call out gently.

No answer. My fear rises. What if Martyn's right? What if she's lying in the shadows, ready to spring and attack? I quickly put down the food and kick the door shut behind me; at least she can't escape, even if she pounces.

'I've – I've brought you some food.'

My eyes begin to adjust to the dark: smudges take on line and form. The wine racks. The boxes. And a figure, crouched in the corner, eyes flickering. I realise then that she is the one who is afraid.

'Would you like some water?' I say. 'Anything?'

'Which one of them are you?' her voice sounds strange: thin, as though it comes from a spirit, not a human. 'I can't see you.'

'I'm Jon. You – you know me . . . so . . . I'm here to help you,' I say loudly. I kneel down on the floor, cross-legged, folding my arms. 'I'm here to tell you about the Hebetheus religion and why you should turn your back on your wicked ways, so that you can understand why you should join us. But first you can eat.'

The shape shuffles forward. I steel myself and resist the urge to pull away. To my surprise, I see that her eyes are wet.

'Are you hungry? Please – eat.'

'I – I can't with these on.'

I don't even know where the key is. Then I stop myself – surely this is more cunning? Oh yes – I'll take off her cuffs and then she'll embarrass me again. There are limits to the compassion I can show her.

'You have to just try. Bend down, use your mouth. It's fine.'

She sniffs and leans down. Her hair falls forward; she shakes it back. She takes the bread in her mouth, trying to chew a bite off; half of it breaks away and the other half remains hanging from her lips. I make a mental note to cut it into small pieces next time.

She chews and chews, quickly, swallowing it down hard. She leans down to eat the next half, when emotion seems to overcome her. She sits up, tears falling in cascades, trickling into her hair, dropping on to her cuffs. A little bit of bread is still hanging from her mouth.

At the sight of her tears, my compassion becomes real, no longer an maxim but a pain in my heart. I realise that, for all her evils, she is human too.

'Don't worry,' I say, 'I know this is all – this is – I mean – look.' I gulp. 'I . . .' What should I do, what should I do? *Improvise.* I'll speak the words of Hebetheus; that will cleanse and reassure her. '"Hebetheus is a new religion which aims to avoid the mistakes of past religions."' The sound of her crying hits my heart like hailstones until I can't keep the door shut any more. '"Old religions are full of lies, corruption and mistakes –"'

She reaches up to wipe away her tears. Then she realises her hands are cuffed. She lets out a wail of frustration, then wipes her face against her sleeve, sniff-hiccuping.

I can't bear it any more. I crawl a few more feet.

'Please don't cry,' I beg her desperately. 'Look, I know you're upset, but we really do want to help you. This isn't . . . look, I know you think this is some sort of weird cult, and that we're all crazy, but it's not. The Hebetheus religion has really helped me, and it could really help you too, SNAKE . . .' She has, at least stopped crying – but now she is staring at me so intently that I break off, feeling my cheeks warm.

There is a brief, burning silence. Why is it so hard to translate my feelings into words, to explain what the Hebetheus religion has done for me? I've forgotten what it's like to be ignorant. I can't understand why she doesn't leap at it right away. A desperate frustration kicks inside me. How can I make her *see*?

Then I remember the very first words Jeremiah said to me.

'Are you happy?' I ask her. *Stupid question*, I realise. 'I mean – before you –'

'Why do you call me SNAKE?' she suddenly interrupts. 'I don't get why you all keep calling me that.'

'Er . . . It's just a kind of codename.' I pause nervously, wondering if I'm allowed to tell her that.

'Oh really? So what's your codename then? Dickhead?'

I splutter in shock. I realise she has flipped back to the feisty SNAKE again, the SNAKE who kicked and thrashed in the van when we tried to hold her down.

'Look, we're here to help you –'

'*Help me?* Look – I mean – just look at this –' she shows me her wrists. The cuffs have rubbed against the skin, forming red bracelets of pain. 'You've kidnapped me!' Her voice begins to rise hysterically. 'I mean – what is this? Some kind of schoolboy joke? What d'you really want? Money? Is that what this is all about? 'Cos you're crazy, my parents don't have any, we're not rich, you picked the wrong girl!'

In my anger, I forget to be compassionate.

'Yeah, yeah,' I cry, 'just deny everything! Just pretend we're some evil guys who want money. We don't care about money. You know why you're here, SNAKE!'

'What d'you mean? I don't know why I'm here! *You* tell *me*. God, you are going to be in so much trouble. My dad – when I get out of here – he'll *kill* you. You'll be expelled, all of you! You'll be arrested.'

'No, SNAKE.' I shake my head firmly. 'You're the one who's going to be arrested.'

'How the hell WILL I BE ARRESTED? YOU DON'T GET ARRESTED FOR BEING A KIDNAP VICTIM.'

'No, but you *do* get arrested for planning to put a bomb in the school.'

SNAKE stares at me with an open mouth.

'Are you serious? I mean – when you mentioned that last night I thought it was just part of your stupid game – I mean, come on, you're not *serious* –'

'You know I'm serious. Jeremiah overheard your conversation. We know everything. So there's no point in lying.'

There is a long silence. Tears fill her eyes again, but she blinks them away fiercely.

'You really believe this?' she asks. She shakes her head incredulously. '*What* conversation?'

'You know the conversation, the one you had in the

changing room when you thought nobody else was around. He heard every word.'

'Oh really? Oh really? And where'd d'you think I was going to hide this bomb? In my pencil case? 'Cos yeah, sure, I had an exploding pencil sharpener.'

'It's not a laughing matter!' I cry. 'These are people's lives we're talking about – how you can *joke* –'

'I'm not bloody joking! You know the attacks on London last year? The bus which blew up? My cousin was on that bus. She lost her legs, she's stuck in a wheelchair now for life, and so sure I don't find this funny one bit.'

I swallow, shocked. This isn't going the way I'd imagined it; I had anticipated a gradual unpeeling, until finally she would spill a confession which I then carry out to Jeremiah like an offering in both hands.

She almost sounds genuine. But then I remember Jeremiah's words of warning: *The most dangerous thing about SNAKE is not that she lies. It's that she's deluded. She thinks she's doing good when she is doing great harm. She does not realise how dangerous her actions are. Remember, this is the nature of evil. Nobody who does evil can ever imagine, can ever digest the fact that they are doing it – they always persuade themselves that it is the right thing, that they are doing good, that they have no other choice.*

I open my mouth to try another track, when she says, 'So do you have any idea why someone would want to become a terrorist? Can you think of why?'

'Well – I mean – you'd know best,' I say without thinking. She gives me a look of such deep fury that I hurry on, humouring her: 'I mean – they're evil, aren't they? They're a long way from undergoing a Soul Shif –' I break off, realising such concepts will go over her head.

'Crap,' she says emphatically.

The word hangs in the air, diffusing a nasty smell. I feel my cheeks burning; I can't believe she's getting the better of me.

'You think that terrorists become terrorists for a laugh? Of course they don't! Don't you even watch the news! A typical terrorist is some young guy who's lost his family and is burning up with rage against the West. Well, what do I have in common with that? I'm happy. I was happy. I was enjoying life, I was doing my homework, going out – I mean, I don't have any drum to bang, I don't have any message to get out there, I don't want to harm anyone, I wanna get good grades and become a doctor and I want to go to Cambridge so why – *why* – the fuck would I become a terrorist? I *like* the West. I love my country. And as for bombing St Sebastian's – as for killing my friends, my teachers, the people I love – well, it's just insane. I'd never do anything like that.'

'But – but – well – you're a Muslim,' I point out.

'So now you're saying all Muslims are terrorists? I mean, how prejudiced is that?'

'Well – no – but –'

'I'm not a Muslim.'

'What?'

'I'm not a Muslim.'

'So what are you then?'

'I'm a Hindu.'

'Oh.'

'Yeah. Oh. But even if I was a Muslim, I would still be innocent. God.'

'I know, I know. Tell me about Hinduism then,' I say quickly, still shocked by this new twist of her character. *Is she lying?* I wonder. *Is she teasing me?* 'Isn't that the one where you have lots of funny gods?'

'No. We worship *one* God, only our God expresses himself in different forms.'

Suddenly she withdraws, turning away, in on herself. 'It's hopeless. You're crazy. I'm scared.' Her voice breaks.

'I –' I feel upset at our broken connection. 'Have – have some water.' I pick it up.

'How am I supposed to drink out of that?'

'Well – here – I'll hold it,' I say.

'D'you remember?' she suddenly says. 'About a year ago, when you were new at school and you were behind in RE? And Mr Abdilla asked me to help you out with some homework about ethics, and I came over to your place and I helped you?'

I swallow. I haven't mentioned this to the Brotherhood, afraid what they might think if they knew I'd once fraternised with a terrorist.

'And then we watched *The Simpsons* and we sat in your room listening to music and we had such a good time.'

A flash of memory: sitting on the sofa together. Padma suddenly rolled up the *Radio Times* and playfully hit me and I tickled her and then Mum came in and thundered, 'What is this noise?' and we both cracked up. After that night, she gave me her number and I always meant to call but I was never sure if she just wanted me to call about homework or if she wanted to be friends, or something more and I was too shy to risk finding out.

But that happened in the past, to a naive and deluded and sinful Jon.

'I've forgotten,' I say quickly. 'Just have a drink, okay?'

I am about to let her drink, when she whispers something.

'What?'

'Kiss me.'

My eyes dart to her lips. A deep red rosebud. Then I realise that my mouth is hanging open and I quickly snap it shut. I get up, walk a few feet away and sit down cross-legged.

'I'm going to tell you the ten rules of the Hebetheus religion.'

'Okay.' Her voice is pale but there is almost a sing-song in it. 'But I'm thirsty. Can't I just have my water first?'

I pick up the glass at arm's length and hold it to her lips, letting her drink. I watch the water bead on her lips, the pink flick of her tongue as she licks them off. If she tries to kiss me, I'll teach her a lesson. She drinks a little more, then lifts her eyes to mine. If she tries to kiss me, I'll throw the water over her. All the hairs on my skin seem to quiver upright with static energy. It almost feels like that day when we went on a school trip to a National Trust property and Martyn eyed up the sign saying DO NOT TOUCH THE ORNAMENTS and the teacher said 'Martyn!' but we all knew he would do it as he always breaks the rules. Just before he reached out to stroke them, I felt my stomach tickle with a kind of angry pleasure.

'How can you do this?' she asks me. 'How can you take away a person's freedom? Isn't there any love for other people in your religion?'

I stumble back in shock, tipping over the water. It flows across the grain, seeping into the floorboards, soaking her thigh. I step back, then forwards, pick up the glass, set it upright. Only a little remains.

I tread back to the centre of the room and sit cross-legged. I stare at a patch of wall, about a foot above her head, where there is a mark in the shape of a question, and I recite for what seems like hours, my eyes blinking in strain, my voice becoming scrapy. As the words flow, I feel as though I am coming back; as though I have been venturing out into a forest, pricked by thorns, and now I have found my path again; all is well. My voice becomes cracked and hoarse, but I will not drink her water.

Suddenly: a loud bang at the door. SNAKE and I both jump. I rise, my legs shaky with cramp. It's Martyn and Chris. Martyn peers round the door at her, as if peeking a thrilled glance at a dangerous creature in a cage. Then they pull me out, quickly closing the door behind us.

'So have you found anything else out?' he hisses.

'What?'

'A confession? Stuff about her plans that we can use for the next video?'

'Well – not yet – but –'

'Well, Jeremiah says we can have a go,' Martyn cries excitedly.

'But I thought . . .' I trail off, looking at the teeth marks on his hand, now a faint blur of bruises. I feel irritated; I shrug it off. To be honest, SNAKE was tying my mind in knots and it's a relief to escape. 'Okay,' I say. 'Sure. See if you can learn anything from her.'

'Oh we will,' Martyn says, nudging Chris, who blushes and chuckles, 'oh, we will.'

I take one last glance in – to reassure her Martyn and Chris will treat her well – but she is huddled in a corner like a spider, her face a vague smudge.

They go in, slamming the door behind them. I jump. *We will . . . we will . . . we will . . .* sing-songs behind me. I turn back uneasily, then shrug and hurry upstairs to see if Jeremiah wishes me to take more divine dictation.

# 4 P.M.

'Is that someone coming?'

Thomas frowns and screws up his eyes.

We are in the front garden, fortifying our base. The landscape around is barren with winter: fields of hard brown, anorexic trees, sinister packs of forest. There are no houses nearby, though we can just about see the humped back of a local farmhouse and a spiral of smoke wreathing from its chimney. And then – a black shape. A figure? Heading our way?

'No – it's just a crow,' Thomas says. 'Look.'

The black shape spreads and soars into the clouds. I feel my heart follow it.

'It must be a good omen!' I say.

We return to laying out the stones.

When Jeremiah passed us a heavy brown sack and told us to fortify the cottage, I pictured metal mantraps, the type hunters use, with big fierce teeth that will snap an ankle like a twig.

I felt ashamed when he drew stones out of the bag, each painted with a Hebethean symbol.

'I want you to lay them out in a circle. You must make sure each stone is touching the other one. That's very important, d'you see? This way, we'll create a sacred circle, a linked chain of God's blessings, and nobody will be able to touch us.'

It is a joyful task: simple and neat. Back and forth we go, laying them out, stone on grass, stone on grass, stone on earwig, stone on dust. Suddenly, for the first time since we've arrived, I feel a sense of usefulness. The mental splinters SNAKE left in my mind are slowly eased out. For the past few weeks, everything I've done has felt spineless. Homework, lessons, riding my bike, playing my Gameboy. I've felt like an actor playing a part, waiting to be here, to become myself. Now my heart sings; I relish the pain in my muscles, the ache of my back as I stoop and stoop and stoop. Every stone I lay is a stepping-stone closer to Him; every stone is a bridge towards peace for all mankind. As each stone chinks against its brother, I feel a shivery feeling inside, and I can almost see the sparkles of magic leaping and fusing –

Suddenly: in the distance, the rumbling sound of a car.

We dive down. At the front of the garden is a thick wall of bushes. We push through their prickly softness into a green cave and kneel down on the hard earth. We stare through the zigzag gaps, watching the car swish past.

We wait a few more minutes. I fiddle with a twig, ripping off its arms and legs.

'Thomas, did you have to undergo an Initiation ceremony?' I whisper.

That's what I like about Thomas. A few weeks ago, I made the mistake of asking Martyn what his Initiation had involved and he'd merely replied, 'I can't tell you, but I can guarantee yours will never be as testing as mine was.' Chris too, was secretive about his. But I always feel that Thomas is on my side.

Thomas, however, doesn't reply. He is staring at a patch

of earth in deep fascination. He pushes his finger in, twists it, frowns deeply. He lifts his finger to his mouth and licks off the crumbs of earth. He looks at me and giggles.

'It tastes like God,' he whispers.

I laugh in faint confusion. I almost want to push my finger in and copy him. But I feel self-conscious; Thomas made it look perfectly normal but I worry I'll look crazy.

'It's warming up a bit now,' I whisper.

Thomas doesn't reply.

'What do you think of SNAKE?' I whisper.

He doesn't reply.

I give up. Maybe Jeremiah has ordered Thomas not to talk to me because I am not yet a proper member of the Brotherhood. Maybe I am tainting his higher purity in some way. Though that doesn't make total sense, as Thomas has been chatty in the past. I stare at a whorl of earth. It looks like a mountain; the spray of a dead feather above it forms a cloudy backdrop. Is this what the world looks like to God?

I become aware that Thomas is shifting beside me and I get up too, examining the circle. As we follow it round, I am dismayed to realise we have been working as two people. The line is jagged, looping out too far on the left side of the cottage. At the back we have a gap about a foot wide – and no stones left to fill it.

I turn to tell Thomas –

– but he has disappeared.

I hurry back to the front garden. Has he gone back inside the house?

Then I catch sight of him. *He is walking down the road.*

'Thomas – Thomas – where are you going?'

Thomas doesn't look back. He shoves his hands in his pockets, whistling.

'Thomas!' My whisper becomes a hiss. 'Thomas!' I risk calling out. 'Thomas!'

'I'm going for a walk,' he declares, without looking back, and walks off.

What's he playing at? Scenes from this morning's celebration flick-flack through my mind like a set of playing cards. Thomas not joining in with the footie. Thomas's weird, sad smirk. And what about last night, when he seemed to be crying? What if he's a mole? Like in those movies where a criminal pretends to be a policeman or a policeman pretends to be a criminal? What if he's going off now to update the police with a report about us? To collect a reward? I turn, ready to run into the house and tell Jeremiah.

But. What if Jeremiah told him to walk off and leave me here? What if I go and tell on him and leave the house unguarded and then Jeremiah tells me Thomas has been sent on a secret mission and then just at the moment I leave the house vulnerable someone comes along and catches us out? My stomach burns with savage frustration. Why am I always the one left out, the new boy, the one whom nobody tells anything? Jeremiah hasn't told me when my Initiation will be yet, I'm still waiting; and I'm waiting, and if Thomas walks off now and tells the police, it won't be my bloody fault.

Minutes pass. Oh, God, what should I do? *Improvise.* But how? Oh, God, please give me a sign, please guide me. I crouch down and pick up a small, blackened acorn. If it lands with its green cap facing me, then God is telling me that Thomas is on our side. But if it lands with its acorn facing me, then God is telling me that Thomas is a traitor.

I am just about to throw up the acorn when through the bushes I suddenly see someone walking by. I duck down sharply. *It's the woman who came by yesterday and banged on the door.*

As she passes, she looks at the house and walks on.

She stops. She looks at the house again. This morning we closed the curtains so that nobody could see in. She frowns. I tense, ready to run and raise the alarm.

Then she walks on. I let out a sigh of breath. My heart slows but refuses to settle; Thomas's absence keeps itching away until my heart feels raw and red with worry.

Finally, I see him coming back.

He crouches down beside me behind the bushes. His cheeks are ruddy, his breath short. He grins at me. Will I hear the sound of sirens now?

'Here.' He uncurls a red palm. A squashed fir cone.

'It looks like God,' he says. Then, as I blink, he checks his watch, suddenly switching back to being normal Thomas again, brisk and together and in charge. 'Hey, our time's up.' He checks the road is clear, gets up and walks to the house. As I get up, I suddenly notice the acorn. It landed sideways.

# 9 P.M.

(A CLOSE-UP OF SNAKE. THE BOTTOM HALF OF
HER FACE IS HIDDEN BY A WHITE BANDAGE.
HER BREATHS SOUND RAGGEDLY MUFFLED. HER
EYES ROLL.)

MARTYN voiceover:

This is the terrorist, SNAKE.
Take a good look at her. We
have interrogated her at
length and learnt that she
planned to put a bomb in the
lockers in St Sebastian's
School. We intervened and
prevented SNAKE from taking
this line of action. In the
meantime, we saved the lives
of hundreds of innocent boys
and girls from our school. We
have reason to believe SNAKE
is not the only one out there.
We have learnt that SNAKE is
just part of a whole network
of forty-five dangerous

teenagers in schools planning
these acts. We would therefore
like you to listen to us and
take us seriously.

(A CLOSE UP OF THE SWASTIKA SYMBOL ON THE
WALL.)

MARTYN voiceover:

We belong to the religion of
Hebetheus. We believe in peace
for all mankind. We are watching the news on a daily basis.
We are waiting for a response
to our demands. We want the
government to promise they
will have a vote in the Houses
of Parliament to amend the
Prevention of Terrorism Act
and make it tougher! We want
the police to promise they
will investigate SNAKE and
smash her ring of forty-five
terrorist friends. We want a
million pounds to build a
temple to spread our message.
Time is running out. If we do
not hear of this action happening within the next two
days, we will kill SNAKE.

This is not a lame threat. We
will act in the name of peace
to wipe out all terrorism on
the planet.

# 11 P.M.

**I feel weirdly close to crying,** but I won't cry, I won't, because then I'd be like a girl and maybe being too much of a girl is why I'm not allowed in.

I tug off my polo neck and pull on my school shirt, my substitute for pyjamas. I lie down in our bedroom, alone in a sea of musty mattresses. I open up the *Book of Hebetheus* and try to focus.

The rest of the Brotherhood are in the Prayer Room. Jeremiah told me I couldn't join in because I 'wasn't ready' for the knowledge they were discussing. Because I hadn't been Initiated yet. I nodded and smiled and said *Sure, fine, I understand*. But I don't understand.

*Be patient*, I tell myself. Jeremiah knows what he's doing. Just read.

A member of the Brotherhood of the Hebetheus should avoid reading books, watching TV or reading newspapers at all times. Books are dangerous because they encourage us to enjoy evil as entertainment. Examine the hypocrisy of our nation. A man will buy a newspaper on his way to work which details on the front page the horror of a child who has been taken by a killer; he will express inner dismay and then, a few minutes later, begin reading and enjoying a book about a killer who abuses children. We express dismay when terrorists blow up our buildings, then run to the cinemas to watch disaster movies where people perish in falling buildings. All art is evil, because it feeds on our lower and baser instincts, telling us to extract pleasure from pain, thrill from fear, security from watching others suffer whilst knowing we are safe. Too often, they encourage us to worship villains (Hannibal Lecter) etc. and blur the boundaries between good and evil, creating complex moral messages which in turn cause audiences to feel confused about what is good and what is evil. But the Hebetheus states that good is good and evil is evil and all art is evil for suggesting black may be white or white may be black. Read only the *Book of Hebetheus*; all else will pollute and confuse your mind.

Why aren't I ready yet? What's *wrong* with me? It is because I messed up and let SNAKE nearly escape? When I first met Jeremiah, he said that I was special. The word seemed to stretch out in my imagination like a beautiful gold cloth I wrapped around myself and whenever I thought of my dad and Celine, I'd remember: Jeremiah thinks I'm special. God thinks I'm special. But a few weeks later, when he was teaching about the Dangers of Women, he told me I was 'fragile'. I didn't understand what he meant by that. He said, 'What I mean is, Jon, you're sensitive. The world is too harsh for you to really exist in it. In this survival of the fittest, you're not going to go far.' I was stung. Did he mean I was weak? A wuss, a girl? But then he shook his head and explained: 'Those who thrive in this survival of the fittest are those who are cruel. Look at the richest and most powerful people in the world. They deal in arms; they make huge profits by running sweatshops and forcing children to work twenty-hour days. People who get ahead do so by trampling on the weak. To be weak in this world is to be noble. But I didn't use the word weak: I just said you were fragile.' There was Jeremiah again: pulling words out of a hat like a magician, turning lead into gold, making us see the whole world in a different way.

I think I know what they're discussing: SNAKE's shocking links to a network of forty-five terrorists. When Martyn announced he'd extracted this confession from her, Jeremiah acted as though he'd performed a bloody miracle. He's been treating Martyn like a deity ever since. I keep trying to push my jealousy away but I can't help it. Martyn's triumph feels like my failure. Why didn't she confess this to *me* in my interrogation? I wish I'd been stronger with her. That was my problem – I felt sorry for her. I was *too* compassionate. I should have been more tough. But no, instead I let her weep all over me. I was weak.

Because actually that *is* what fragile means.

And is that why I haven't been asked to join in –

*Shut up Jon, shut up*, I tell myself fiercely, miserable and weary with tying my mind in knots. I pull my sleeping bag over my head and bury my face in my pillow and eventually I sleep.

Dreams come. Hot, poisonous dreams. Dreams of SNAKE . . .

I wake up suddenly, weak, shuddering. My first thought is: *Oh, God, I'm going to have to wash my sheets without Mum noticing*. Then I remember.

The bedroom is still empty. I reach down and feel my

spent cock, limp like a dead seahorse.

Then in the gloom I am aware of a moving light. A figure at the door. He beckons me gently, then puts a finger to his lips.

I rise up, glad of the darkness to hide the damp of my trousers. I come closer; Raymond smiles. Then, suddenly –
– he grabs hold of me.

At first I think he's play-fighting and I kick him gently, feigning a tussle. Then Jeremiah comes at me. A black bag veers towards my face. Then – wham – I am in darkness and I am screaming but the cloth soaks up my screams –

# MIDNIGHT

– *It's okay, Jon. It's all right.* His voice is very close, tickling through the stitching of the bag. *Trust me, okay. Trust me.*

I feel his hand slip into mine. The feel of his long, cool fingers reassures me for a moment before the panic flares up again.

– *Walk forward.*

I'm being punished. Was it the wet dream? Because I let SNAKE escape? Are they going to – hurt me – are they going to – My hand splays out, feeling the painted brick of the wall. Are we going forwards towards the front door or backwards towards the cellar? A breeze – a door opening? A feeling of space. We are entering a room. I can smell fresh paint and incense – the Prayer Room?

– *Sit down.*

I collapse on the floor, my palms feeling feeling . . . A floor, a wall. A texture of paint, the dried gloop of brushstrokes. Yes, the Prayer Room. Surely they wouldn't hurt me in the Prayer Room?

Can I take off the bag, I try to say, but the cloth slurs my words into a drunken-sounding spool.

– *Trust me, Jon, be still and be calm. It's all right. This is the first part of your Initiation. Be still.*

My body falls slack with relief. A trickle of sweat slithers down my cheek, soaks against the cloth, dribbles back salty on to my lips. My Initiation; thank God. *Thank God!*

Footsteps; whispers; the flare of a lighter.

– *Take off your clothes.*

– What?

– *Take off your clothes. It's all right. Trust us.*

I pull off my black school trousers. Dampness smears my fingers and I am glad of the darkness to cover my shame. My fingers brush my boxers, then flit to my shirt, feeling my way down my buttons. I take off my shirt, the cool air caressing my chest. No command is spoken but I can feel it heavy in the air: I pull off my boxers.

– *The Hebetheus God . . .*

– *He waits and . . .*

– *Time for . . .*

Whispers, too quiet for me to decipher.

Fingers, skin against my skin. I yelp and hear their laughter. Are they laughing at me? Is this all a joke? Did they ever mean to –

Someone pulls the bag from my head. My eyes wince, then widen, flitting.

Jeremiah is kneeling in front of me, a candle and a small saucer of water by his side, a knife – *my knife* (they must have taken it from under my pillow) – in his hands.

The others sit in a circle, cross-legged, their faces smudged with shadow.

Goosebumps prickle over my skin; I feel more naked than naked. I almost want to pull the bag back over my head.

– *Relax*, Jeremiah whispers.

– *You're ready now, for your Initiation ceremony.*

I look up sharply. He looks at me with eyes of love. Then with the tip of his forefinger, he pushes my head back down and wields the knife.

I freeze in terror. I think of Abraham, whom God asked to kill his son as a test. I know that if I am meant to die now before God, I must accept my fate. I think of my mum, the way I left her crumpled on the stairs before I ran away, and my heart cries a silent apology to her. I think of Dad too, but I feel only hatred for him.

I feel the knife slide against my scalp. I screw up my eyes tight. I think with a strange, detached curiosity: so this is what the moment feels like just before death strikes.

I wait for the pain.

But there is none.

Just a light scrape. A lock of dark hair falls like a feather.

I realise I have been holding my body taut, every muscle stretched to screaming point. I sag; my muscles turn to liquid trembling jelly. As I feel the cold knife coming down again, the words sink in. *My Initiation ceremony.* My cleansing. I am not worthless; I have not failed him. Jeremiah feels I am ready, that I deserve to belong. Oh, thank God, oh, thank you.

Every scrape of the knife causes a warm bubbly feeling to break a path through my heart. The fingers on my skull pause, as though sensing the feeling. Tenderness seeps from his fingers back into my skull. My heart beats, and swells.

Jeremiah begins to chant softly, as he bathes my head with water.

I silently echo back each word until my body is a choir of singing cells. His voice becomes sleepily hypnotic and at times I almost pitch forward into the cradle of his lap. I open my eyes and watch the last fluff of hair separate like a puffclock and swirl to the ground. I notice a few splats of blood on the floor; I relish them; I want him to cut me, to cut himself, to feel my blood mingling with his.

– *Jon?* Jeremiah says.

Water trickles from my hairline, damps my eyes.

– *Yes?*

He hands me something. I recoil, thinking it's a snake. It drops to the floor.

He picks it up, laughing, and I laugh and then our eyes meet and he holds my gaze steady. As I stare into those blue eyes, I feel unspeakably touched. As though I have just received a medal. As though Jeremiah has cut away all my sins and worries. As though some inner war that has been raging inside me is now over. The past is truly past. I am a new Jon and God is my new father.

Then he sits upright, his face a beautiful mix of sternness and serenity and I know then that his soul has opened to God and he is about to impart some knowledge of great profundity. His voice is so light and cool it seems to float through the air, ephemeral as the candle smoke.


– You helped to kidnap SNAKE; that was the first test of your faith to the Brotherhood. Now your ceremony has been performed. And now is time to tell you what your final Initiation will involve.

– What is an Initiation? Jeremiah asks. – It is a step into the Sacred Circle of the Brotherhood. A door opens and you enter it. But the door also closes behind you. Once you enter, you never leave. Are you sure you're ready for this, Jon?

I nod.

– In order to open the door, you need a key. You've been waiting for this key, Jon, you've been wondering about its shape and size. And now, finally, you're holding it. (He points to the coil of rope I'm holding.) This is a special key. A golden key.

I nod.

– You understand, Jon, that we would never ask you to do something small or trivial. The whole point of an Initiation is that it should be a challenge. It should stretch your soul to its very limits. Expand the soul; and allow God to fill it.

– Yes.

– If you want to be great in the eyes of God, if you want to prove your love for Him is great, then you must do something great. Something that will change your life for ever, will change others lives, will change the landscape of the world around you.

– Yes, yes, I want to be great.

– Our hostage, SNAKE, is a threat to humanity. But we must also show her compassion. She is after all, a human being, nearly. As you know – a soul as ruined as hers cannot go to Manu. And yet there is hope for her. There is a way we can save her soul, a way *you* can save her soul, Jon. You can do this. You can release her soul.

– Can I . . . I can?

– This will be your Initiation – to release SNAKE's soul. Are you ready?

– I'm not sure . . . d'you want me to pray for her?

(A faint ripple of laughter, fading into the darkness.)

– Jon, God wants you to act, not just talk about acting. Millions of people all over the world pray every day, and does it really make any difference? For them, prayer is the lazy opium of the human soul. They treat God like a servant; they expect him to rearrange the whole world to meet their needs. No – God wants us to be *his* servant, to act for him. To pray – and then to do! And you have the answer. Right in your hands.

– I look down at the rope.

– I . . .

– It's the kindest thing to do, Jon.

– You mean . . .

– Jon, look at me. We live in a terrible world. All our values are upside down. Including our ideas about good and evil. Yes, the Bible says *Thou shalt not kill.* But the Bible is full of lies – we know it to be the deluded ramblings of spiritual wannabes. Think about it. What's right? That SNAKE should be allowed to walk free and plant another bomb? A hundred people may die as a result. And think of the pain that spreads from that – the hundreds of people who knew those hundred people. The boy who never gets to grow up and become a doctor. The woman who loses her precious daughter. It could happen to you. It could be one of your family.

– But if the government r-responds to our terms . . .

– Yes, they may respond. And if they respond we may think about allowing her to live – if we feel that we can convert her. But though we must show her compassion, we must also face up to reality. Sadly, her heart is possessed by a *raptor* and it has coiled tight tentacles around her heart . . . whether or not we can remove them remains to be seen. Martyn spoke to her for over four hours today and she would not back down or apologise once, or show the slightest sign of remorse. Instead, she bragged of her other plans, her fellow *raptors*, as you well know. However. There may be hope for her; if in the next few days she shows signs of being receptive to a Soul Shift, then we may respond. *But* – but – she may not. And then, Jon, we will call on you to be great. Are you ready for this call, Jon?

*

– Jon, each of us are put on this earth for a purpose. Sometimes it takes us a while to discover what that purpose might be. You know (soft laughter) I remember that when I first asked you to join the Brotherhood, you were surprised. You didn't think you could be a chosen one, you didn't feel you could be special. So humble, I thought. You told me you weren't sure what you wanted to do after school, that your grades were average, that you didn't feel God had given you any talents. You seemed almost sad. But I knew then that you had a purpose, a great and grand role to play in God's divine plan. That you were destined to be a hero. To save innocent people. To cut down evil. To be great! Are you ready for this Jon? Are you ready to be great?

– Jon, you may feel it is a sin to kill but let me tell you it is not. God kills all the time, every day. Earthquakes erupt; rains fall, waves wash entire nations away. Death is a part of life. We cannot shy away from it. And why should the evil be allowed to live when so many innocent and sweet souls die? We live in a twisted society that says every man should be allowed to live, even if he or she plans to spread destruction across the globe. It is not a sin to stop this! It is not a sin! It is a *duty*. A responsibility. Because if SNAKE lives and people die as a result, then every single one of those deaths will be a bloodstain on *your* conscience, will be stained there for ever, and your chances of a Soul Shift will wither; perhaps you will not even reach Manu . . .

– Remember that it is not *me*, Jeremiah asking you do this. It is God.

– You are not alone, Jon. We will all be with you when you

perform this great duty. You will act for all of us. Can you do this, Jon?

– Can you do this, Jon?

– I asked, can you do this, Jon? If you cannot, you should leave this house tonight and you will have failed your Initiation.

– Can you do this, Jon?

– *Yes*, I say.
   Yes.

# 1 A.M.

**My trainers thwack and drum** against the road. My lungs claw air. I turn, look back at the cottage. Did they see me run? A yellow light gleams in the window; the cottage looks so cosy, as though it belongs in a fairy tale like Hansel and Gretel. I push on a few more feet but the stitch biting my side sinks its teeth in too deeply. I double over, clutching my ribs and spitting. I watch saliva gloop over the side of my trainers. I run my hands over the bristle of my shorn head, feeling the nicks where the knife cut too deep. I hear myself moan lightly. Oh God, what am I doing here?

I'm a coward. That's my problem. I'm too kind, I'm too girly, I'm too whatever, because all of them could do it but I can't. I can't kill someone.

I can't do it.

So I have to run now. Or my Initiation will come and the rope will be liquid jelly in my hands. My arms will freeze the way they do when you're in a nightmare with a monster and I won't be able to put the noose over her neck. To kill her will crack me open like a nut; I'll splinter, fall into pieces.

I run a little further. I wonder if there's a phone box nearby, where I can call home. What will my mum say?

What if the police pull me into an office like they do in movies and shine a searing spotlight into my eyes and force me to give them all the details of our secret chants and prayers? It will break my heart to betray Jeremiah; I can't do it, I can't.

There is a light ahead; a farmhouse. I creep along a line of hedgerow, peering through the gaps. A woman comes out of the door, her white hair shining in the moonlight. She whistles and calls, 'Here, boy, here, boy!'

I could stand up now. I could ask to borrow her phone. I could just say I'm lost. And when my mum tries to take me to the police station, I can refuse to go; I can lock myself in my room and tell her I'll starve myself if she makes me go.

'Here, boy, here, boy!' A collie dog comes bounding up and she pats it gently.

A smile breaks open on my face. I remember the dog I had, a red setter called Isaac. My mum bought him as a puppy and I loved Isaac and he loved me. When I was fourteen and turned against Christianity in a period of doubt my dad took him back to the dogs' home. I didn't speak to him for a week, until he persuaded me that it was God's punishment, not his.

The woman goes back into the house. The door closes and the lights go out. I sit by the hedgerow for a while and look up at the stars with bitter sadness. I've been waiting so long for my Initiation, I'd always pictured it would be the happiest night of my life – and now this.

I don't make a conscious decision to go back to the cottage; I just find myself getting up and slowly walking back. My legs feel weak and every so often my body breaks out in a shaking fit. When I get to the gate at the bottom of the cottage, I stop and hesitate. Nobody seems to have noticed

I ran; I guess they're all asleep, thinking they're safe with me on guard duty. I feel a sudden rush of shame; my Brothers are counting on me. They believe in me. And here I am trying to run away.

I look up at the stars. I think of God looking down on me and even though I still don't know what to do, I feel a rush of comforting warmth.

Thanks to Jeremiah's compassion, SNAKE has been brought up from the cruelty of the cellar to the library, now known as the Hostage Room. A light shines from the window. It tempts me. For a moment I struggle and try to walk away but with a shudder of fascinated revulsion, I find myself going up to the window to peer in. I hope I don't catch her at work. I keep worrying that she might find something, some little thing in the room – a knife, or a fuse and somehow make a bomb during the night. I wouldn't put it past her; I still feel stunned by Martyn's revelation about her network of forty-five terrorists. I realise now that I've underestimated just how dangerous she is.

She's awake. Her skin shines silver in the bright moonlight. An echo of my wet dream sings through me and I flush.

Suddenly she looks up at me. When I look at her, she drops her eyes. Almost as though she's – ashamed. Maybe Martyn's interrogation did some good. Maybe by forcing her to admit everything, she had to face up to who she is.

I know that I should hate her. I know that I should crave her death. But when I search my heart for blackness, I find myself thinking instead of the night she helped me with my homework. I remember feeling a little sulky about having a *girl* bring me up to speed. I was half-expecting her to flounce in and make some clever remark about girls being more brainy than us thicko boys. But she didn't patronise me once. She explained everything clearly and kept telling me how intelligent I was, how quickly I was learning. She seemed so kind. I can't understand how she changed from that considerate, fun-loving girl, who tickled me and told me she had a silly crush on Bart Simpson, to this – this *animal*, whose head is churning with fantasy explosions, who is hungry for bodies to burn.

Her look of shame suggests she is becoming human again. Maybe she is remembering her old self. The girl she was before she got sucked into terrorism. I wonder who recruited her; she must have been trained by someone. Maybe it was some charismatic, older guy, who had a way with words, who encouraged her to go against her heart and deny her nature?

And doesn't shame imply regret? Doesn't regret imply the desire to repent? No – not repent, that's a wicked word. To *revow*. Doesn't revow imply the beginnings of a Soul Shift? Doesn't a Soul Shift imply she should be forgiven?

A sudden noise in the distance.

I tense, searching for an interruption in the darkness. But – nothing. I think, I hope. Just the wind, cool on my cheek. And a feeling I am being watched.

I turn and look at SNAKE.

But she's not looking at me.

Aware of my gaze, she looks up just as I look away.

I fiddle with loops of laces, then look again.

She looks back at me.

Our eyes lock.

Self-consciousness drops away. We eye each other curiously. I feel her eyes rake my face and a small frown dips her forehead. For a moment it feels strange, as though I am the animal and she is the innocent victim. Then I shake myself and smile awkwardly.

She frowns.

I smile more widely.

Suddenly a smile breaks across her face. Her eyes become huge and luminous. Her cheeks apple. I notice her smile has a goofy sing to it, with pokey front teeth.

Her smile hooks my heart. I find myself laughing, my eyes on her, feeding from her, and she giggles too and for a moment we are lost.

Her laughter dies out before mine. Her face sinks back into sadness, her lips pinch. She stares at me with terrible eyes.

I look away again quickly, then look back at the window. I see her moving and I panic, ready to jump up and tell Jeremiah she's trying to escape. Then I realise she is crawling towards the window. She moves in sideways undulations, a cross between a snake and a crab. Then her head pops up at the window. She can only balance by leaning on the ledge, her nose squashed up against the glass. I squash my nose up too, trying to make her laugh again. But she just stares at me. I stare back, drinking in her face. I haven't noticed how she has freckles, or big eyebrows, or dark circles of misery under her eyes.

She breathes on the glass and reaches up. I see her struggle with her roped hands and I reach instinctively, but my fingers bang the glass. She pokes one finger at a stiff angle and writes:

*Help*

She looks at me again.

What can I do?

I picture myself putting the rope around her and kicking away the chair. The gurgle of air squeezing out of her throat. I feel sick. I stare down at my trembling hands. I can taste bile in my throat. I start to chant silently in my head, trying to make it go away. Her gaze feels like a laser and I want to shout at her to go away. I look at my hands and still she keeps staring.

I'll speak to Jeremiah. That's the right thing to do. I'll tell him that SNAKE seems different, that the *raptor* in her heart is dying. Tomorrow, I'll speak to him.

I look up at her and see that my yes or no is a cliff-face that she is clinging to. When I nod, tears fill her eyes. I mouth, *I'll try*. I nod again, each nod a rub of her shoulder, a wiping away of her tears, a smile. I mouth goodnight and go to join my Brothers in sleep.

# Day Three

# 9 A.M.

*I realise that people might classify* our religion as extremist. But those are the type of people who don't really understand what a religion is. Jeremiah explained to us that religion comes from the Latin word *religere*, which means to bind your soul back to God. For most people religion is about tweaking their souls as a little hobby – half an hour singing pretty songs on a Sunday to make themselves feel better for the rest of the week. But our Brotherhood believes that *every minute* matters to God. Every single minute is a chance to sin or to soar, to save the world or chip away a little more at it.

The word *extremist* is really just a way of putting us down, making us all sound like loonies. If we're extremists, then they're all *smallists*.

I remember when I was fourteen years old and I had a crisis of faith about being a Christian. This was even before you left home, Dad. I remember asking you about the word *repent* and what it really meant. And you said it wasn't just about saying sorry. I got confused. You told me it came from the root word *metanoia* meaning 'to change your mind' or 'change your direction'. So *repent* wasn't really a black-and-white term but one with shades of meaning. In fact, it might not have anything to do with being sorry at all. And I said to you, Dad, what about all the other words in the Bible? And you said in a vague sort of way, don't worry about it, they're the words of God.

That was when I began to doubt everything. If just one word can be twisted in translation, surely the Bible is just the echo of an echo of an echo of a once clear and sweet religious song? Later, you persuaded me that the Bible was God's message and I should trust it rather than question it. I came back to Christianity. But now I know better. I don't want to worship the religion of a dead man, whether he is holy or not. I need – we all need – a voice of God who is alive today.

And that voice is Jeremiah.

He might only be sixteen. But Buddha was once sixteen; so was Jesus. Age doesn't matter. We all have these stereotypes in our minds; we think a prophet ought to have grey hair and look wise. But God could have chosen anyone to speak his message – he could have chosen a young girl with blonde hair, not that women are allowed to be his messengers. But he could have. The point is, people only really respect great leaders once they're dead and then it's too late. Like William Blake. He was a poet and he drew angels and people thought he was a loony (though Jeremiah says he spoke some words of wisdom and he was close to a Soul Shift). People only liked his stuff hundreds of years later; when he was alive, they couldn't take it.

Last night Jeremiah said that I may have to kill SNAKE in order to save the world from her evil. But this morning we are sitting in the Prayer Room, blessed by a beautiful dawn, fragile as an eggshell, and I don't feel sick or worried any more. In fact, I feel ashamed that I ran; I'm glad none of them saw me. Jeremiah is just making a threat. He has to be strong in order to slap awake all these stupid people out there. But if I look at any of my Brothers, I know they wouldn't really want to kill someone.

And Jeremiah is right that we should aim to do great things for God. *Smallism* pollutes every area of society. A few months ago, for example, Mrs Kay called me in for a Careers Advice session in school. She said, *What do you want to be when you grow up?* I said a pop star. I just blurted it out because I couldn't think of what to say. And she said, *Don't be silly, Jon.* So I said: An astronaut. And she sighed and said, *Try to think a little smaller, Jon.* What she was basically saying was: be an accountant or work in a bank. Because that's what adults all seem to think becoming an adult is about. Giving up on greatness. Being practical. Not being disappointed. But I tell you, God is GREAT and life is about BEING GREAT and DOING GREAT THINGS and that's why teenagers are better suited to being God's messengers than adults. We, the New Generation, the Next Generation, will be the ones who change the landscape of this world.

I'm trying to focus on prayers but instead I find myself talking to you, Dad. I don't know why I keep doing this, keep letting you into my head, when I hate you so much. But I'm not talking to the bastard you are now, but the dad you once were. Don't think I've forgiven you. And don't think I'm doing the wrong thing now. I don't even need to defend myself to you. I feel calm. I know I am right. I had a vision this morning, on waking: a vision of a beautiful *zapor*, with flowing fair hair. She slipped into No. 10 Downing Street, into the prime minister's bedroom and gently whispered into his ear, her voice as sweet as the sound of the sea. So he will respond to us. He will . . .

And if he doesn't . . . and if they do ask me to kill SNAKE . . . well, then . . . I need to speak to her . . . I need to speak to Jeremiah . . . I need to speak to him . . . and then . . .

# 1.30 P.M.

**After lunch, Thomas and I** are sent to educate SNAKE.

The moment we enter the room, Thomas thumps himself down on the floor, opens his exercise book and begins to read from his copy of the *Book of Hebetheus*. I feel frustrated; I wanted to speak to Padma on her own.

'"Imagine for a moment that human beings are in a cave. From childhood, each human has their legs and necks in handcuffs so that they can only stare straight ahead of them at a light reflected on the wall – which comes from a fire burning far above and behind them. On the wall, they see dancing patterns of life like shadow puppets."'

Thomas's voice sounds like a spring tightly compressed into a jack-in-a-box; at any point it might break open and burst into laughter or tears. Padma, too, senses something feels wrong and she looks at me.

She looks beautiful this morning.

'"Imagine that one of these men was released from his handcuffs. He's compelled to stand up, walk and look up at the real light above him, outside the cave. His eyes are dazzled and he cannot believe what he is seeing. He wants to turn away from the light and put his cuffs back on.

"But then someone drags him by force towards that

light. The man might shout out in protest, but still he is dragged. Then the light shines on to him and he can't see anything.

"But slowly, slowly, his eyes grow accustomed to the light. And then he sees the true nature of things."'

The sun gleams through the window, forming red fire-flies in the dark sea of her hair.

'"But imagine if that man were to come down again, back into the cave. Even though he has seen the sun, his eyes would be infected by darkness.

"Now he is a stranger amongst the other prisoners. He knows the truth about the fire and shadow patterns on the wall, but they will only laugh at him. Perhaps they will say that if he went up and came back with corrupted eyes that it wasn't even worth trying to go up."'

I look at the brown curve of her neck, imagining the harshness of the rope against the silk of her skin.

'ARE YOU LISTENING TO ME?' Thomas suddenly shouts at Padma.

'Yes,' she says quickly.

Thomas puts down his exercise book. He stands up and walks around the room. Padma and I exchange glances. Thomas stops, pauses, stares down at a patch of floor. I slide his book over to me and read quickly,

'"– perhaps they were able to get their hands on the man who had released him and led him, they would try to kill him –"'

'Have you read any of these books?' Thomas shouts.

Padma's eyes widen and she presses up against the wall. Thomas gestures angrily towards the bookcase. He pulls out a random book, thumping it.

'Have you?'

'No, how can I –'

'You know that reading's evil, don't you? How can we purify you if you read –'

'How can I read with these stupid cuffs on?' Padma demands. 'Besides, there's nothing wrong with reading.' That note in her voice again, that sound that unnerves me: defiance. 'Reading is fun. It helps you learn stuff.'

'In the Hebetheus religion we don't agree with books,' I say quickly.

'You don't agree with . . . ?' she screws up her nose, shaking her head as if to say *Another one of their crazy ideas.*

'Books are dangerous,' I explain, giving Thomas a nervous glance. 'They give people ideas. It's like – imagine if when you'd been born, nobody had ever told you about the word, say, *hate*. If you didn't have the word for it – would you feel it? It's only because you see a film or read it in a book that you're tainted with it. Some time in the future, when we've taken over everything, the word *hate* will be banned, you see. Because it just won't be needed. We're all going to be too happy.'

'But . . .' Padma shakes her head. 'That doesn't make sense. Sometimes you can feel an emotion and it's such a mix of all the other emotions, like all the colours in a paintbox mixed together – that there isn't a word for it. But you still feel it. And . . . books make you think –'

She breaks off, looking at Thomas. For he is staring at her as though she's the most terrible *raptor* he's ever seen in his life.

Then he reaches into the bookcase and lobs a book right at her. It hits the wall. Slams to the floor. Pages flutter by her feet. Padma catches her breath, appealing to me.

'Thomas,' I begin, 'what are you doing? Violence isn't our way, you remember what Jeremiah said –'

A book arrows in my direction. It skims my ear and hits the wall. Another book sails towards Padma, hitting her foot; another yelps against the ceiling. Pages roar through the air; spines rip; Thomas howls – I go to him, begging him to stop, calm down, what's the matter, but he screams in my face *There's raptors in the bookcase, little raptors, screaming and jumping up and down and* and I grab his arm as he reaches for another book and he smacks his fist against me, banging me back against the case. Pain zigzags down my spine; I cry out. Books tremble, as though drawing in a shaking breath, then topple to the floor like broken buildings. Thomas falls among them, loose pages taking flight like birds, his hands clawing his face, tears soaking his cheeks, his mouth a black hole of howls.

'Thomas!' I turn back to the door just as it bursts open. Chris and Martyn pile in, gaping. Raymond enters, then steps aside for Jeremiah.

'Thomas – he's upset,' I stammer.

'He just went mad,' Padma bursts out. 'He just went crazy!'

'You shut up!' Raymond orders. He stands over Thomas. 'What the hell's the matter?'

'He's cracked,' Martyn says in an awed voice. 'He's –'

'He just lost it,' I say.

'Let me see him.' Jeremiah cuts through us, kneeling down by Thomas. He tries to remove his hands from his face but Thomas claws them back.

'Get them off me, get them off me!' Thomas screams.

'It's all right, it's all right,' Jeremiah shushes him in his angel voice. 'There's nobody here, it's just me, it's Jeremiah, you're okay, you're okay.'

I look at Chris who looks at Martyn who looks at me.

'She's put a bad spell on him,' Martyn whispers and nods at Padma. Padma frowns.

Thomas lets go. Jeremiah finally succeeds in taking his hands and Thomas rolls on to his side, head crumpling a printed page, sobbing. He looks like a little boy. I feel frightened, watching him. What's happened to him?

'I think,' says Jeremiah, a benign softness warming his face, 'I think Thomas may be on the verge of a Soul Shift.' He smiles down at Thomas with honey eyes and gently touches his face. 'Go – all of you,' he commands. 'Leave him alone.'

We all hang about in the kitchen, talking, trying to work out what's gone wrong with Thomas, whether it's madness or divine illumination, though Raymond jokes there's a fine line between the two. I feel angry with him; he acts as though a Soul Shift is a concept from a comic. But I have to admit, I feel confused and, I admit, a bit jealous. Why is it that Thomas, with his good grades and fancy house and nice parents, has all the luck with God too? I'd thought that a Soul Shift was all about being happy, which shows how far off I am.

Some time later, we hear a creaking and Jeremiah's soothing voice becoming loud and then distant. We edge to the kitchen door, peering surreptitiously into the corridor. Before Jeremiah leads Thomas into the Prayer Room, I hear him say, 'It's all right, I can see you need them, it's all right, I'll sort it out for you . . .'

Jeremiah shuts the door and then turns to me and instructs me to tidy the books up.

# 2 P.M.

**Back in the Hostage Room,** I quickly shove books back into the case. I hear a sob; Padma is crying again. I turn back to the bookcase, feeling panicky. I never know what to do when she cries. I turn Plato up the right way, then the King James Bible. The cover is white; the letters gold italics; the paper fine as tissue. It fits snugly into my hands like a white dove. And suddenly I am overcome with the strangest urge: to open it up and read one of the Proverbs. I always used to do that when I was feeling troubled.

I take a deep breath. I walk up to her, intending to stop at a safe distance, but my heart compels me forward and I find myself kneeling by her side. I reach for a tissue – but I have none. I offer her my sleeve and she laughs through her tears and I laugh too.

'Sorry about Thomas,' I say. 'He's just going through a Soul Shift. You see – a Soul Shift is when you – you know – you go into this like amazing state and you're with God.' I don't know why, but my words only increase her weeping.

As she looks up at me, I can't help picturing those huge wet eyes blank and glazed. Every time I've played out a fantasy of killing her, my mind has vomited at the sheer thought. But now, in reality, with Padma just flesh and blood beside me, it suddenly seems . . . My heartbeat thumps with the shock it of it: *I could do it*, I realise in excitement. *If someone passed me a rope now, and said: do it, I almost feel I could.*

Then, like a snap of the fingers, the revelation vanishes. One of her tears hits my arm in a salty trail; suddenly she is human again. I feel ashamed and I find myself speaking to her in a sharp tone:

'When you spoke to Martyn yesterday, you told him you had a network of forty-five other terrorists. Can you tell me more about their plans? I mean, I know you don't want to grass anyone up, you don't have to mention any names, but if you can just give me some clues . . .'

I will her with all my heart to confess. I don't care how long it takes. I'm not going to make the mistake of being too compassionate this time. I'm going to keep chipping away; I just need something, even if it's one bullet of information that I can carry back to Jeremiah, to prove I can be a good interrogator too.

'What do you care?' she says in a choked voice. 'You just want me dead. You're all animals . . .'

'Animals! No – that's not true. I don't want you dead – none of us do!' I cry, flushing, wondering if she used her evil powers to see into my mind. 'It's not like that!'

She shakes her head, sniffing, tears falling and plopping into her lap.

'I've been thinking . . . that I want to convert to the Hebetheus religion,' she says. 'I don't want to be a Hindu any more, I want to join Hebetheus.' She lifts her liquid eyes to mine.

'Are you serious?' I ask.

'Well, I've heard your rules, I've heard passages from the *Book of Hebetheus*. I might be new to it, but it really – it fascinates me – I'm really, really interested. I think you may all be right about a lot of things.'

'Well – that's great.' I feel an odd disappointment – does this mean it's all over? But then I am excited. I was right: she *did* want to *revow*. Perhaps I was her inspiration; Jeremiah will be so pleased – I want to leap up and tell him right now!

'If you go and tell Jeremiah now, will he let me go home?'

I hesitate.

'Yes.'

She suddenly kicks the floor with an animal sob of rage.

'He won't though, will he? He'll never let me go. None of you will just LISTEN to me. Why won't you just all BELIEVE me? Instead I have to PRETEND to be interested in your BULLSHIT . . .' Her words disintegrate into moans.

'Maybe you're not ready for a conversion just yet then,' I say sadly.

'So which one of you is set to kill me?' she sobs.

'I – well – I was,' I begin and stop, for her eyes enlarge with horror and a fresh film of tears. 'But – I – I –'

She wriggles up next to me and squeezes her fingers into my arm, so hard it hurts.

'Please don't kill me,' she begs. 'Please. I'm seventeen next week – my mum's organised a party and everything and I haven't done anything wrong, and you won't do it, will you, I know you won't, you're nice, you're good, I can see you're good –' she looks me in the eye fiercely. 'You are good, aren't you?'

My eyes hold hers, then slide to her lips, then swiftly jerk back up to her gaze.

'Yes, I'm good,' I say, but my voice sounds weak. I

frown, remembering. 'I'm a member of the Brotherhood of Hebetheus. Of course I'm good. We do good. It is our role in life to bring peace to mankind.'

She moves in even closer, her arm hot against mine, and I can feel the faint brush of her breast against my elbow as she forces me to look at her.

'You know I'm not a terrorist, don't you?'

'I . . .' I drop my gaze but the ferocity of her attention forces me to look her in the eye once again.

'Come on, Jon –' her voice rises with a hysterical edge and I shush her quickly, nodding at the door. 'This is my life we're talking about, I mean, for God's sake, I've never even spoken to Jeremiah the whole time we've been at school. The *only* time he ever paid me any attention was when we got our essays back in English and I came top and he was just behind me and he turned and gave me such a dirty look, he's had it in for me ever since then. I don't know, maybe I pissed him off so he made up some story about me talking about a bomb on my mobile when –'

Suddenly I frown, pull away from her body heat.

'No, Jeremiah's not like that,' I say sharply. 'He'd never do something so petty –'

'No – of course not, I know that, he's really amazing. But you know I'm not a terrorist? I never, *ever,* ever planned to plant anything anywhere.'

'Well, well – I mean, maybe,' I give in, trying to ignore the panic thrashing about inside me.

'Please don't kill me,' she repeats. 'Please.'

'Look, the reason your death sentence came up is because of your confession to Martyn and – the thing is – if you could just tell me about wanting to turn things around, get out of the terrorist network, *really* convert to Hebetheus – not with just a few words so you can escape –

but *really* understand what we're telling you –'

'I'm trying, I'm trying,' she sobs, 'but how can I leave a terrorist network I don't even belong to?'

'But yesterday you told Martyn that you did! Don't lie to me, you're playing games now. One day you tell Martyn you have a network of forty-five other terrorists and the next you say you don't belong to anything. I'm not weak and stupid, you know!'

'I didn't tell him that – he *forced* me to say it,' she cries. 'He put his hands on me and he hurt me!'

'What?' I cry. 'You're lying. Come on, Martyn wouldn't do that! He's a member of the Brotherhood of Hebetheus and we're not allowed to – we don't – we don't put our hands or our attention on women,' I recite.

'Oh really? So this is just my imagination? I mean – just look at my shoulder!' She wriggles angrily in her cuffs, swivelling around to show me a ring of nasty bruises.

'You might just have – you might have banged yourself . . .'

'No – he *forced* me! He *threatened* me!'

The word *force* echoes in my mind, with whispers of thrilling fear.

'W-what happened?'

In a quiet, dejected voice, she tells me the whole story. At first I am not sure whether to believe her. But as she goes on, certain details ring true. Martyn's bullying; his threats. I feel instinctively that she is telling the truth. By the end of her tale, I look down and realise my hands are fisted; I feel ready to smack him one. *For God's sake*, I cry inside, *she's just an innocent girl* –

Well, nearly innocent. But we – Jeremiah and I – are trying to help her, and Martyn is undoing all our good work. What did Jeremiah say? That we ought to be *whiter than white*. That we ought to show *compassion*. I look at her bruise again. That is not compassion. I feel a sudden urge to hug her, to hold her tight and say *Sorry, sorry, this isn't what we're about, none of us will hurt you, I promise.*

'Right. I'm going to tell Jeremiah about this right now.'

'Okay,' she whispers, and a ghost of a smile passes across her lips. A pause. 'Thank you.'

I am about to get up, when she digs her fingers into my arm again and nuzzles her head against my shoulder like a pussycat.

'We're friends, aren't we, you and me? We're friends?'

I am about to give a formal 'Yes', for the Brotherhood are friends to all humanity. But the pleading in her voice touches me.

'Yes,' I say, 'we're friends.' And we grin and in that moment all our troubles are forgotten and it's as though we've just shared another homework session and might watch TV or spend the afternoon slouching in the swings, taking the piss out of the younger kids, swopping CDs. 'I'd – better – go and speak to Jeremiah now.'

I stand up. I feel unsteady; I press a palm flat against the wall. My head is reeling with confusion; suddenly I am desperate to leave the room, breathe my own air, close my mind to her thoughts. What if she's lying? If she's realised that she's in the wrong and now she's trying to paint over her past? Does that make her good or evil? Oh God, I wish there is a test for goodness the way there was for lies; a detector we could strap around her wrist to measure precise recordings of her heart and conscience; then I might know if she deserves to die.

# 3 P.M.

A fly is buzzing in the Prayer Room, lashing angrily against the closed windowpane. Thomas is lying on the floor, dreamy-eyed. His body looks limp and exhausted, as though he's just had flu. Jeremiah is sitting in the middle, on the Ring Symbol, still and serene as the Buddha. I give Thomas a nervous glance but Jeremiah beckons me and I kneel down opposite him.

I look up into Jeremiah's cool blue eyes. In the black holes of his pupils I have a sudden vision of myself: laying the noose around her neck, like some ancient necklace placed on a virgin to be sacrificed to the gods. Can he really want me to, can he really mean it, is it a test? Is he sorting the *zapor* from the *raptor* in my heart?

'Yes?' Jeremiah prompts me gently.

At first I can't get the words out, I stutter and stumble like Chris, until Jeremiah puts a cool hand on my shoulder. He tells me to calm down.

I explain everything to him.

Well, nearly everything. I do leave a few things out, I admit. I keep worrying that Jeremiah won't believe me; I keep telling him that I know it sounds crazy but it's the truth. But, to my surprise, he accepts it all at once. He calls for Raymond to bring Martyn in. I rise to go, but to my horror Jeremiah orders me to stay.

'Sit down,' Jeremiah motions. 'Martyn, Jon and I have just been talking about you . . .'

Martyn sits. He gives me a glance that is almost conspiratorial. As though we're back at St Sebastian's and we've just been called in to see the Head and we'd better make sure our stories tally.

'Jon has interrogated SNAKE just now and he informs me that not everything you say is correct.'

'What?' Martyn jumps. He swivels an innocent, injured gaze on me. 'What?'

'Let me explain. Jon interrogated SNAKE at length and SNAKE confessed that she is a terrorist. She is not only the head of a network of forty-five other terrorists across this country but is the mastermind behind a worldwide organisation of forty-five *countries* – I open my mouth to object but Jeremiah flickers a sidelong glance at me and I play along with his game. 'So, what do you think about that?'

Martyn shifts uncomfortably.

'Well, that's really bad,' he says. 'She's, like, really evil.'

'So you think SNAKE – a sixteen-year-old schoolgirl – could really mastermind a worldwide terrorist organisation?'

'I dunno. I mean, she could use the internet, couldn't she, and that sort of thing.'

'You don't think that Jon might be exaggerating?'

Martyn twists his lips up to one side, then lets them spring back.

'Er, yeah . . .'

'What do you think the difference is between exaggerating and lying?'

The fly buzzes incessantly in the background.

Martyn frowns. He knows what this is all about. Beneath his casual shrugs, I sense his guard is up.

'Well, they're kind of the same, only one's a bit worse than the other. Lying's really bad, it's just telling something that's false, whereas exaggerating . . . I mean, that's just adding a little extra bit on, and everyone does that, all the time.'

'So you don't feel guilty about the fact that yesterday you interrogated SNAKE and then exaggerated her confession?'

'I didn't –' Martyn's voice is close to shattering into a shout – 'I didn't – she said –' He breaks off, clenching his fists and jumping to his feet. 'That fucking fly is driving me mad!'

He strolls over, but Jeremiah's voice stops him.

'No. Leave it. None of us have a right to kill God's creatures. Sit down. Come on, Martyn,' he says gently. 'This isn't a trial.' He spreads his hands. 'This isn't a courtroom, this is a holy room. I'm your leader. It's not my place to judge or punish. I am merely a conduit for the God of Hebetheus. If SNAKE didn't really say the things you claimed, then you can tell me in all honesty. I'm not going to hurt you, I'm not going to throw you to the lions.' Almost parental now, almost tender, as though Martyn is an errant child. 'You're one of us.'

Martyn fixes his stare on the floor.

'I wasn't *lying*,' he says flatly.

'So, Jon, why do you think SNAKE is telling the truth? What makes you think you can trust her over Martyn?'

I jump as though he's suddenly spun a torch on my face.

'Yeah, Jon?' Martyn spits out acidly.

'I – I –' I swallow, still trying to blink away confused patches of light. 'I just think she can open up to me a bit more than, say, Martyn, or . . .'

'Why's that?' Jeremiah asks.

Suddenly I feel a cool sweat sticking to my brow. I thought Martyn was in the dock. Or is this all just a test to probe me? Is Martyn just the decoy?

But I've done nothing wrong. I have nothing to hide.

'Look, Padma likes me,' I say.

'Padma?' Jeremiah mocks me. 'But I thought our terrorist's name was SNAKE?'

'Yeah, yeah, I know, SNAKE trusts me.'

'Ooo, SNAKE *trusts* you. SNAKE *likes* you,' Martyn sing-songs under his breath.

'I think she trusts me,' I burst out in a temper, 'because I don't go around threatening to rape her!'

My words burn the air.

'Martyn.' Jeremiah's voice is cool with astonishment. 'You threatened to *rape* her?'

'I – no,' Martyn says, but the blush on his cheeks suggests he may be 'exaggerating'.

'Chris was there, at the interrogation, wasn't he?' Jeremiah says sharply. 'Raymond! Call in Chris.'

It only takes thirty-odd seconds for Chris to come, but it feels like three hours. The silence fills the room like choking smoke. Jeremiah's aura becomes arctic-cold. The fly reaches a pitch of hysteria. I can feel Martyn punching me with furious, sidelong glances. I can hear him screaming silently: *Traitor! My Brother, the traitor!* I sit up very straight and tell myself I'm in the right, Martyn's in the wrong. Then – at last – the door opens.

Chris is sensitive enough to smell the scent of trouble the moment he enters the room. He kneels down. Martyn gives him a Brother's look but Chris won't return it.

'Chris, did Martyn threaten to rape SNAKE yesterday?' Jeremiah asks.

'Y-y-yes,' Chris admits at once. 'But it w-w-was h-his

idea n-n-not m-mine.'

'You bloody –' Martyn curses him, then breaks off. 'Okay. So I did. But how else was I going to get her to tell us? I wasn't really going to. It was just a threat, right? Because she's evil! It's not easy getting the truth out of her. I didn't lay a finger on her!'

'Chris, I want you to tell me exactly what happened. Now it's very important that you explain without any exaggeration,' Jeremiah says. 'Okay?'

Chris nods frantically. Martyn is in torture.

'We j-just tried to get her to talk but she wouldn't.' Chris breaks off to suck from his inhaler and Jeremiah waits patiently. 'She j-just kept denying everything. So th-then Martyn said we had to make her talk and so he told her we'd rape her if she didn't c-c-confess and then she con-fessed really quickly but the p-p-point is, we didn't mean it, because none of us in the Brotherhood are allowed to t-t-t-touch a w-w-woman or even think about th-that.'

There is a silence.

'I presume that SNAKE did admit that she was going to plant a bomb in St Sebastian's?' Jeremiah asks.

'She –' Chris breaks off. 'W-w-well we didn't t-t-t-t-talk about th-th-that –'

'Well, everyone knows that anyway!' Martyn says sharply. 'So what was the point in asking?'

'True,' Jeremiah says. He turns to me. 'But I presume she did admit it to you?'

The words are there. There on the tip of my heart. *The truth is, she said that she is innocent. She says she didn't plant a bomb. She says she's not a terrorist.* But if I say that – then what? It's too much for them to take. They'll think I'm in cahoots with her; Jeremiah is already suspicious. It will undermine the victory I've just scored for her. And besides, even if she did deny it – she must have planned to plant the bomb – or what are we all doing here?

'Yeah,' I say quickly, 'of course she admitted that. But that's the *only* thing.'

It seems strange to lie, for the sake of holding up a bigger truth. For a moment I feel snagged in confusion. Why does it seem so hard to be white, to be good, to always tell the truth? Why can't things just be black and be white, why does the world keep on smearing the two colours together?

'But,' I cut in, just as Jeremiah is about to speak.

'Yes?' he asks, searing me with his gaze again.

'I think she's sorry. I really do. She seems really different over the last few hours. She actually said to me that she's interested in repenting, in coming over to the Hebetheus Brotherhood –'

'As a woman, she couldn't be part of our Brotherhood,' Jeremiah says coolly.

'Well – yeah – but what I mean is – she is sorry, I think she wants to change and I don't think she deserves to be . . . to be . . . you know . . .'

'But we've sent the video out now!' Martyn cries. 'If we back down now, we'll look weak and stupid, nobody will take us seriously, they'll think the Hebetheus is a load of shite . . .'

'You see the position your lies have put us in?' Jeremiah asks coldly.

Martyn quails. Chris is tearing off his nails with his teeth. He looks as though he's about to cry. Jeremiah stares at them stonily.

'I'm sorry,' Martyn mutters, picking at the stitching on his trainers.

A silence. Jeremiah presses his hands into a flat steeple and rests his chin on them. He ponders. Behind him, the sun breaks through the floating clouds and arrows white rays through the curtains, falling on his hair in divine sparkles, shadowing the thoughtful curve of his brow.

'She must die,' he says at last.

'What!' I cry, jolted. 'But . . . but . . .'

'As you say, she has confessed to planting the bomb in our school.'

'Well, she seemed to say that, yes.' I squirm in hot entrails of panic. 'I mean – but she might have been intimidated by me interrogating her, I mean I know you lot think I'm in cahoots with her but I'm not, I was tough with her – I mean –'

Jeremiah lays a hand on my shoulder.

'Jon, you have a compassionate heart. But we knew before we came here that she was going to plant the bomb.'

'But you said that her soul could be saved! And we've been reading to her and it's all been going in – today she said she was close to coming round! We've done all this good work on her soul and now we're just going to kill her! That's not very compassionate!'

'So I did,' says Jeremiah. 'So I did. But I feel that, even though we have educated her, her soul is black in its very core. Besides, we have not just kidnapped an *individual*, Jon. You have to see beyond that. SNAKE is a *symbol*. A symbol for all terrorists, a symbol of the ignorance of the government and the police who allow people like her to thrive. And how we deal with that one symbol shows how we will save the world.' He sighs, and a faint sadness seeps into his voice. As though he is weary of trying to save an ignorant world. 'We'll give them until tomorrow to see if they respond. SNAKE's life will depend upon the enlightenment of this country.'

'And . . . what about us?' Martyn asks unsteadily.

'You must be punished,' says Jeremiah, to my surprise. 'You will undergo a Sacred Cleansing.'

He and Martyn stare at each other for a minute.

'You may go,' Jeremiah says.

'Okay, fine,' Martyn snaps. 'Come on, Chris. We'd best go now, since we're in the doghouse.'

Chris stands up, gangly and uncertain. They are just about to leave when Martyn suddenly spins back, saunters over to the window and, with a fierce *thwack!* kills God's precious creature. Thomas lets out a faint moan. The bluebottle thuds to the sill, its wings moving stickily. I wonder how much pain an insect might feel when it dies; if, in its own small world, it suffers as much pain as we do.

Martyn stares at Jeremiah, waiting. Jeremiah doesn't respond. Martyn leaves. Chris trails behind him.

Jeremiah lets out a sharp exhalation.

'I'm sorry,' I say. I feel as though I have taken a knife to the protective sheen of our Brotherhood and made a gentle incision: just a hairline crack, but dangerous enough for it to split and spread into an earthquake. 'I'm sorry . . . I'll talk to Martyn, I'll tell him I'm sorry . . .'

'There's no need,' says Jeremiah. 'Tomorrow morning, he will undergo a Sacred Cleansing and things will be different.' He sighs. 'You know, Martyn was Initiated a long time ago, long before you, Jon, and yet he has so far to go in his understanding of the Hebethean principles. You, Jon, have overtaken him.'

I feel as though I've just scored a goal or a piece of homework has landed on my desk with a grade *A+* slashed across it.

'I want you to watch him,' Jeremiah continues. 'Record in your notebook everything Martyn says or does. Be subtle, no need to trail him. Just note things down and report back to me.'

'Of course,' I say, with a thrill of excitement.

I get up to go but as I face the door I hear Thomas moan again and the sound is familiar. I realise it's an echo of a nightmare: a scream I imagined Padma might make. I picture the noose around her neck, pinching the skin. I turn back and kneel once more.

'Jeremiah – I just – I just wanted to ask – you know about Padma – about SNAKE, I mean – you said you overheard her on her mobile, talking about her bomb plot – but what if – what if you didn't hear it – you know – completely – what if you got the wrong end of the stick and she was just . . . you know . . . joking. Or something.'

Jeremiah stares at me for a long time. I look at the symbols on the wall; at Thomas; at the dead fly; at the symbols. I'm aware of my cheeks growing very hot.

Finally, Jeremiah says, 'Jon, I think perhaps I've underestimated you. I'm sorry if we forced you to say yes last night – but I can see you're not capable of killing SNAKE, you're not ready yet for your Initiation. Perhaps if you'd like to go home –'

'No, no, no,' I cry. 'I can do it, I can – I can do it. I just – it's fine. I can do it.'

'I want you to know, Jon, that I would never lie. *Never.* Not to you or any of my Brothers.'

'Yes. I know, I know . . .'

'Good. Now sit with me awhile,' Jeremiah smiles.

I open my mouth to speak again, to tell him Padma is waiting for me to return, to reassure her. I shut up and obey him. Jeremiah's anger has seeped away; his expression is tranquil now. Just to sit with him is as soothing as listening to the sound of the sea. Slowly, my worries dissolve away. I realise that the best thing to do is avoid Padma from now on. I can't cope with her mind-games so it's best not to speak to her. I don't need to worry about her any more, about right or wrong, black or white. It's not my place. Jeremiah knows best; I just have to put my decisions in his hands.

# 6 P.M.

**The six o'clock news.**

First: a suicide bomber has killed forty-five people in a blast in Iraq.

Second: a boy has been murdered in a knife fight in a school in London.

Third: us.

'Police are still searching the country for the missing girl, Padma Laxsmi, who was kidnapped from her home three days ago by a group of young extremists,' the newsreader says.

Then: a detective. Not dark and craggy like the detectives on TV dramas, but balding, with a plump face and a silly brown moustache.

'We are doing everything in our power to track down these boys. A woman in Kingston has identified the van the boys were travelling in on Kingston High Street last Thursday. We are following CCTV footage which suggests the van headed in an easterly direction. I'm afraid I can't give you any further information at present, but I assure you we are doing everything in our power to find them.'

A rapid flash of our photos again, though there isn't time for all of us: Raymond's and mine are missed out. I feel quite relieved. Then Martyn is saying we will kill her if our demands aren't met. Then Mr Abdilla is saying Padma is innocent. The weather girl concludes that temperatures are expected to drop in the evening, with a possibility of snow in the south-east of England.

Jeremiah lowers the sound until her voice is humiliated to a murmur.

We all stand about with slack shoulders as it sinks in.

The government haven't responded to us. Our slice of news pie is shrinking every day, nibbled by newer and fresher horrors. The wild shock, the slam-punch of our actions have gone; the repetition of the news (our sixth time on this station in three days) has diluted the pain; this report will only bruise people's minds faintly, fading quickly as they return to cooking and putting their kids to bed and sinking back into their selfish lives of cosy houses and cars and careers.

Rage kicks my stomach, rage and confusion. Just how far do we have to go to get ourselves taken seriously? Just how much more do we have to do to shock them? How many other terrorist suspects do we need to kidnap before they'll care? Isn't one life enough? And God, now I really will have to kill her, and I don't want to kill her, but what else can we do if they won't take any notice? It will be their fault, they'll have driven me to it, only I can't do it, can I, I can't?

I just can't understand the indifference of people. So much suffering in the world and yet still we drift through our lives oblivious. Suddenly I see how truly selfish we all are. We're all heroes in our own blockbuster films; everyone else just has cameo roles. No wonder the world keeps on churning out suffering and nothing ever changes. But how can we change it, *how?*

Martyn opens his mouth as though about to pontificate, then quickly snaps it shut.

Jeremiah is locked into a tense pose: shoulders hunched, fingertips pressed to his lips, brow furrowed. Then he flicks the sound back on, skipping channels, showering us with blasts of sin: a blonde sex-temptress cajoling us to buy butter with a heavy wink; a programme telling us how to improve our homes, inflaming capitalist greed; a celebrity singing contest feeding the hollow thirst for fame. The Houses of Parliament: a debate. Or maybe it's the PM's Question Time. Everyone heckles and shouts clever things at each other. It reminds me a bit of school.

'Look at them,' Jeremiah jeers in disgust. 'When we sit and discuss problems, we work together. But all they do is score points off each other. It's not a debate, it's an ego circus. And they're running the country!' His voice rises to a shrill pitch. 'We're going to make them listen to us. We'll make them. Oh yes, they're going to listen to us.'

# 7 P.M.

(A CLOSE-UP OF RAYMOND)

RAYMOND voiceover:

We were amused to see that the
police are planning to come
after *us*. This explains just
why terrorism will never be
wiped out. You decide to
condemn a group who are trying
to do good and write them
off as a bunch of Christian
fundamentalists – which, by
the way, we're not. But when
it comes to a real terrorist,
you decide she's innocent –
without even bothering to
properly investigate her.

SNAKE may or may not be in a
network of forty-five terrorists. But that is not the
point. She planned to plant a
bomb in the school and there

are many out there like her. It is time to declare a true war on terror. The Prevention of Terrorism Act needs to be changed. Suspects should be held indefinitely. Furthermore, we believe that if someone is proven to be a terrorist, they deserve to be hung –

[CHRIS whispering:
I th-think this sounds too e-extreme –

JEREMIAH: We *have* to be extreme. The terrorists are extreme! We have to fight fire with fire. If they are prepared to end human lives, we have to show we can match them and end their lives!]

RAYMOND: All terrorists must be hung in Trafalgar Square. This bill – which we christen 'The Peace Bill' must be debated in Parliament right away.

We want to hear action is being taken, or tomorrow SNAKE dies. At midnight – tomorrow.

# 11 P.M.

Notes on Martyn's behaviour, Day 3

8 p.m.: Dinner. Jeremiah asked M to say Thanks To
God before eating and M did so. We're running out
of tins of beans so we saved some & just ate
toast. Raymond had to cut the mouldy bits off the
corner of bread and it tasted hard. Martyn made a
remark about being tired of toast, toast, toast.
Thomas was not present; T was in Prayer Room. M
asked if he should take him some food. Jeremiah
agreed and thanked M for his kindness.

8.15 p.m.: M was in the Prayer Room with T for a
long time. I stood by the door, listening, but I
couldn't hear what they were saying. Then Chris
came out. C mentioned he feels bored.

9 p.m.: A phone started ringing. We all went crazy
– funny, I didn't even stop to think that there was
a phone in the house, I'd almost forgotten the dead
old woman. We couldn't work out where the ringing
came from at first. Then we realised out it came
from the dead woman's bedroom. We stood outside,
listening to the message. The voice was cheerful, a

woman's – maybe the woman who knocked on the door? R and M went in to delete the message. Then J ordered R to tear the phone out of the socket and destroy the wires so nobody could call in. 'Or out,' M added – cheekily I thought.

10 p.m.: Glanced in the bedroom whilst others were meeting in Prayer Room for evening Love to God and noticed a sheet of paper sticking out from under M's pillow. Noticed a cartoonish-picture. Looks like a zapor, only you can't get male <u>zapors</u>. Is M suffering from lustful thoughts?

There's something else that I feel I ought to write down before I show this to Jeremiah. Something I ought to confess:

10:30 p.m.: I found myself going into the Hostage Room briefly and removing the Bible, quickly telling SNAKE we planned to burn it. Instead of setting light to it as I should have done, I found myself going into the bathroom and removing the loose tile just beneath the sink and seeing if the Bible fitted in. I found myself picking it up again, filled with a craving to flick through, like some alkie nourishing a bottle of gin in his hands, begging his body to obey him, to put it back down. But: I drank. I polluted my mind with some proverbs. I don't know why I did it. I guess sometimes I read the <u>Book of Hebetheus</u> and I feel as though my soul is being squashed into one of those Russian dolls and the more I read, the smaller and smaller the doll becomes. The Bible made me feel fluid; I felt I could pour through it, let it pour through me. I savoured the Proverbs: 'My son, do not despise the LORD's discipline and do not resent his rebuke, because the LORD disciplines those he loves, as a father the son he delights in.' I sat there, the words settling softly in my mind and I thought of my father without hate, but with a kind of sadness. Then I felt rotten inside. I remembered that Jeremiah had once warned me: 'There are those who lurch from one religion, one belief, one new age claptrap to the next like drunks. Those people are not desperate for the truth. They just want to believe in <u>something</u> – anything – that they can lean on like a crutch.' I quickly shoved the filthy book away, full of regret that I had tried to take the cheap and easy route. The Hebetheus might be a hard and narrow path, but it is the only one to God.

I read through my words and then tear off the bottom of the sheet and flush it away before I take the report to Jeremiah.

# MIDNIGHT

**I wake up suddenly in the night,** heart pumping: tomorrow you're going to have to do it, tomorrow you're going to have to kill her, you realise that, don't you, you realise that the government aren't going to respond and then it will be murder –

They will respond. They will.

*You're going to have to kill her.*
*You're going to have to kill her.*
*You're going to have to kill her.*
*You're going to have to kill her.*
*You're going to have to kill her.*
*You're going to have to kill her.*

– Shut up, shut up, let me sleep, let me sleep –

*You're going to have to kill her.*
*You're going to have to kill her.*

*You're going to have to kill her.*

Let me sleep. I'm too tired, I'm so tired, just leave me –

*You're going to have to kill her.*

*You're going to have to kill her.*
*You're going to have to . . .*

# Day Four

# 10 A.M.

**At the end of Morning Prayers** Jeremiah asks Martyn to sit beside him at the front. We all sit upright; the air becomes rich with the scent of danger.

Silence. I don't know why but Jeremiah just sits there; it's almost as though he wants the silence to build up until the room screams with it.

Finally, he says, 'Martyn, we all want to help you reach a Soul Shift. It's what we all want for each other – we're your Brothers. So now we feel you should undergo a Sacred Cleansing.

'We've discussed this and we're all going to help you with this. Aren't we?'

Jeremiah nods at us and we all agree, chorusing nods and grins, though Chris shoots me a quick, bewildered glance.

Martyn isn't fooled, though. He sweeps a glance over us, frowning, and his shoulders droop a little.

'Martyn, why did you first come to the Hebetheus religion?'

Martyn looks startled; then he says quickly, 'Because God called me to be with the Brotherhood. Because this world is totally fucked up and we have to sort it out, it's a mess and we're gonna save it.'

Silence.

Martyn carries on hastily, 'And anyway, you were the one who told me I should join – you said you'd had a dream about me . . .'

I start: when Jeremiah first told me about the Brotherhood, he said the same thing: that God had spoken to him in a dream. I didn't realise Jeremiah had dreamed of other disciples too.

'And do you feel, as a member of the Brotherhood, that you should tell the truth at all times?'

Martyn knows what he's referring to. We all do. Martyn's mouth bunches up tight and he digs the end of his lace sharply into his trainer.

'Oh, because you're doing such a good job as our leader, aren't you, and only you know the truth,' Martyn snarls.

Even Jeremiah looks taken aback.

'Because it's all going so well, isn't it?' Martyn carries on. 'The government have responded to our demands, haven't they? And you said it would work, you said the God of Hebetheus would go into the politician's dreams and guide them. And that woman who knows the dead old woman keeps passing by the house, looking in, sooner or later she's gonna want to be let in, and Thomas's sick – and he needs medicine and you know it.'

We all stare at Jeremiah. He looks helpless.

'Look,' he says quickly, 'Thomas is undergoing a Soul Shift and he's not here with us in prayers this morning because he needs to rest – it's a big adjustment for his body to make –'

'*Because* he's a schizo!' Martyn shouts. 'And he needs his medicine! And you told him before we came to stop taking it, he didn't take it for a week and he didn't bring his pills and he needs them and now he's sick and look

174

how much good it's done him!'

Thomas? Thomas a *schizo*? Thomas can't be a schizo. Schizos are the bad guys in movies who hear voices and have six different *raptors* in their bodies, fighting for their soul. Martyn's lying, isn't he, Jeremiah, isn't he?

'Thomas is . . . mildly schizophrenic,' Jeremiah says, turning to us. 'But he is still one of our Brothers. We don't discriminate against schizophrenics. And I feel we all need to pray for him –'

'Pray for him?' Martyn cries. 'He doesn't need prayers, he needs medicine and he needs it now. One of us has to go into town and break into somewhere and get it –'

'No.'

'*Yes*. It needs to be done –'

'This is your Sacred Cleansing,' says Jeremiah. 'We will discuss Thomas later. I am praying for Thomas –'

'But –'

'I have asked God what to do and I am waiting for an answer. Now is the time for your Sacred Cleansing.'

'But how come you're the only one who God can talk to?' Martyn yells. 'What if I had a dream and God said I was the one he wanted to speak to? How can you say your dreams are any more special than mine?'

'Either you undergo a Sacred Cleansing now or you leave the Brotherhood. We have discussed this and agreed this is the time for your Sacred Cleansing.'

Martyn turns to face us, his eyes narrowed.

'Who here thinks I should undergo a Cleansing?'

There is a silence. Jeremiah's eyes hold mine like a laser.

'I do,' Raymond says.

'I do,' I say quickly – anything for him to stop looking at me like that.

Jeremiah's spotlight spins to Chris. Chris flushes the

colour of a tomato and quickly nods a *Yes*.

Jeremiah lets out a sharp breath. Briefly, his expression looks almost stricken but it quickly smoothes out to normality again.

'Good,' he says. He turns back to Martyn, who is also looking shocked. Martyn gives Chris a murderous glance. Then he swallows and mutters, 'Okay, I'll do it then . . .'

'So let's go back to when you first joined the Hebetheus.' Jeremiah's voice is gentle. 'Do you remember the dream I had about you? And at first you didn't believe me – you doubted me, d'you remember you told me that? No – don't bristle – you don't need to defend yourself. Your doubt was understandable. It would have been strange if you hadn't felt doubt. But do you remember the words I said that touched you, that made you believe?'

Martyn starts and looks slightly nervous.

'I saw your father in my dream,' says Jeremiah slowly, 'and he was a *raptor*. I told you he was evil and you suddenly went quiet and realised that if I knew that, I must be telling the truth. He is a *raptor*, isn't he, Martyn?'

Martyn nods slowly. His anger seems to have dissipated; now he looks wary, vulnerable, almost boyish.

'And do you remember when you had to perform your Initiation? Yes, I know the details are always to be kept secret but for once we will share them with your Brothers. I told you to burn his clothes, didn't I? I told you to take all the bottles from his drinks cabinet and pour them into the ground, didn't I? To release him from his suffering and his anger?'

Martyn nods.

'It was a test,' says Jeremiah, 'and you suffered for it. You knew from the beginning that you would. But it showed, it proved, that you would do anything for the

Brotherhood; it proved your love for God. You were so brave, Martyn, so brave, and I felt so proud of you.'

Martyn gives a gruff, lopsided smile, his face dreamy with memory.

'And you remember what your father did when he discovered you had burnt his clothes and poured away his drinks?'

'Yeah, he hit me,' Martyn says lightly, shrugging as if to say, *So what?*

'You were black and blue. He put you in hospital. But that wasn't the first time, was it?'

'He doesn't mean to do it, he's not a bad dad, he just drinks too much,' Martyn says frowning. 'He's not a bad dad – it's just like you said – he's nice but the *raptors* in his drink take over him and then he goes a bit crazy and he turns nasty on me and . . .'

My heart burns for Martyn; this is like watching him undress; I almost feel I shouldn't be here. But then again, he has seen me naked, and we're all Brothers, aren't we?

'And your mum . . . ?' Jeremiah coaxes him.

'Yeah, she left three years ago.'

'She left you a note, didn't she?'

'Yeah, on the table . . . she left a note . . . she'd left me a bit of money too, my lunch money for that week, but Dad had already taken it, he was already down to the supermarket . . . and . . .'

'Or maybe you drove her away?'

'*What?*'

What? we all echo in silent shock.

Jeremiah's face suddenly twists into a sneer. It looks so unexpected, so out of place on his features, that for a moment he almost looks as though a *raptor* has wriggled beneath his face and taken hold.

'Maybe you drove your mum away. Maybe she and your dad were happy together, and then she got pregnant, you came along, and you put a strain on the family, and then your dad started to lose it and to drink and you drove her away.'

'What!' Martyn's voice rises. 'I didn't drive her away! Is that what this is all about, is that what you're getting at? You're saying I'm a liar, a liar who drove his mum away! My dad did it, it was him, it was him, you should have seen the way he treated her – beating her up – I wanted her to go, I TOLD her to go, to be free of him –'

'But you wanted her to stay too, didn't you? You still felt deserted when she finally did leave?'

'What is this?' Martyn's voice breaks; his whole body is stretched taut, his fists perched on his knees like grenades. 'I don't want to talk about this; I want my Sacred Cleansing to begin.' He sniffs, jerking his palm across his face.

'And your father? Didn't you feel as though you'd failed him too?'

Stop, I want to shout, stop this, Jeremiah. What are you doing to him, what is this?

'Failed him?' Martyn's eyes flash.

'Come on – you tried to convert him to the Hebetheus that night he beat you, but you couldn't bring him on to our side. Now he'll never reach Manu – you failed your own father –'

'You try telling him!' Martyn screams. 'You don't know what it's like, he won't even listen when I ask him to give me my lunch money, I can't go home half the time, I haven't got a home, he's not even a real – dad – I don't have – you – fucking –' He sees another sneer on Jeremiah's face and *wham!* thumps Jeremiah across the face, sending him flying back on to the floor.

The silence blazes. Raymond jumps to his feet, shaking. Chris is white. I half-stand, then collapse back down on the floor.

'Jeremiah?' Raymond whispers in an icy voice.

Martyn goes to stand up, poised to fight. But Jeremiah sits up, rubbing his raw cheek and – to our amazement – he laughs softly. Martyn stares at him, appalled – and then, as though cut down – he suddenly breaks and starts to cry. Raymond blinks. Martyn goes to strike out again through the blur of his tears but Jeremiah leans in and hugs him. At first he struggles in shame and fury but Jeremiah says, 'It's all right, you don't need to care about that bastard, we're your family now, we're your family now, we're here with you and we want you to be with us,' and Martyn lets go, lets the tears flow though he's probably never cried in front of anyone in his life before. My heart ties up into a knot and I feel as though for the first time I understand Martyn, I've had a glimpse into his soul and I say silently: *I'm so sorry, Martyn, I'm so sorry.*

'We can't all be leaders,' Jeremiah says, 'we can only have one, but Martyn, this doesn't mean you don't have a place here in the Brotherhood. You have a place,' he says fiercely, 'you have a place and you have no idea how important you are, how every minute of the day God beams with pleasure that you are doing his work. God is your father now and he is so proud of you. We couldn't have done this, we couldn't have saved our school from SNAKE's evil, without you, without anyone here. You must never forget that.'

Martyn nods, sniffing, embarrassed by the tears he's shed. But a pride burns in his eyes and he nods again, bowing his head before our Great Leader.

# 12 P.M.

As I enter the Hostage Room, carrying Padma's food, she picks up her glass and hurls water at me.

Her cuffs ruin her aim; the water sails past me in an arc, spraying me only softly. I wobble; her plate of baked beans nearly pitches to the floor. She thumps down her glass, glaring at me with wolfish eyes. I put down her plate, next to the last night's plate: uneaten, the beans congealing in a pyramid of orange gloop.

'I hate you,' she seethes.

'Padma –'

'You didn't tell them, did you?' she tries to kick me as I sit down next to her. 'You lied to me! You said you'd talk to Jeremiah about Martyn and then come back and tell me, you lied to me!'

'No – no – you've got it all wrong. I did – I did! I told them and Jeremiah believes you, he knows you're telling the truth.'

'So they're not going to kill me now?'

'No – I –'*Oh God, forgive me.* 'No. It's okay.'

She blinks several times, then breaks into tears of relief. My heart knots. I put my arm around her and she leans in and lets out a choked sigh. I run my hand over her hair. It feels like a sheen of black water. I know I should stop right now; the others are waiting for me in the kitchen and they might come in at any minute. But I stay there, holding her, feeling her warmth seep into me. I need that warmth; ever since Marytn broke down this morning, I've been feeling strange . . . *tainted* . . . I stroke her hair, over and over and it's as though her hair is like Samson's, as though there is magic in it, not strength but softness, a healing, soothing softness; I feel human again. I remember the look on Jeremiah's face as he sneered at Martyn and then I remind myself: Jeremiah did it out of love; he was cruel to be kind.

Someone could come in any minute. I make to move but she clings to me tightly and suddenly the silence between us is alive, prickling and tingling like the air before a storm. She looks at me and I look down at her and then I pull away quickly and tell her I must go; I will be back some time after I have eaten to educate her.

# 4 P.M.

**God, I'm sorry. I need to confess.** I need to tell you what just happened with SNAKE. I need to clear my conscience. I just hope you can forgive me.

I *kissed* her. Or she kissed me. I don't know how it happened; it should never have happened, but it happened. And now I feel sick with guilt.

I didn't even go into the Hostage Room alone. To begin with, Jeremiah came in with me. I felt uneasy about him coming, which I guess is a bad sign; the *raptor* in me craved to be alone with her. The moment we entered the room, he and SNAKE locked eyes. Poison danced in her retinas. Jeremiah walked right up to her and stood looking down at her with a sneer. He waited for her to speak first.

'I'm not a terrorist, you know,' she said, her back pressed tight against the wall. Her voice was shaking slightly; I realised just how terrified she was of him, though she tried desperately to hide it. 'Come on, if I was white, I wouldn't be here, would I? I just happen to fit your nice little stereotype of a terrorist. You're the type of guy who sees anyone who's Asian or from the Middle East with a rucksack on a bus and immediately assumes they're carrying a bomb.'

'Oh, am I?' Jeremiah looked ruffled. 'Because anyone

who wants to combat terrorism is really just a racist, aren't they? I'm racist because I want to live in a world free from terror? I'm racist because I want to live in a world of peace.'

'Look – I'm the same – I'm a Hindu. I love God, I love the world, I believe in peace.'

'A Hindu.' Jeremiah rolled his eyes. 'And I suppose you believe in reincarnation. I read about that. How when you're dying your last thoughts determine where you go in your next life because hey, man, we all get recycled.'

'Do you want to know why we believe in reincarnation?' she spat out. 'Because we believe in karma. If you do wrong, it comes back to you, in this life or the next; if you do good, it comes back to you. And when you're free from karma then you get enlightenment, the ultimate freedom but you wouldn't understand that because this karma is on your head, all that you're doing to me now – you'll have to suffer it yourselves, you'll have to pay for this!'

Jeremiah stared her down and said, 'I'm not afraid.'

'You know, people like you – you're all Devil Worshippers!'

'Devil Worshippers!' Jeremiah mocked her.

'You do, you worship the Devil. It doesn't matter what words you use – if you kill in the name of God, then it's not to please God, it's to please the Devil. In fact God does just become a name, a meaningless name, a word. You – you give religion a bad name. It can help people so much, do so much good, but when people read about people like you they think religion can only do harm and bring more suffering into the world –'

'It's not killing if you're stopping other people being killed!' Jeremiah said in a voice of ice. 'It's our duty to help people live their lives in peace and freedom.'

'Freedom!' Padma cried, 'that's a joke coming from a fascist like you.'

'No. We're a democracy. I'm not forcing anyone to be here, SNAKE. Any of us can just walk out when we please. You want to go, Jon? You can just go, can't you?'

I nod quickly, jumping as Padma glares at me.

'Come on. In your cult, people aren't allowed to read, they're not allowed to think – it's fascism.'

'No, we simply believe in democracy where people do as we guide them for their own good.' Jeremiah shook his head. 'Don't tell me, SNAKE – I suppose you disagreed with the war in Iraq? I guess you opposed the introduction of democracy there?'

'Yes,' Padma hissed. Then suddenly she turned to me. 'D'you agree with the war in Iraq?'

'I – I – no –'

'Not what *they* tell you to think, not their brainwashing – what *you* think!' she cries.

'I – I don't know enough about it –'

'It doesn't matter if you don't know anything!' she grabbed my hand and to my horror, right in front of Jeremiah, she pulled me down beside her and put her hand on my heart. 'Here. This is how you decide if something's right or not. This is how you know. You can't listen to arguments, to crap, to evil thoughts, you listen to your intuition – to your heart and then you feel what's right!'

I stared at her, gaping, and then looked up at Jeremiah, terrified that he would sense everything, would know how I held her just a few hours ago. But he knelt down on the other side of Padma and pressed his hand to her heart. She shuddered, curling away from him, but he held her gaze and smiled.

'I can feel the most terrible *raptor* in the world in here,'

184

he said. Then he reached out into his pocket and pulled out a noose.

'No!' she cried. The colour drained from her face. 'No.' She turned to me. 'You said – you said –'

'Hold her down,' Jeremiah said. 'Hold her down while I put it on.'

I grabbed her arms. I couldn't look her in the eye. I couldn't bear it.

She didn't fight back. She didn't scream. She froze; Jeremiah tightened the rope, checking it with scientific scrutiny. My whole body became clammy with sweat. My heart was screaming out that this is all wrong, I can't do it, oh, God, I thought I would be able to go through with it, but I can't, I can't –

'Good.' Jeremiah took the noose off and stood up. 'It fits.'

He walked over to the door. 'I'll leave you to educate her. We'll wait until the ten o'clock news tonight to see if the government responds. In the meantime, try to save her soul, Jon. Remember: if she dies unsaved . . .'

I turned to Padma. And then – she kissed me.

But that's a lie. And I cannot lie to you, God. I was the one who leant in and – I don't know why, God, I don't know why I did it. Maybe it was the evil of sheer lust. But it felt like more than that. I think it was the look of pain on her face. I couldn't bear it. I wanted, simply, to make her feel better.

I kissed her and at first she didn't respond. And then we were kissing and for a moment it was surreal: everything was forgotten, past, present and place. It just felt as though I was kissing this wonderful, golden angel and I wanted to drink in her kisses like nectar . . .

A little *zapor* climbed on to my shoulder and whispered

into my ear: *She's a terrorist. You're kissing a terrorist. What are you doing?*

But when I broke off and looked down at her she gave me a look of such sweetness . . . I don't understand, God – how can such evil be wrapped in such beauty? Have you done this to test us? To tease us?

I don't understand. And then there was more. It got worse than just a kiss.

She said to me: 'How can you believe him? How can you believe all this Hebetheus shit? You seem so *nice*. So intelligent.'

I should have defended you then but instead I just changed the subject. I told her I was going into town tonight with Chris to get some medicine for Thomas to help with his Soul Shift; I told her I could get her chocolate.

'What – but – but – can't – can't I come? If you're going at night, I could sneak out, I could escape.'

'Padma, I *can't* –'

She interrupted me with a kiss. I kissed her back, and I admit it, I wanted more, I ached to touch her, to feel her skin beneath my fingers – but she broke off and whispered, 'Please. You could find the key to the cuffs and hide it under a floorboard. Then when you go, I'll climb out of the window –'

'But someone will be on guard. They'll call Raymond and we'll only get away three feet before they'll catch us. I mean – there are five of them – and just me – don't you see –'

'We could just try! We're running out of time!'

The *we* made me jump. It was so authoritative that I felt scared, angry: didn't she realise I was a member of the Brotherhood? Didn't she see the risk I was taking; what would Jeremiah say if he walked in right now?

Then I looked into her face and realised she was desperate. That I was the only one she felt she could trust. Her last hope.

'Look, we'll think up a plan, I promise,' I whispered, hardly able to believe what I was saying. 'But it has to work. I'll think it up tonight, when I go. I promise.'

'Okay.' She looked so sad that I put my arm around her again, kissing her hair. I kissed the smooth ebony of her cheek, the edge of her lips, but she shook her head, pushing me away. I heard a creak outside in the hallway and I quickly recited:

'"The Hebetheus is a new religion which aims to avoid the mistakes of past religions." Look, I'll get you a Coca-Cola. Anything you want.'

Padma fixed her gaze on the sunlight square that formed a barred window on the boards.

Suddenly the door opened. I was too close to Padma and I stumbled back.

'Jeremiah w-w-wants to see you,' Chris said.

'Jeremiah w-w-wants to see you,' Padma imitated his stutter perfectly. Chris flushed in outrage. For a moment I was taken aback by her cruelty. Then I realised she was saving me.

'Shut up, SNAKE, you stupid bitch!' I cried harshly. 'Okay, Chris I'll just be a minute. I'm on rule nine and I want her to get it. If she can.'

Chris left without closing the door properly.

'I have to go,' I whispered, my eyes flitting from the door to Padma to the door.

'Please when you're out can you just call my mother,' she whispered.

'What? "The Hebetheus states that every member has a duty to expel evil and cleanse the world."'

'Call my mother, please let her know that I'm safe. Please. Please.'

'I –' I was about to say *I can't* when Padma raised her eyes to mine. I saw the pain deep in her pupils. I thought of how it must have been, that night that Jeremiah sidled up to her in the nightclub, of those lonely nights of terror, sitting here, wondering what we might do to her. I whispered *Yes*, and then I sinned again; I leant in to take another kiss and this time she let me and bliss burned through my body. Then there was a creak and I saw Chris at the door and my heart turned upside down – *Did he see?* – but his expression was neutral. I informed Padma coldly that next time I would expect her to be able to recite the ten rules of Hebetheus back to me and she rolled her eyes very lightly, a tiny smile at her lips, before assuming a contrite expression.

What have I done, God? What am I doing? I keep on re-tasting the sweet honey of that kiss, but I know it's poison. And what did I do, offering to help her escape?

I shouldn't have promised her I'd call her mother. I shouldn't have promised her. What am I going to *say*? And how will I find a phone box, what excuse can I make? Oh, God, I feel as though she has wriggled into my heart and is still writhing there. Please destroy her. Please save me. Please keep me pure and forgive me.

# 10 P.M.

**I give Chris a sidelong glance.** Snow is falling: entire fields of white stretch out before us and fresh flakes begin to billow from the night sky. Now that my hair is shorn the cold bites into my naked scalp with vicious teeth. Beside me, Chris squints at the little map Raymond drew when he stole into town earlier this afternoon. Raymond said it was 'straightforward' – just follow the road down for two miles and then when it meets the big main road follow the signs to 'town centre'.

But 'straightforward' is the wrong word. The future feels jagged with what-ifs; with traps and pitfalls and wrong turns we might take. We're jittery with nerves. What if CCTV picks us out in town? What if someone recognises us and calls the police? Every so often we find ourselves looking back and peering at the cottage, watching it grow smaller and smaller until it is just a smudge on the horizon. And in the meantime the big wide world out there gets closer and closer.

I start to worry about Padma's call again, when suddenly something wet splats across my head. I jump and turn on Chris, who grins wickedly.

'Ow, you bastard, now that really hurts!' I reach down and gather a ball and Chris yells and runs on. As I aim to throw, we share a nervous look: *Should we be doing this?* But we have to do this; it's the only way to stave off our terror. I toss the ball at him and cheer as it explodes against his sweater.

From then on, all the way into town, we fight. We pass houses, woods, yelling and screaming with hysterical laughter, and for half an hour, everything is forgotten, it's as though we're just walking home from school together, having a laugh.

Then we hit the first main road into town. That sobers us up. Even though all the shops are shut, there are still a few people about – mostly our age. I'm wearing a tracksuit Raymond lent me and I quickly pull the hood up over my face. My senses feel torn in a hundred different directions. It's as though we have been locked away for months and months. The world seems a technicolour dazzle; we pass shops, drunkenly feasting on commerce; horns and screeching tyres scrape our senses.

And every so often we see someone.

An elderly tramp, his face graffitied with life's sorrows, trudging past with a bottle of gin. A girl with a bouncy walk and red hair like a fox and a nose-ring. I stare at her in fascination and she bigs her eyes at me as if to say *What are you staring at?* I quickly look away. I feel strange. Something is wrong, something is different.

I realise that usually I look at people as though I'm behind a glass cocoon. Usually I pity them, feel sorry for their ignorance, for their doomed and silly souls. But now – I feel almost . . . a sense of kinship with them. Like an echo of the feeling I had earlier today when Padma kissed me. Has my lust corroded my spirituality? Is she turning me into one of them?

'When w-we get to B-Boots, c-c-c-an you be the one to

smash the glass?' Chris stammers as we pass a newsagent.

'I – I –' I stop, wheel back to the billboard outside. 'Hang on, that's us!' I point at the headline: *HOSTAGE DEADLOCK WITH TEEN BOYS*.

Across the road, a newspaper is lying on a bench beneath a soggy bag of leftover chips. I run over, shoving the chips aside so that they splat to the pavement in a yellow bird's nest. I flip through the paper frantically.

'W-w-we should go, w-w-we don't have m-much t-time,' Chris says.

Jordan . . . drugs . . . footballers . . . where are we? I feel a strange twist of disappointment. So nobody's noticed us; nobody cares. A risk of jail – all for nothing.

Then I turn to the front page of the *Mirror*.

*WE WILL KILL HER*, the headline screams. Underneath there is a photo of Martyn: a grainy black-and-white smear cut from the video.

'Jesus!' Chris cries.

I scan the article, phrases leaping out: . . . *none of us can understand what these boys are doing . . . we all know Padma Laxsmi is a kind and innocent girl . . . these boys are deluded and dangerous criminals . . . Padma Laxsmi is the victim of an insane mistake* . . . It feels odd, as though we are reading about other people, another version of our story where everything has been simplified, like a movie: six evil boys and one victim.

'Here – listen to this!' Chris jabs the page. 'It ss-says they are t-trying to tr-track us d-down from o-our computer and e-mailed v-video threats but they c-can't b-because one of us must be a c-computer – genius! I'm f-famous.'

'We're going to end up in jail –' I say, my voice breaking. Then I look at Chris quickly. 'Only we won't, our God will save us. We'd better go to Boots.'

We slip down a dingy side alley to the back of the shop. As Chris passes me the crowbar, I don't even feel nervous any more. What we are doing now seems trivial compared to the horrors the *Mirror* described. We're doomed anyway, so what would a robbery charge matter? I wield the crowbar and crash it against the window. The smash shocks me out of my numb state: as glass tumbles to the floor, my heart yells *What are you doing?* But there's no going back now. I swallow, watching Chris prise open the doors. His face looks vivid with adrenaline; as he yanks them open, he whoops with pride.

Earlier on, Raymond cut the wires to the alarms. But I don't trust him; I steel myself, waiting for alarms to scrape my ears.

But: a safe cocoon of silence. Chris and I stumble in. A shelf of chocolate bars sing to us. All we've eaten in the last few days is toast, or beans on toast, or beans. We grab handfuls of Twixs and Marses and Flakes and Caramels, Topics, Lion Bars, Twirls, shoving them into our pockets. Chris dives for a can of Coke –

'We'd better get going,' I cry.

'Yes –'

'The pharmacy – it's over there –'

The pharmacy is cool and grey, a toyshop of coloured boxes with fancy Latin names. Chris starts panicking, pulling out cough cures and flu elixirs, tossing them on the floor. A bottle of cough medicine spins over and breaks, emitting a sickly syrup with a cherry smell.

'Chris – calm down! Just be cool, try those shelves –'

'H-Here is it!'

'Is it? You've got it?' I run over to him. 'No – that's not it, Chris, you're panicking –'

'I don't know where the h-hell it is!'

'Calm down. Look – here – here – this medicine is serious stuff, they'll have locked it up at the back, okay? I think we should try these cabinets.'

'They're l-locked.'

'Well, smash them then!'

Bad idea: several of the medicines topple out, smash-crashing on to the floor.

'Shit!'

'Look, we just have to focus.'

We squint at the array of concoctions. Minutes squeal past. My eyes burn; it gets to the point where I start read-ing a name without reading it.

'We could just take some Valium!' I cry, picking out a box. 'Just give him a double dose.'

'What about th-this?'

'No – that's not it – hey – this one at the back –'

'Y-you've g-got it –'

'Yes. *Yes*. Come on! We have to get out of here!'

As we leave, Chris knocks against the door and suddenly an alarm comes to life.

'I knew Raymond would –'

'J-just GO!'

We slip through the alley and dash back on to the main street. A man walking by stares. He's wearing a neat grey overcoat and an eccentric black hat – a wide-brimmed one, the sort you see on gangsters in 1920s movies. He spots us and roars:

'STOP!'

Chris tugs my sleeve, wheeling behind me. I grab him and we run.

'COME BACK HERE, HOODIES!'

Shops and benches streak by. My hood flies back off my face with a blast of freezing air. The ground is thick with snow, my trainers skidding all over the place. I look back; he is gaining on us. His hat flies off and he lets out a bellow, then leaves it behind. I notice his head is entirely bald and for some reason this suddenly strikes me as hysterical and laughter bubbles in my torn lungs. Then Chris stumbles, half-falling in the wet snow. I yank him up and yell, 'COME ON!'

*Oh, God, please don't let him catch us, Oh, God, please don't let him catch us*, I cry inwardly to the rhythm of my thudding feet. My legs begin to tremble as though the muscles will snap; my lungs swirl with acid. The shops are coming to an end; we hit a main road, looking left right left right which way and then Chris lets out a cry and I turn and suddenly the man is right behind us and he reaches out, yanking my hood and I cry out and he pulls my tracksuit top clean away and slips forward into the snow. Chris and I stare down at him. Then we run.

Across the road, a car is screaming and tooting to a halt. We run down a suburban street, then another. Chris is flailing, wheezing desperately. I pull him into a front garden. We leap over grass and gnomes, down a side path, crouching behind a fat green recycling bin. He fumbles, pulls out his inhaler and gulps it in, shaking violently. A Twix slips out of his pocket and falls to the ground. I pick it up.

I peer round the side of the bin – the man is walking on the other side of the road – and pull back with a heart-skip of shock. Chris sees the look in my eyes and freezes, silently sucking on his inhaler as though it's a dummy. I press my face against the plastic, peering with narrowed eyes. Cars; houses; a yellow-lit living room across the street with a cosy TV set scene. I wonder if my mum is watching TV right now. We wait. Snow falls; cars toot. The man comes back the other way. There is a small trickle of blood running down his forehead. I crush the Twix to pieces beneath the shiny paper. The man looks right at us and I am terrified he will spot our prints in the snow but then again they could have been anyone's. He dabs his forehead with a hanky and walks on.

Chris and I wait another ten minutes. We share a Twix, cramming the chocolate into our mouths, gorging ourselves on the comfort of sugar. After the Twix we have a Lion Bar, then a Twirl. Chris smudges chocolate on his cheek and I want to tell him to dab it off but I don't.

'We'd better save some for the others,' I whisper. I peer out from behind the bin. No sign of the man.

We get up and slink to the edge of the garden, creep from car to car, winding back to the main road, where we pause behind an illegally parked Fiat.

'We're l-lost,' Chris stammers.

'We're not – we just head down the main road and then it goes back into the country, right? Look, we'll get up on the count of three and then we RUN, okay? As fast as we can?'

We streak down the main road, looking back every three seconds to see if the man is following. But there is no sign of him. The main road thins and we stop outside a country pub and Chris breathes in more of his inhaler. A drunk woman comes stumbling out of the pub and I duck my face.

'W-w-we sh-should go through the w-w-oods,' Chris says. 'I kn-know the w-way.'

I frown.

'Are you sure?'

'Y-yeah – I w-w-went w-walking th-there with Martyn y-yesterday – we j-just w-went for a w-walk –'

195

'Okay –' I break off. For, a few feet down the road is a phone box.

An old-fashioned red one, quaintly preserved.

We walk on, right by it, and I tell myself I'll just tell Padma about the man who chased us and how there wasn't time to stop –

And then I remember the feel of her lips against me.

'I have to make a call.'

'What?' Chris cries.

'Just wait here. I'll be one minute.'

Chris stutters some more but I ignore him and run.

Earlier, when I was on a guard shift, Padma breathed on her window and wrote her mother's number in the mist. I memorised it, too nervous to write it down. I pick up the receiver, fumble in my pockets for the last dregs of my change. I slot in 30 pence. Chris bangs his fists against the glass, shaking his head in astonishment. I wave, mouthing 'Wait!' 0 . . . 2 . . . 0 . . . 8 . . . 5 . . . what was it – yes, 44, my mum's age, that's how I fixed it in my memory . . . 6 . . . 61, 6 for the 6th of May, the date I first spoke to Jeremiah, then 1 . . . and was it . . . 03 or 30 . . . oh God, what was it . . . ? Chris walks off, turns, throws up his hands. Wait, wait. 30. It was 30. It rings. What am I going to say? It keeps on ringing, on and on. Finally, someone picks up.

'Hello?' A man with a voice like elderly apples.

'Mrs Laxsmi – is that Mrs Laxsmi?'

'Who? Who is this?'

I slam down the phone. Chris stares at me. I squeeze my hand in my pocket, shoving savagely past tissue and chewing gum. Another 30 pence tumbles into the phone's throat. Chris throws up his hands again and begins to walk away. I tap it in quick: 02085446130. It rings. I push the door ajar with my foot and cry, 'Wait!' But Chris keeps going. Someone picks up.

'Padma?' I cry without thinking.

'Padma? Padma's not here . . . she's . . .'

I know instantly that I will never forget that voice. That for days and nights to come I will lie awake and re-taste the raw anguish of that voice: a voice more dead than alive.

'She's alive she's okay she's okay.'

'Oh, my God – oh, my God – you've got my Padma, are you the boy who has my Padma –' The stench of her anger is so intense that I cut in pleading:

'Please don't worry, she's alive, I'm going to get her back to you, I promise –'

She bursts into tears.

'Oh, my baby, oh, my poor baby . . .'

I find I am crying too. I smear my face with my fingers. I can't see where Chris is now; I don't care.

'I'm so sorry, I'm sorry,' I sob, 'I'm going to bring her back to you.'

'My little girl, oh, please tell me you haven't hurt my little girl –'

Beeps. I shove my hand in my pocket: no change left.

I stumble out of the phone box and down the road as though drunk.

'Oi, you!'

A cool car swerves past, boys and girls waving and whistling out of windows, bass-line pumping, the night is still young. I stare at them as my tears dry on my face. As they catcall, I think: I could have been in a car like that right now and now I'll probably never get to ride in a car like that again.

The car passes, the music fades.

Chris appears. He stops a wary two feet away.

'Yeah?' His anger steamrolls through his stutter. 'Have you finished telling the police?'

'You think I just told the police back there? You think I'd do that? Chris, I'm your Brother. I was calling my parents, okay? I called my mum. I didn't tell her anything. I just wanted to hear her voice.'

It might be a lie but my pain is palpable. Chris falls silent.

'Oh,' he says quietly. 'Okay.' Then: 'I won't tell Jeremiah. I think we sh-sh-shouldn't tell him about the m-man either.'

'No, we shouldn't. Thanks,' I say gruffly and we gaze at each other as Brothers.

# 11 P.M.

**We have five different symbols for God** in the Religion of
Hebetheus. The highest symbol is the circle. The circle,
Jeremiah told me, is an image of pure, simple, divine per-
fection. The perfection of God. No kinks in its smooth
infinite curving. And in the centre: the empty space that
God fills. Jeremiah, our Great Leader, is a human circle.
Empty, allowing the messages of God to fill his space. *So
God's message to Jeremiah can't be wrong, she must be
a –*

I push the thought away, focusing hard. It is another
hour until we will reach home. We walk in silence. The
air becomes more and more pure, until finally the cold
reaches a climax and bursts in another dizzy flurry of
snowflakes. My eyes water and my nose stings with cold.

*Padma Laxsmi has been kidnapped by a gang of evil
criminals . . . are you the boy who has my daughter . . .
what have you done with her?* I keep trying to push it
down; I keep trying to squeeze it tight into the corner of my
mind; my brow sweats and inwardly I recite Hebethean
chants frantically but it bursts through them, finally: the
Truth. Padma Laxsmi isn't a SNAKE. She's not a terrorist.

We've made a mistake.

We've taken a girl and we've locked her in a cellar and

we've starved her and put cuffs on her and bated her and bullied her. And she's innocent.

We're animals. Like terrorists. We have become that which we hate.

How could there be kinks in Jeremiah's circle? He can't be racist, like Padma said, and he can't be jealous of her high marks, and he can't be doing this for a joke, or for spite, or for attention, or madness, so, how, how can he have got it wrong?

I think of my father, the way he stood in the pulpit on Sundays, lecturing. I would sit beneath him, drinking in his words like they were honey pouring from bees in heaven. When I knelt down for prayers, the God I saw in my mind had a fluffy beard, like an older, more wizened version of my father. But Jeremiah isn't like him, I argue fiercely before the thought can even form. My father is a stupid, pathetic fraud who pretended he was perfect when he was living a lie and fucking a floozy. Jeremiah isn't a fraud, he can't be a fraud, he's divine. But –

Maybe God is testing him. Or . . .

Maybe God saw something Padma might do in the future. Maybe we didn't stop her doing something, but we stopped the possibility of something, a kind of pre-emptive threat. She might not be guilty now but she might have been guilty in the future and now we've prevented that future guilt and actually saved her –

I mean – wouldn't it have been better if someone had killed the snake before it tempted Eve? God would have killed an innocent snake but he would have saved a race from ruin . . .

Oh God. What will the headlines be the day they catch us? We'll pass from boys into myths, sixteen-year-old demons. We'll stand in court and everything we say will be cut and pasted, stretched and shaped into legends. They'll never see I was a real person. They'll never understand that it was all more complex than just six boys who wanted to torment a girl, that there was good in the Hebetheus, that we meant well. We'll be sent to jail, lost in metal cages, when we should have been drinking beer and meeting girls and having sex for the first time and all that forbidden adult stuff that sounds so scary but exciting. We'll have to change our names, like those boys who killed James Bulger. How strange, I think, I remember the day the newspapers wrote about that tragedy; Dad was driving me to school and it was on the radio. I remember the look of disgust on his face and how he shook his head. I could never have imagined then, never, that I might end up in the same boat.

'Hey!' Chris suddenly points. A horse appears, white as the falling snow. He neighs, snorting mist, before galloping off across the fields in lightning beauty.

I want to climb on his back and be carried away for ever.

Chris says, 'I know a short cut.'

I don't care where we go; I follow him numbly. The woods are white with silence, stretching out like the land of Narnia before Aslan comes to redeem it. At one point Chris stops to scorch his lighter against a tree, telling me he's branding a Hebethean symbol. As the flame highlights his face, I wonder: doesn't he ever doubt? Hasn't it hit him? Then I remind myself: he's my Brother. And the Brotherhood *is* good. Even if we made a mistake, we are good.

And tonight my Brother and I will return to the cottage and the deadline will be up. My Initiation will begin and I will be asked to kill her.

I watch Chris carry on scorching tree after tree and I feel like tearing the flame from him and holding it against my own skin.

# MIDNIGHT

'Jon,' Jeremiah says. 'I think you should narrate the video tonight.'

'We're not – we're not going to kill her?' I stammer.

'Why – d'you think we should?'

'No – I – *no* –'

'Chris has given Thomas his medicine. Thomas is not well yet, though he joins us this night. But he will be better tomorrow and I would like to see the Brotherhood united as a group. Besides, I feel we owe the public one last chance. This is about their redemption as much as hers. We must show them compassion; we must be patient. So Jon – your turn has come.'

I see Martyn's face crumple with disappointment; he has been looking for ways to please Jeremiah all day. I look at Raymond, who is playing about with his steel bar, his favourite toy of late. I think of being in the phone box, Padma's mother pleading with me. Suddenly a deep weariness rises up inside, filling me with black, choking smoke. I want to empty the Prayer Room and curl into a ball and sink into a bath of deep prayers. I want to wallow there and offer up my twisted heart to God and beg him to untangle it. But instead I have to stand here whilst a needle of headache begins to prick my temples.

'I'm feeling a bit tired,' I say, dropping my eyes.

'But not too tired to begin the first part of your Initiation, surely?' Jeremiah says in a very calm voice. 'To narrate this video is an honour.'

Suddenly I am aware of five pairs of eyes on me, watchful.

'Yeah, of course,' I say. 'Sure. I'll do the video. It's an honour. Yeah.'

I remember how desperate I once was to speak before the camera. To stand there and feel God's words flow through me. I once imagined that when I looked into the lens, I would see a minute world, a blur of faces and minds my words might seep into. Now all I can see is the glint of glass and a big blue eye behind it. It feels as though I am standing in front of a loaded gun.

'We of the Hebetheus religion are so compassionate that we are giving you one last chance.' My voice sounds flat and I try to buoy it up. 'We will not kill our hostage tonight.' I wonder what Padma's mother is doing now. Is she weeping, is Padma's father holding her? I realise I have lost my thread. Where was I? 'The Hebetheus religion believes in peace . . .' . . . and . . . what? What do I say next? I've forgotten the creed, I can't believe I've forgotten the creed.

I realise that the room has gone very quiet. I can hear the faint tap of Raymond's iron bar against his steel toecap.

I begin to panic. It's like being in an exam with a white sheet before you and a blank mind and everyone around is scribbling and oh God – thank God – the words rush back into places and I recite them by heart. My voice seems to detach from my doubts and take on a survival instinct of its own.

' . . . in peace for all mankind and Soul Shifts for every soul. If our demands are not met by 10 a.m. tomorrow, I will kill Padma.' I hold up the coil of rope for the camera to zoom in on.

I think of my mother's face when she switches on the news tomorrow and sees my face. I think of Mr Abdilla. Of Padma's mother.

'That was good,' Jeremiah says warmly, clapping me on the back. 'But you stumbled a bit – it's fine to be nervous in front of the camera. Try again.'

'Yeah, I was just a bit camera-shy,' I say, feeling strange again, as though I am in a room full of actors and I have to keep remembering to slip into my part. 'Cool. I'll do it better this time.'

I stand and wait. The headache begins to spread, its needle-prick expanding and blurring into a temple-thump. One of the candles flickers out and dark shadows seem to gather in the corners as though listening to me too. I think unsteadily: *Is God really here, sitting in this room, listening? What does he really think of this?* Remember Jeremiah's words, I tell myself fiercely, quick, remember:

'We of the Hebetheus religion are so compassionate that we are giving you one last chance.'

My voice is stronger this time.

'We will not kill Padma tonight.'

As I stare into the lens, it seems to spin like a white bird flying in a circle. I can see Padma's mother. Her fingers claw her cheeks as she breaks into a scream and she won't stop screaming and her screams knife my ears and I put my hands over my ears, folding in.

'Jon, are – are y-you okay?' I look up and see Chris. 'It's o-o-kay, it was just a s-s-siren.' He laughs nervously. 'It w-wasn't for us.'

'Don't worry, if they do come, we'll deal with them,' says Raymond, caressing his iron bar.

'Sorry – I just – I panicked –'

'The stone circle outside will protect us; God will protect us,' Jeremiah says coldly. 'Have more faith, Jon. Try again.'

*It's all right*, I keep telling myself, just do it again. How many goes did Chris take? At least eight. But a paranoid fear stings me. As Chris sets up the camera again, I feel my cheeks burn and my knees start to tremble and I'm certain they can see inside me, see every atom of fear and doubt. Oh God, why did I make that stupid call, why did I do it? My faith is too fragile, I've broken its shell and now it will take weeks to form a new one, oh why didn't I trust Jeremiah and listen to him?

I glance beyond the camera. Through a crack in the curtains I can see falling snow. An urge grips me: to run. To push past them, to head down the hallway, burst out of the door and just run, pound down the road, into the open sky, into the snow. I half turn, then slap myself and stand up straight. *Just do it, just get through this, just get it over and done with. Don't think about Padma, don't think about her mother, just push it aside and do this. You have to do this, Jon. If you don't: what will they do to you?*

'We of the Hebetheus religion are so compassionate that we are giving you one last chance,' I say. 'We will not kill Padma tonight . . .'

'Good one,' Raymond says, giving me a thumbs up, and I feel close to tears of relief.

'Nice,' says Martyn, nodding, giving Jeremiah a cautious glance. 'What do you think, Jeremiah?'

Jeremiah stares at me with a strange expression in his eyes.

'I think Jon should do it again,' he says.

'What was . . . okay,' I say, shrugging. 'It's cool. I'll do it again.'

I swallow. We do it again. I speak more quickly this time, the words tumbling out, and as everyone stares at me they seem to come closer and closer until they are gathered about me in a circle, their breaths stifling my breaths, their eyes boring into mine, and the urge comes again to curl into a ball but I fight it.

Then it's over. Raymond says it's perhaps not as good as the time before but it's still good.

'I think he should do it again,' Jeremiah says.

I look at him; he looks back.

'Sure,' I say, very lightly. 'I'll do it again.'

I do it again. Every word feels as though it limps, staggering, from my heart and I have to push it up my throat with both hands and force it out of my mouth. It's over and Jeremiah smiles and says do it again. The room fades and it's as though I am hanging in white space, just me and Jeremiah, my voice floating above me, and he asks me to recite it again. I do it again and this time the space cracks and the room becomes too real and there is sweat sliding long fingers down my back and I know I can't last, I feel as though I'm holding a table high above my head and my hands are shaking and I can't last out before my spine bends and breaks and I *snap* – and then Jeremiah says, 'Enough', and turns away.

I walk out into the hallway; Chris calls me and I wave my hand: *coming*. In the bathroom, I lock the door and break down into sobs. I collapse on to the floor, my head against the lino, as the sobs batter me like fists, punching my stomach until it is sore, wrenching wetness out of my ribs, bruising my eyes. I try to keep as quiet as possible.

I keep thinking they have stopped, but every time I try to rise they deal another blow. Finally, I stagger weakly to my feet. I flush the toilet just in case anyone is outside listening.

I turn to the sink, spin the taps. I look at my broken face and a curious voice whispers: *Who are you?* Then I cup the water and cleanse my face, over and over, until it is soft.

I find myself reaching down beneath the sink and yanking out the Bible. My hands are shaking violently; I flick through pages so quickly the fine paper tears like tissue. I read a proverb, a parable, a revelation. I want it to fill me up and take away the pain, to tell me the Hebetheus is wrong and this is right, but I only feel more and more desperate and empty and I find myself ripping out pages and tearing them into shreds. I open the window and throw the Bible out into the darkness and heave in breaths.

Outside, I feel as though I am barely capable of speech. But I don't have to talk to anyone, for Jeremiah orders that I won't be getting much sleep tonight; Martyn has been released from his watch and I will have to guard the house for the next two hours.

# 1 A.M.

**I guess you're laughing at me now,** aren't you Dad? It's 1 a.m. and I'm sitting out here with Raymond in the freezing cold on watch, shivering, feeling *sick* inside, knowing this is all rot, all a waste of time, oh I bet you're laughing at me now.

On impulse, I tell Raymond that I need the toilet. He frowns but says nothing.

The others are all asleep. Padma must be asleep too, for when I pause outside her room the door is framed with a dark slit.

The key sits in the locked door. I twist it slowly, open the door very gently, step into the room, and close it behind me. It's so dark that her body is just a hump on the floor, like a piece of driftwood that's washed up from the sea. I can hear her snoring gently. The clouds in the night sky part and a shaft of moonlight washes over her face, lies in pools around her plump mouth. I sit down in the shadows and red thoughts slither into my mind, burning hot inside my face. I see myself crawling across the floor and lying down against her. Waking her gently with a soft, moist kiss. Tasting her sleep in her kiss. Her desire. A look of sweet surprise on her face. More kisses. In my fantasy, her cuffs fall away by magic. She unbuttons my shirt and kisses every moment of my chest. I tear off her top and run my tongue over her nipples. I've never touched a breast before. The thought electrifies me, hot charges gushing through my body.

And then:

A knife of shame slams down, cutting my snake-desire into two. To lust is a sin. She is a female viper, luring me, tricking me. I remember those wicked words she spoke earlier: *How can you believe all this Hebetheus shit, Jon. You seem so nice. So intelligent.*

And suddenly my desire is replaced by hate. It pours through me like acid. I remind myself that she is innocent but it only makes me hate her even more. Her innocence feels like a mockery, a deliberate joke to ridicule our Leader.

How *dare* she defy the God of Hebetheus? What's her religion? Just a load of silly gods. And as for enlightenment – it sounds as though she just copied the term Soul Shift and gave it another name. She's just manipulating me, tying me in a cat's cradle of lust, tearing at my faith, tearing me to pieces. Bitch. Bitch, bitch, *bitch*.

I look up at the square of sky framed by the window. To imagine that the God of Hebetheus is only a product of my imagination, to accept that he is not a force singing through all things in this world, pushing the earth round, arranging the swing of the sun and the moon, suddenly knocks the air out of my chest. I feel cold inside; my heart goosebumps in misery. How pale the stars look. And what is beyond them? Darkness, and more dying stars, and planets whose atmospheres are too cruel for life to exist. I stare out at the faintest twinkle of the distant town lights, where people are, this very minute, committing crimes and sins. The big bad world that I must now face without armour, without a shield.

My fist clenches in my lap. I picture myself storming across the boards, waking her with a harsh kiss and then *wham* smashing open her face, punching away her lies –

'Jon?' she whispers. She is awake. Suddenly. 'Jon? Did you call –'

I get up quickly and run out, closing the door behind me. I run down the hallway and sit outside quietly beside Raymond while my heart freezes, by degrees, into a cold hard ball.

Guard duty ends; Martyn takes over. Inside, I lie awake for hours, voices yelling in my mind, until finally a nightmare grabs me and pulls me under.

I dream that I am lying out on the front lawn, the snow seeping into my naked head. I am staring up at the stars and I am calling out to God. I am yelling at him, screaming at him, *Are you there God, are you there?* I can hear my voice echoing around the stars, through the empty heavens and back to me. Echoing through emptiness. But I keep yelling, I keep screaming and –

I wake up hearing myself scream and I'm aware of a voice beside me, telling me it's all right Jon it's all right and for a moment I think I am back home with my mum.

And then I remember.

I lie there, shaking, and Jeremiah keeps telling me it's all right, I'm all right, go back to sleep. He lies beside me, not touching but close enough so that the warmth of his body seeps into mine.

Every so often I wake up in the night and I am aware of that warmth close to me, a balm that soothes me and sends me back to sleep . . .

# Day Five

# 8 A.M.

**The next morning I wake up** feeling tired. I'm aware of
Chris and Martyn whispering across a mattress; I turn
away to face the wall. I picture what I would be doing in
the real world right now if I wasn't here. I'd be getting
up, getting ready for school. Mum would be shouting at
me to hurry up as she needs the bathroom, followed by
shouting at me to hurry up and come down before my
breakfast gets cold before shouting at me for not eating
it. Then I'd be on the school bus and in for registration
and I'd be starting Geography with Mr Tims who has a
twitchy eye which always makes me laugh. I miss it all,
even Mum's shouting.

I think perhaps that the God of Hebetheus might not
exist. And I don't know what to do or think. I feel ashamed
of my fury for Padma last night. It feels now as though
hatred took me over like a *raptor* and I became another
person. But this isn't the first time I've felt like this. That's
the worst thing: the repetition of it all. I remember what I
went through when my belief in Christianity came crashing
down: the sleepless nights, the tastelessness of food, the
brick I threw through the church stained-glass window in
a fit of rage, only luckily Dad didn't find out and blamed it
on vandals. Isn't there anything worth believing in? It

doesn't seem so. I feel white with despair. Useless. With no energy to even feel any more.

In the hallway, I hear the sound of Jeremiah's cheerful voice ringing out, telling Thomas he looks much better, instructing him to prepare breakfast before prayers.

I decide I'm just going to lie here. I'll tell the others I'm ill. Yes, I'm just going to lie here and let the days disappear into nights and let my Brothers carry on with their crazy stupid stuff, let the world spin on with its wars and loves and highs and lows, let time go singing by . . .

And then the godsend comes.

# 9 A.M.

**Thomas calls out that we are on the news.**

I want to carry on lying in bed but Martyn and Chris jump up, yelling, 'Come on Jon!' I try to ignore them but Martyn grabs the end of my feet and pulls me across the mattresses, sleeping bags carpet-burning my back. I yell out and then he tickles me and I dissolve into laughter. Tears burn behind my eyes; then, before he can assault me again, I quickly get up.

'Okay, okay, I'm coming,' I mutter. Even speaking seems to take too much effort; my vocal cords feel as though they have been slashed.

Martyn and Chris exchange glances. Then Martyn turns to me and asks if I'm happy.

I quickly reply sure, I'm happy. Then I look into his eyes and I see an unexpected compassion. And for a moment all my fears nearly come flooding out. I wonder: *Does he ever doubt? Does he ever wonder if we are really saving the world?*

But, no. I can't imagine Martyn or Chris ever do. Because to doubt, to take away everything you believe in, to leave your mind without a structure, is too unbearable. If only I could wind back the clock, if I only I could walk back from experience to innocence again. But I can't undo the damage: it's too late. So I smile again and say I'm fine and Martyn just shrugs.

As I walk into the kitchen, a deep sense of loneliness overwhelms me. I look round at my Brothers and they seem like strangers. Long before I joined the Hebetheus, I felt as though I never fitted in anywhere. Even the Christian Church felt slightly false, as though I was wearing my father's second-hand persona. At school I never felt cool enough for the hards or sad enough for the squares. The Hebetheus made me feel as though I finally had an armour, a texture, a colour that made me more than plain old Jon. And now, once again, I'm an outsider. And I can't even tell any of them or they'll just say I am insane and order a Sacred Cleansing for me.

I slump down on a kitchen chair. Up above, Mr Abdilla appears on the screen.

His face looks haggard, as though the skin is slowly sliding off the bones, causing his eyes to appear unnaturally bulbous.

'Boys – Jon, Jeremiah, Thomas, Martyn, Chris, Raymond – I have some good news for you.

'Firstly, thank you for trying to make contact. We appreciate this and we would like to hear from you again.'

*Contact?* He must be talking about the phone call I made.

I sit frozen in my chair. Fear exhales an icy blast across the back of my neck. I wait for Chris to tell them everything. But he remains silent. And nobody else says anything. I realise in shaky relief: they probably think he's just referring to the video.

I feel so nervy that for a moment I don't realise what Mr Abdilla is saying. I look up at the screen in disbelief. Then I tune in. 'I am pleased to announce that the police have taken your allegations about Padma Laxsmi very seriously and have investigated your claims, but at this moment in time they have not yet found any evidence that she is a terrorist. Her home and locker have been searched and we have not found any bomb-making equipment. Perhaps it is time for you to pass Padma over to the police, however, and let them question her, which they will be able to do more fully at a police station. You also made some very compelling and interesting points about changing the laws and I am glad to report that last night I spoke directly with the prime minister himself and he has assured me that they are thinking very carefully about holding a Commons debate regarding the length of detention of terrorists this week.

'May I suggest now that your demands are being taken seriously and that we could arrange to meet? If you could telephone the following number, I will be able to talk to you and arrange for a safe place that we can all meet to talk together? I can assure you that if we meet you will not be in any trouble and that we are merely anxious for your safe return and to see that Padma Laxsmi is also safe.'

As he reels off the number, Thomas grabs a pen and hastily writes it down.

An icy gush of euphoria floods through me. Oh, thank God, oh, thank God, we can leave now and Padma will be safe. I open my mouth. A squeak comes out. Chris turns and laughs. His face is such a bright red all his freckles look neon. Martyn does a monkey jump and punches me on the shoulder and I tussle him and Raymond cheers and joins in and Chris starts tugging all our legs to trip us up and even Thomas laughs and joins in jumping on top of us and we turn into a roaring joyous tiger-tangle of legs and arms and laughter.

'Wait!' Jeremiah orders.

Martyn jumps up, spins around and then punches him breathlessly on the shoulder.

Jeremiah merely flinches.

'It's a hoax,' he says.

'WHAT!' Martyn screams. 'It's not a hoax – you heard him! Mr Abdilla SAID they are taking our demands SERIOUSLY!'

'It c-can't be a h-hoax,' Chris whispers, his freckles dancing back on to his face as the colour drains away.

'It's a hoax,' Jeremiah says dully, turning back to the TV and flicking it off.

'Oh yeah, right, come on, how would you know?' Martyn yells. 'You're just power hungry. You just want to stay out here for ever telling us what to do!'

Martyn walks up to him, eyes blazing. Jeremiah stays very cool, his fingers slack by his side, but his eyes become slits.

'He's right,' Thomas says suddenly. 'Jeremiah's right.'

Martyn wheels round.

'Whose side are you on?'

'If they were really *seriously* debating the terrorist act, we'd hear it on the news,' Thomas says earnestly. 'The prime minister himself would be commenting on the new Commons debate, or saying yes, he felt the law needed to be changed. Not Mr Abdilla. Since when did he make the rules? He's just been given a script. What did he really want? For us to meet in a "safe" place. I think he is really referring to a place where we will all be arrested.'

'Oh what would you know, you're bonkers anyway!' Martyn cries. 'You're on mental pills!'

There is a stinging silence. Thomas flushes red. Chris bites his lips as though forcing back a terrible laugh; Martyn looks at him and giggles as if they are sharing a private joke.

I expect Jeremiah to be his usual calm and soothing self. But instead he looks uncharacteristically angry. His eyes flash and his fists clench.

'And what about Mr Abdilla saying we've made *contact*? What's that? Was that you, Martyn?'

'What!' Martyn is furious. 'How the hell could I have contacted him? Jesus, Jeremiah. If Mr Abdilla's just winding us up then he's a bloody patronising jerk and we should bloody go and do it now. Let's stop standing around talking about it and delaying – let's do it. Well? Are we going to release SNAKE's soul or not and show these fuckers that we are for real.'

Jeremiah stares at him coldly and then says, 'You and Chris will now go to the Prayer Room and paint the Redemption Symbol on the floor. Thomas – guard the house. Raymond – please prepare a final meal for our hostage. And Jon – I suggest you pray. You need to purify yourself to prepare for your Initiation.'

# 10 A.M.

**My heart wakes up.**

I'm going to help her, Dad. I'm going to help her. I know my future's over, I know I'm going to end up in jail. I've ruined my life but I want to save hers. I want to do something good, one last good thing before they catch us. I'm going to keep her alive. Oh God help me, I'm going to keep her alive –

# 11 A.M.

**But I don't know what to do.** Oh God, I wish I hadn't thrown away my Bible. I used to open it up in times of trouble, pick a random place, and hope God would speak to me through it. How much time do I have left – an hour, maybe two? The paint has to dry and she has to eat her last meal. The thought of Padma sitting in the kitchen, eating burnt old toast makes my heart snarl. We can't do this to her, we can't, I have to stop them. Oh God I don't even know which God I am praying to, maybe the Christian God, maybe her God but please hear me now and reach down to earth and fiddle the hands of time, slow it down, stretch out each minute for me, give me time.

Okay, what do I do, what do I do? She's in the Hostage Room. I could just grab her now and we could try to run. But Thomas's on guard duty; Raymond's in the kitchen, watching out through the window. A dead end. I could make a run for it alone. I could just say I need a walk to prepare myself, I could run, run, run like lightning down to the phone box to call 999 but it would take an hour. By the time I called it would be too late. They'd hang her anyway. Another dead end. *Come on Jon, think Jon, think.* You can't let them kill her no matter what happens, you can't let them. I need to call the police somehow but my mobile's dead. Raymond cut the lines in the house. And I don't even know where we are – somewhere in Suffolk that's all I know. Maybe I could just talk to Jeremiah, just beg him but somehow I don't think I could persuade him. I picture the disappointment on his face and my heart clenches because I never wanted to disappoint Jeremiah. In a funny way I almost love him even though I don't understand how he got it all wrong when God was speaking through him. I could try to talk to him but he seems so set that he is right and if only I had a weapon, yes, a weapon, I could never use it but maybe like in the movies I could threaten them, tell them to back off, grab her, run away with her. My knife – yes *my knife* but no, Jeremiah took that for my Initiation. My mind swings from room to room searching for ammunition – *Come on think, Jon, think*

# 12 P.M.

**I have an idea. It's not a very good one** but it might just work. The trouble is, Thomas is outside on guard duty. The air is cold; the sky dispenses lazy, careless handfuls of flakes. Then: a godsend. Thomas decides he needs the toilet. He sees me lingering and asks if I can take over for five minutes. The moment he's gone, I bend down, pretending to tie my shoelace. It seems so long ago that we made the stone circle of protection; I was a different Jon then. I pick up a stone, shake it off, slide it into my pocket. Then another. Then another. They jostle clunkily and a faint wet patch seeps through my trousers. I stop, staring at the horizon. Oh God, is this a stupid idea? David may have killed a giant with a stone – but what if that never really happened? Who knows what bits of the Bible are true or what bits are stories to inspire us, not meant to be taken literally?

Suddenly the front door opens. I jump up guiltily.

Martyn and Chris come out, Padma sandwiched between them. My eyes flit to hers. A flash; a morse code of irises. A thrill shoots down my spine. Oh Padma, I will save you, I will, I will. I look away quickly, checking their faces, seeing if they saw our glance, translated it. Martyn is blank, preoccupied. Chris, however, has noticed something. A tiny smile trembles on his lips, then passes away. Or maybe it's just my imagination.

I stuff my hands in my pockets, frowning hard, hiding my inner panic.

'So where are you going?'

'Oh, Jeremiah told us to take SNAKE for a walk,' says Martyn. There is a smudge of black paint on his face from painting the Prayer Room. 'Before she – you know.'

My hackles rise. Martyn had better not lay *one* finger on her, or I'll kill him.

'That's a bit risky, isn't it?'

'Jeremiah said w-we should just take her for one minute. Just round the house. We're k-keeping an eye on h-her,' Chris says.

'Jeremiah is so considerate,' Padma interjects.

A ghost of a smile flitters on my lips and Chris gives me a strange look again.

'Well, okay, I'll go inside. I'm going to be busy praying for a bit,' I say.

Inside the house, I hurry down the hallway. Raymond is in the kitchen, preparing Padma's final lunch: several pieces of burnt toast. I can hear Jeremiah in the dead old woman's bedroom; there are scrapy sounds as though he is looking through drawers or moving furniture; just what is he doing in there? Then Raymond looks up at me through the doorway. I give him an innocent grin and slip into the Hostage Room.

I eye up the spot where Padma normally sits. The corner looks strangely bare without the glint of her cuffs and her brave smile above them. A plate sits, from her breakfast this morning, with a leftover half-eaten apple, now browning at the edges. I take a bite, my lips brushing apple skin her lips have brushed, and it feels like a secret kiss.

The noose is lying on the floor beside her plate. I pick it up and go to the bookcase. I give the door a nervous glance, then yank out Plato and Milton. I bunch up the noose into a coil and hide it behind them, then tidy the books up again. A sense of despair hits me – it's a useless gesture – Raymond will just go and find some more rope. But at least it will buy us time.

Now for the catapult. Chris brought it along as his weapon, though Martyn kept teasing him that it was a naff one. I go to the bedroom, figuring Chris must have hidden it under his pillow. And then another idea hits me. I wheel back, my head thumping with dizzy solutions *Come on, Jon, hurry up come on.* I hurry on to the Prayer Room. If I can just open a window, leave it on the latch, then that could be an escape route. I'd never make it through the door, Martyn and Raymond would just pummel me to the ground – but the window – they wouldn't expect that! The element of surprise would shock them. Yes, I'll fire stones at them, shock them, grab my few precious seconds, take Padma out through the window. But can that work? Oh God, if only I had more time –

I open the Prayer Room door and stop short.

Martyn and Chris have painted across the floor. But their symbols look more than a little subversive.

'Jon!' Jeremiah bursts into the room.

I move in front of his vision, desperate to hide the cartoon from him, dreading his anger. But he pushes me aside, gaping in shock.

'Where is she?' Jeremiah demands. He breaks off and does another double-take at the cartoon, drinking it in. A flush burns his face. He spins back to me. 'Where IS she? For fuck's sake, SPEAK! Where's SNAKE? DID YOU LET

'THE JOYS OF THE SOUL SHIFT'

HER GO?' He comes up to me and shakes me. 'SNAKE?'

The force of his anger blazes through me, leaving me stunned.

'Where. Is. She?'

'She went for a walk, with Chris and Martyn, just like you told them. A nice little walk to cheer her up before you – you make me – make me –'

'WHAT! They took her? And you let them!'

'They just went for a walk, that's all . . .'

'Did they say where they were going?'

'No.'

'What direction were they going?'

'I don't remember –'

'Oh God – can't you see? For days, Martyn's been brewing and now – *this* –'

'What, what are you saying? That they've got Padma?'

'Of course they've got her, you idiot. Yes.' Jeremiah throws up his arms. 'They've taken SNAKE. They've stolen our hostage!'

# 2 P.M.

**I forget my doubts about Jeremiah;** I forget the cartoon; I forget my Initiation: my desire to bring her back blots them all out.

Jeremiah pulls me into the kitchen. He tips over the table, sending six plates of old scraps of beans on toast crashing to the floor in a scatter of china and slop of sauce.

'Hey –' Raymond shouts.

'They've run off with our prize! They've got our terrorist!' Jeremiah screams. 'They went for a walk –'

'Oh shit – I gave them permission – I thought they were just –'

'Get the weapons! Get them all now!'

Raymond runs out, shoving past me. I grab hold of the doorframe and steady myself. Jeremiah is breathing in and out very quickly, smoothing his fingers over his chin, blinking hard.

'What do they want with her – what will they do with her?' I cry. 'Maybe they just want to save her from being killed. Maybe they've just taken her to the police.'

'No.' Jeremiah looks at me blankly. 'They won't do that. If they go to the police, they're the ones in possession of SNAKE, they're the guilty culprits. All the blame can fall on them; we can say they were the leaders, nothing to do with us. No. It's Martyn.'

'But why, why would he –'

'Because he's a son of a bitch, that's why! He just wants to challenge me, he's jealous of me and he wants to bring me down and if he thinks he can get away with it, well then he can't –'

He breaks off as Raymond enters, with Thomas by his side. Their arms are groaning with the weight of the long soil boxes from the bathroom. The ones that hold the seeds for spiritual plants. They dump them on the table. Thomas looks quizzical but Raymond knows what he's doing. He flings up handfuls of earth, drawing out a plastic Sainsbury's bag. He rips it away in white shreds to reveal . . . a rifle. From the next box, he parts the soil to reveal two guns wrapped in cellophane. He hands one to Jeremiah, then one to me.

I stare down at it.

'This is a toy, right?'

'What we do is this,' says Jeremiah urgently. 'We spread out. We'll go down the road – no wait.' His eyes narrow. 'They won't have gone down the road, not to where people are . . .' He snaps his fingers. 'They'll have gone to the forest. Right, now we go, go, GO –'

'But – the spiritual seeds – and . . .' The gun is still lying flat in my palm in a spray of dirt. I flex it wide open, balancing it there, afraid to curl my fingers around it. I look at Thomas, who stares back at me with dazed eyes.

'Give me the gun back,' Raymond cries. He nods at Jeremiah. 'I told you he wouldn't be able to handle it.'

'It's not that!' I cry. 'The Hebetheus – we were meant to stand for peace! What the hell are we doing with guns? Where the hell did they come from?'

'A few mates of mine,' Raymond smirks.

'Listen,' Jeremiah hisses, 'we brought them along only in the case of the worst emergency. In case the police invaded and tried to steal SNAKE.'

'But –'

'We didn't bring them for attack, we brought them purely for defence. And that's why we're using them now.'

'I can't take this,' I say, shaking my hand, holding it out to him.

'We don't have time for this,' Raymond interrupts impatiently. 'Just leave Jon behind – take Thomas instead – we have to *go* –'

'No – he has to understand, I want Jon to come and I want Jon to understand,' says Jeremiah fiercely. 'Look, Jon. I'm not asking you to shoot anyone. We're just using them *in defence*. Just to scare Martyn and Chris. Hell, d'you want them to get away with Padma?'

'No,' I stutter. 'No – God – no –'

Jeremiah comes up to me and takes the gun. Then he takes my hand. He slots my gun into my palm.

'This is how you put the bullet in, see?' He looks at Raymond, who nods reassuringly. 'You can put up to six bullets in. This is how you cock it. And you pull the trigger like this. It's simple, see?' He curls his hand around mine, fusing my skin with the cold metal. His eyes hold mine. There is a desperation in them that shocks me.

'We have to get her back,' he says. 'We have to. You don't want Martyn to get his hands on her, do you?'

I nod slowly.

Jeremiah holds my gaze and keeps his palm locked around mine until the warmth of his hand becomes an insistent heat.

'Okay?' he whispers softly.

'Okay,' I whisper back. 'Okay.'

'Should I come?' Thomas asks in a trembling voice. 'I'm sorry I wasn't on guard duty – I just needed the toilet –'

'No,' Jeremiah spits out, 'you stay here and guard the cottage.'

Jeremiah grabs me, dragging me towards the door. Then he swings back to Thomas.

'If Martyn and Chris come back here – with SNAKE – then – then keep them here. Act as though you're on their side. But whatever you do, don't let them leave the cottage, okay? They're traitors.'

'Okay.' Thomas still looks stunned.

'Okay,' Jeremiah cries, hitting me, 'come on, let's go!'

# 2.30 P.M.

They could have gone anywhere. Into town, to a farm-house, out across the fields. It's only the snow that gives us a trail: a jagged trio of footprints leading across the road, across the field and out towards the woods. Just by the rim of the trees, Jeremiah stops us, frowning, bending down and examining. The intensity of his concentration burns off him like a laser. The footprints are smeared into a muddy confusion; Raymond asks worriedly if they might have called the police and been caught here.

'No,' Jeremiah says in a low voice, shaking his head, 'I think maybe they just had a tussle here.'

My fingers clench tight around the gun. I'm going to kill Martyn.

I'm going to kill Martyn and Chris. The bastards. The *bastards*. I picture them dragging her into the forest, kicking and punching. I hear her screams in my ears. I see Martyn holding her tight, telling Chris to climb a tree, to tie the rope around it. I picture the dangling noose, caressed by a gentle breeze . . . But they wouldn't do that, I keep telling myself, they wouldn't want to kill her. Except: maybe Martyn's jealous of me. Ever since his Sacred Cleansing, he's been desperate for Jeremiah's attention. Maybe he wants my so-called glory. Maybe he wants to usurp my Initiation, maybe he wants us to chase him, to find him with a dead terrorist, to hear Jeremiah cheering him. I remember the bite-marks lacerated across Martyn's hand; I hear Jeremiah's voice, *You don't want Martyn to get his hands on her, do you?* I hear Padma's voice, *He told me that if I didn't tell the truth, he'd rape me.* I let off a shot without even realising.

'Jesus!' Raymond shrieks. 'What the fuck are you doing?'

'I'm sorry. I'm sorry.'

I'm shaking violently. When I let off the bullet the gun knocked me back and my arm burns with a twisted pain.

Jeremiah stares into my eyes and I push my hatred down and stare back at him.

'I'm sorry,' I repeat.

'D'you want to shout out to them that we're coming?' Raymond asks suddenly. 'Are you on their side?'

Jeremiah's eyes narrow.

'Of course I'm not, of course I'm not,' I cry desperately. 'I just want to find her. Can't we get a move on, I want to find her. Please, *please* can we just get a move on before it's too late, please?'

Raymond looks at Jeremiah.

'It's okay,' Jeremiah says softly. 'Jon would never betray me. He is the most loyal of them all. His devotion to the God of the Hebetheus knows no bounds.'

And despite everything that's happened, I find myself dropping my eyes in guilt.

# 3 P.M.

**The forest is our enemy.** As we go further in, the undergrowth thickens. The tree-sieved snow is too thin, the forest floor a dirty chaos of old leaves and melting slush. The footprints become finer and finer, like those of a ghost, until finally they disappear altogether beneath a heavy bush.

'Shit!' Raymond curses.

*Oh God,* I find myself praying to the Christian God for the first time in a year, *Please, please help me.* I know I've betrayed you, I know I've turned my back on you and worshipped a false God. But hear me now, please: I want to come back to you. And I want to beg you to keep her alive and safe and well. And I promise you in return . . . I promise I'll pray to you every day. Even if I end up in jail, in a cell, I'll pray to you. Just please let her be safe.

'Maybe we should separate,' I say.

'Keep your voice down!' Jeremiah hisses. 'No,' he whispers, 'we stick together.' He bends down by the bush. 'It looks as though they went through here – look.'

He points to a clump of black hair, cruelly stolen by green thorns. I curl my palm away, resisting the urge to claim it for myself.

Jeremiah and Raymond dive into the bush. As I slither

behind them, earth and leaves rip my belly and twigs claw my hair and the gun keeps thumping and catching in the mud and I can't work out if the safety catch is on or not and I just wish I was God, wish I could spot the ant-like figure of Padma running and reach down with a giant pink palm so she could run on to it and I could curl my fingers around her and lift her up safe.

Jeremiah bursts up through the branches into a clearing. Raymond follows. A twig viciously digs into my hair and I struggle to tear it out. When I pull myself up, the gun shaking, I find there is only us in the clearing.

'Jesus, we're never going to find them,' Raymond mutters.

'No, we are,' Jeremiah snaps sharply. 'God is on our side, Raymond, not theirs!'

My eyes fall upon a tree: a burn mark flushing up its trunk.

'Keep going,' Jeremiah whispers. 'Just keep going –'

'But they could be anywhere –'

'Go.'

We move on a few more feet. The forest seems to stretch out for ever: black trunks in endless rows of mocking pillars. Even though it's only afternoon, it already feels like twilight; the heaviness of the undergrowth creates a veil of murky gloom.

And then divine inspiration strikes.

'Hang on,' I whisper.

'Ssh –'

'No, I know – I've got it – I know where to find them!' I cry in excitement. 'Look – just follow me – look –'

My heart screams with gratitude for God. I draw them back into the clearing and show them the scorched trunk.

'Look – look –' I compress my voice into a highly strung

**235**

whisper, 'this mark – Chris made it on the way back from the phone –'

'From what?' Jeremiah asks.

'The town – we went – the medicine – I mean, on the way back, we came through the woods – and – and – Chris kept lingering for ages, making marks on the trees – I thought he was just messing about but he must have made them to – to –'

'To show them the way?'

'But where?' Raymond whispers.

'We follow the marks,' Jeremiah says in a whisper. 'Can you remember them all?'

'No – we'll just have to look and follow.'

'You see?' Jeremiah whispers breathlessly. 'I said that God was with us! Our Hebethean Saviour has answered our prayers.'

I open my mouth, stung with outrage. Not *your* stupid god, but my God has saved us, I want to say. My God, who is real, who doesn't give false dreams about innocent girls. I bite my lip. Jeremiah pauses for a moment, looking pale and creased with worry.

'To think,' he muses, 'they've been plotting against me for days.'

# 3.30 P.M.

**We find another marked tree,** another, another. Determination zings through us, glints in our eyes. We're close; we're winning.

'Ssh – listen!' Jeremiah suddenly hisses.

Martyn's voice:

'I can't get the bloody thing open – *thump thump* – you didn't tell me there was a lock –'

'I d-didn't kn-know – I'm s-sorry –'

'I want to go back.' (*Oh, Padma!*) 'I want to go back now.'

I run ahead to save her, but Jeremiah pushes me back.

He glides forward stealthily. I try to jerk into second place behind him but Raymond shoves me back, forcing me to follow him.

'I can't get this bloody thing to open,' Martyn is saying.

'H-h-hurry up, th-they'll find us, oh G-God –' Chris breaks off as he sees us.

They are gathered outside a rickety shack. As we scatter into the clearing, Martyn wheels around. He drops the hammer he was using to burst open the door. I look at Padma, my heart flowing with love and apology. But she's staring in horror at the guns. Chris turns pale; Martyn bends down as though to pick up his hammer, then realises it's useless. Jeremiah sneers and points his gun right at him.

'What the fuck do you think you're doing?' Jeremiah asks quietly.

Martyn looks at Chris who looks at him. Then they both look at the guns.

'We were just having a laugh,' Martyn bursts out. He puts his palms up flat, but the gesture seems theatrical, cartoonish. 'It was just a joke, that's all – we were going to bring her back.'

'Oh, so you think this is funny?' Jeremiah asks, holding the gun steady.

Martyn gives a nervous laugh, then gulps it back.

'Don't you realise,' Jeremiah's voice rises, 'that you're standing before the judgement of God? And that if you don't tell the truth then, by God, you will be sorry!'

Martyn looks over at Chris again. They both start as though to speak, then lose confidence. I feel Padma's gaze on me and I stare back at her with eyes of hope. There seems to be a desperate signal in her gaze. I frown helplessly; she flashes it again. I can't translate it. What, Padma, what?

'We were going to bring her back,' Martyn repeats.

Padma stares at me hard. Then, suddenly, she lets out a scream that slices straight through my gut.

The shock causes Raymond to fire by mistake – up into the sky.

'Fuck!'

Padma runs; Martyn grabs her and they disappear. Chris flees in the opposite direction. As Padma and Martyn escape, Padma glances back with a swish of dark hair and even though their bond is formed on the spur of the moment, a collusion of desperation, a fierce jealousy stabs my stomach.

'After them!' Jeremiah roars.

For a moment, nothing makes sense. We've got guns;

they haven't. They have no advantage on us. But a cartoon moment saves them: Raymond and I make to follow Chris and Jeremiah makes to follow Martyn and we all bang together. My nose hits Raymond's chest; my elbow jabs Jeremiah's ribs. We recoil, stung.

'For God's sake!' Jeremiah yells.

'Jesus, you!' Raymond cries at me. 'You pointed that thing right into my stomach just now! Don't you know what you're doing with that thing!'

'Come on!' Jeremiah yells, starting to run and then stopping and waving at us.

'You shouldn't have that gun!' Raymond cries to me, holding out his hand for it.

'No.' I need this for Padma, for *us* –'

'Just give it, hurry up, they're getting away, you wanker –'

'No!'

'COME ON, GUYS!' Jeremiah screams in fury. 'NOW!'

'Sorry –'

'YOU TWO GO AFTER MARTYN AND SNAKE! I'LL CHASE CHRIS!'

'You shouldn't have that gun,' Raymond repeats as we run across the mud. He slips on a patch of snow and I catch him, heaving with his body weight.

'Thanks,' he mutters. He shoots my gun another furious glance but he knows there is no time for arguing and we run, following flashes of colour and cloth ahead as they flit through the trees.

The trees thin out. Their camouflage is blown. We see them slow, pause, Martyn whisper in her ear. Then they split. Padma to the left, Martyn to the right.

'I'll go after SNAKE, you –'

'No, I'll get SNAKE!' I cry and run before Raymond can stop me.

# 4 P.M.

**Why is she running from me?**

'Padma,' I wheeze desperately, my voice hissing from my lungs. 'Padma!'

She glances back, sees me but – to my shock – she keeps on running. Is this a game? I follow the black swirl of her hair. Maybe she just wants to find a safe place, where nobody can see us?

Finally, she gives in. She bends over, her cuffed palms flat against her knees. She heaves in air, shooting me terrified glances. I run forward, calling her name, ready to hold her.

I am dismayed when she starts, ready to run again.

'Padma! Padma!' I call. 'I'm not with them!'

She turns with an uncertain face. I run up, panting. She takes a wary step backwards. I stop a foot away from her, full of anguish. Then I realise: the gun. I place it down on the forest floor.

'Look – see? I'm not even holding it. You don't need to run –' I can't get my words out, there's so much to say to her and no time to say it. 'Look – I know – I know you're right – you're right about Hebetheus – it's all wrong – it's crap!'

She starts at the word and I repeat it again:

'It's *crap*. You're not a terrorist. We're idiots – oh God – I just – I just –'

A smile of wonder comes over her face and she lets out a breathless hiss that is almost a laugh.

Then she says: 'I need to run, you have to let me go –'

'Yes – run – that's what I mean – just ignore me and run. Go that way – it goes into town – you'll be safe there – you can find a phone – I called your mother by the way – I spoke to her –'

'You did?' her face lights up in exquisite shock.

'I did – she – she – misses you – you should go – you should go –'

I run forward to kiss her goodbye but she turns away from me. She runs about a foot, then turns back, runs up and clashes her face against mine in a clumsy, messy kiss. I cling to her; I want to hold her, smother her in kisses, breathe in her taste and bottle it for ever – but she wrenches away from me –

'I'm sorry,' she cries.

I stand and watch her run away until the forest devours her. I should have been the one to say sorry, but I feel if I spend the rest of my life saying sorry to her, it wouldn't be enough.

# 4.30 P.M.

**Footsteps crunch behind me.**

'Did you get her?' Raymond demands.

'No – I –' I swallow thickly, terrified my face and voice will betray me. 'No.'

But Raymond looks almost pleased that I didn't succeed where he failed.

'Me neither. The little bastard – I had Martyn, I had him, then one minute he was there and the next he'd vanished – into thin air – I just – I mean – I just don't know how the fuck he did it.'

'Shall we go back after him?'

'No, we'll go back to Jeremiah.'

We run in silence. The closer we get, a dread begins to mount that, even though we have guns and the so-called Hebethean God on our side, we still let them get away.

As we enter the clearing, we find Chris lying on the floor; Jeremiah's boot pins down his shoulder.

'Did you get them?' Jeremiah demands, eyes flashing.

'No – we – lost them – they split up –'

'Right – you – Jon – guard the hostage, Chris. C'mon, Raymond. We're not letting them get away.'

'Okay,' Raymond says. 'Jon – keep him under control.' He grins at me and I start at the unexpected moment of solidarity, the rapidity of swing from me versus Raymond to us versus Chris.

Chris starts to scramble up but I point the gun at him. It feels strange – almost ridiculous – as though I am an actor in a movie playing a part. I feel relieved when he lies back down and I quickly point the gun so that if I fired by accident it would miss him by a good five inches.

Chris writhes and wheezes. *Good*, I say silently, *Good. You tried to steal Padma, you bastard, you deserve to suffer.* I try not to notice that his breaths are becoming shorter and shorter. I stand still, listening intently: my heart dreads the pound of footsteps, the swish of leaves, a shrill scream. I close my eyes and pray: *Oh God, please don't let them find her. Please can she make it in time.* I glance into the sea of trees, tempted by their freedom. But I can't leave without knowing she has got away.

' . . . I've lost my inhaler . . . I've lost it . . .'

I open my eyes.

'You'll have to wait until Jeremiah gets back.'

'Please . . . please . . .' Chris gasps.

I look into his eyes and see the flashing panic. And I wonder at myself: what am I doing, watching one of my Brothers writhe in front of me, in pain? What am I becoming?

'Where did you lose it?'

'I dropped it by the tree,' Chris gasps. 'When Jeremiah – when Jeremiah –'

'Okay, okay –'

'When Jeremiah tussled with me, I-I – d-d-dropped –'

'Yeah, I'm looking, I'm looking.'

I kneel down, scrabbling through leaves with desperate fingers. I begin to panic. What if I can't find it? What if Chris is lying, what if I go off to look for it and he runs and I've lost him? I picture waking up and seeing a noose dangling above my bed.

'It's by the tree – the t-t-tree . . .'

Here.

I grab it and kneel down and press it into his hand. Chris sucks in grateful gasps. I stare at his face and the wall between us crumbles; the labels of traitor and enemy. For the last few days, Chris has probably been running through the same mazes of worry and torment that I have.

'Why did you run?' I ask. 'What were you going to do with her?'

'M-M –' Chris breaks off and takes another hissed sip. 'M-Martyn w-w-wanted to s-s-set up a new r-r-religion.'

'A *what*? The Hebetheus is the only religion that is the truth,' I find myself reciting automatically, without even thinking.

'M-M-M wanted us to form –'*hiss* '– a new r-r-religion w-w-where there w-w-would be n-no leaders, no h-hier-archy and we'd all b-b-be equal. It m-makes s-s-sense. J-Jeremiah's just l-lying to us, you know he is –'

'Oh, and Martyn's the Dalai Lama?' I cry. 'Jesus. And Padma . . . what were you going to do with her?'

'A-a-ask h-her m-mum and dad for some m-money and then give her b-back –'

'WHAT!'

'We'd g-g-give h-h-her b –'

'Don't you think her parents have been through enough and then you want some fucking money so you can buy yourself a new Gameboy –'

'N-no – n-not for u-us – t-t-to f-f-fund our n-new r-r-religion . . .'

'Jesus, Chris! And then what? You were going to bully her again? Get more false confessions? Threaten to rape her once more?'

244

'No – *no*!' Chris hisses. 'It's b-because w-we c-couldn't b-bear to s-see her hung that we did it, w-we don't want to m-murder anyone, even if she is a t-t-terrorist, we don't want to be m-murderers . . .' Tears fill his eyes. 'I w-w-w-want to believe, I really want to believe, but I can't any more . . . we wanted to make a religion of p-peace, where nobody is killed – we wanted to save her . . . th-though e-even sh-she didn't b-believe us – b-but we w-were!'

My hand drops to my side. I feel cold and numb.

'What will Jeremiah do to me?' Chris whispers fearfully. 'What will he do to us?'

I frown. I realise we have crossed a line: that we no longer respect Jeremiah; we are afraid of him. And I'm not sure how or when it happened.

'We could run,' Chris whispers. 'We could both just r-r-run now.'

My eyes lock with his in shock.

I open my mouth to speak when we hear voices.

Jeremiah and Raymond come into the clearing with one more hostage.

Padma.

# 5.30 P.M.

**I don't blame God for not answering** my prayers. I know I don't deserve his help. But for Padma's sake, for dear Padma's sake, I wish he'd helped her. As Jeremiah and Raymond drag her back into the clearing, she looks at me with dead eyes. She thinks I told them, I realise in horror, she thinks I betrayed her.

'You found her?' I ask shakily. 'Where? Where did you find her?'

'In the forest. Where else? You should have looked harder,' Jeremiah adds tersely.

I see Padma's face soften.

But knowing that I didn't betray her doesn't help the situation: we're back to square one. Jeremiah orders Chris to get up and tells me to keep the gun trained on him. He commands Raymond to keep the gun trained on SNAKE.

'We're going to get Martyn,' he says. 'All of us. We're going to search through these woods until we find him. I don't care how long it takes.'

And so we search for Martyn.

Jeremiah makes us walk in file: him leading, followed by Padma followed by me followed by Chris followed by Raymond. Hostages sandwiched between believers, as he puts it.

Every so often, Jeremiah gets out his lighter and marks a tree to stop us going round in circles. As he leans over to defile an oak, Padma twists her head and gives me a desperate pleading glance, nodding at the gun at my hands.

*I want to do it Padma*, I talk silently to the back of her head as we carry on, *but I'm trapped, can't you see? If I hold the gun to Jeremiah's head, he'll turn his gun on me. He knows I wouldn't be able to shoot him. And I think he would shoot me; I think he would, I've never seen him act like this before, it's as though all his religious intensity has just exploded inside him and he's out for blood. And there's Raymond behind me with a gun . . . if I could just signal to Chris . . . but Raymond will see . . . it's hopeless . . . oh God there must be* something *I can do . . .*

My mind feels foggy with exhaustion. I can see Padma is tired too; I can see her pushing through it bravely and I want to hold her and kiss her, give her my last drops of energy.

We come to a clearing and Jeremiah stops us. He lifts his head. His eyes narrow and an uncharacteristically cunning smile creeps across his lips. I shiver.

'Martyn,' he calls up. 'Enjoying sitting in that tree?'

No answer. A rustling of leaves.

'Martyn,' Jeremiah sings lightly. 'Oh, Martyn, won't you come down?' His voice thins into an insidious whisper. 'Martyn, Martyn, Martyn.'

'I'm not coming down,' Martyn bellows.

Jeremiah turns to Chris.

'Call him down,' he orders.

'B-b-but –' Chris stammers.

Raymond points the gun at him.

'O-okay. M-M-Martyn!' Chris calls. 'They've – they've got me. P-p-please come down.'

Silence. I stare up through the crazy paving of green. All I can see is a white trainer, sticking out over a branch, laces dangling like liquorice. I look over at Padma. She gazes back. A snowflake floats down and kisses her hair: my dark angel.

'Fine,' Jeremiah calls up. 'We're going to wait here. We don't mind. We can wait all night if you like.' He turns to me. 'Go and get some sticks.'

Padma automatically moves to follow and help.

'Hey.' Jeremiah's eyes narrow. 'SNAKE. What are you doing? This isn't Girl Guides camp.'

Padma moves back quickly and bows her head.

I gather sticks. Not because Jeremiah has ordered me to. I only gather them for her, for her warmth, her comfort. I make a pyramid and ask Jeremiah to borrow his lighter. He passes it over distractedly, his eyes still on Martyn. The look on his face confounds me. It's as though a demon has taken over our leader. Or was it always there, lurking in the shadows of his soul?

I sit down in front of the fire and I shut them all out. I shut out Jeremiah cat-calling up to Martyn; I shut out Raymond, playing the tough guy and wielding his pathetic gun; I shut out Chris, who is whimpering; I shut out Martyn, shitting himself at the top of the tree, no doubt trying to think up some great excuse. I pretend none of this is happening and I just look at her.

She's so beautiful. It's as though she imbues everything in her aura with a sharp clarity of beauty; the plain sparks from the fire turn into shimmering fireflies against the backdrop of her fairy-hair. She turns snow to diamonds, the night to velvet, birdsong to the murmuring honey angels. I remember how I once sat with her, how I looked into her eyes and saw myself killing her. I feel *sick* with

248

shame. I want to pull her into the cocoon of my arms and hold her for ever. How could I have ever contemplated it, ever dreamed of it?

Suddenly it becomes unbearable not to touch her. I stretch out my leg until I feel it brushing her ankle. I look around casually; everyone is gazing up. Millimetre by millimetre, I shift my leg. As I do so, my trouser rides up. My bare skin touches the thrilling scratch of her jeans. I shift closer and find a tiny patch of bare ankle so that our skin connects in a flow of warmth. She looks up at me and a trace of a smile forms on her lips.

I have to lower my face quickly to swallow back the smile, swallow and push it back down into my heart where it breaks in a bubble of bliss.

I love her.

Oh God, I love her.

'We're all very cosy down here, Martyn,' Jeremiah calls up. 'This is a nice little tree. We can wait as long as you like. Let's just hope the fire doesn't spread into your branches.'

I look at her again. I look at her lips, brush them with my eyes, until she blushes.

Then I look away.

I like making her blush.

None of this is happening. We're not sitting in this forest, shivering; we're not in this nightmare. We're in the park by my house, and the sun is setting and we're gliding on a swing, her sitting in my lap. We're lying by the railway that tracks the park, kissing in the bushes with ice-cream wrappers at our feet whilst we feel the trembles of the train passing by rumble in our kiss. We're kissing in the shack on the school fields, the one they keep all the footballs and cricket balls in, kisses in the dusty cobwebbed dark with

**249**

playground noises singing around us but nobody knowing we are there. We're kissing on my bed, holding each other, Coldplay playing in the background, the posters on my wall looking down at us.

'If I come down, will you shoot me?'

Jeremiah ponders.

'I don't know. Maybe.'

Padma's eyes widen and flicker with panic; I hold her gaze steady, silently stroking her hair until she looks away in relief. I will protect her; I will protect her always.

And the more I look at her, the more everything else seems to drop away. Until there's nothing left but this curious sensation in my heart. Like the ice on the streets after winter is seeping into spring. Full of slush and grey dirt and cool running water and sparkling light. I feel as though I want to dance and run a long long way and climb a tree and stand on its utmost branch with the world waving nervously beneath and whoop out how much I love Padma.

Is this what God is? If you take all these moments, all the love beating in people's hearts all over the world, the love of a boy for a girl, a man for a woman, a kid for their parent, a brother for a sister, a friend for a friend – if you put it all together and roll it into one big ball, is that God?

Maybe God isn't the man I have thought him to be, the elderly stern man who sits in the clouds above like a headmaster ready to give cosmic detentions or gold stars. Maybe he is a man, a woman, a thing who loves you always and doesn't even care whether you love him because he just is love so he'll just wait for you for ever until you find him and all the time he'll just love you. The ball of love shines so brightly, it's like staring at the sun and I feel dizzy and strange and like crying and laughing and kissing Padma all at once.

I look up at Jeremiah with wet eyes and I can't even feel any hate for him; I want to jump up and shake him and tell him my revelation. I think: he's just as weak as any of us, only he puts on a better act. I have to keep remembering that. I mustn't let him scare me.

Then Jeremiah sets the tree alight and reality comes crashing back in.

# 7 P.M.

**Within seconds, Martyn cries out** and comes slithering down the tree. We all stand up, exchanging glances. I stand by Padma's side. Martyn edges back to the tree trunk, shoulders hunched, eyes darting, like a fox cornered by hunters.

'Thanks for coming down,' Jeremiah says, then punches him in the face.

The crack makes us all jump. Even Raymond blinks and curses under his breath. I feel Padma edge towards me and with her little finger she takes hold of the edge of my jumper.

Martyn clutches his cheek, staring at Jeremiah with shocked eyes. Next to me, Chris starts to cry. I take a step closer to Padma. The crack of Jeremiah's fist connecting with Martyn's cheek keeps echoing raw in my stomach.

'Jeremiah!' I cry.

Jeremiah ignores me. He carries on staring at Martyn, his mouth thin. *Crack!* echoes in my mind again. Knuckles scraping flesh. This is all wrong, this all wrong. I thought that Martyn would come down from the tree and Jeremiah would order an Advanced Super-Sacred Cleansing or something like that and we would all return home for another session. I thought Jeremiah was a leader who believed in compassion. And I want to open my mouth and say all of this but I'm scared. I'm scared that if Jeremiah doesn't beat up Martyn he'll beat up me. But I don't want to see Martyn hurt either; he might be stocky and a good fighter but he is no match for Jeremiah and his cold, leonine strength. Oh God, I pray, please calm Jeremiah down, please calm him down.

'I'm sorry,' Martyn says quickly. 'I'm sorry.' He bends down on his knees. 'I'm sorry, I'm really sorry . . .' He bows down until his nose is in the mud.

I wince and lower my eyes.

Jeremiah stares down at him and his face softens.

'Get up,' he says. 'Get up and take off your clothes. And you –' he points a finger like a bullet in my direction and I say, 'What? Me?'

'Not you. Her. Let off your loverboy's jumper and take off your clothes.'

Padma shrinks back towards the trees but Chris grabs hold of her.

'No,' I say. 'Chris – let her go. Chris! For fuck's sake – a minute ago you were trying to get me on your side –'

Chris stares at me, shaking his head. His tears are dry now and I see the desperation in his face: desperation that he doesn't cross the line to the victim's side.

I turn back to Jeremiah. My heart is pumping and my head is spinning with prayers. Out of the chaos comes a voice of reason: keep cool. Keep very cool. It's the only way you might win.

'You can't hang her,' I say. 'You said I was going to be the one to hang her. For my Initiation.'

'I'm not going to hang them,' Jeremiah says. 'Now. Get SNAKE. Over here. NOW!' His voice rises to a shout.

Martyn takes off his jacket. Padma stands next to him,

staring at me wildly. I turn to Raymond. Even he looks uneasy.

'Raymond!' I cry. 'You can't let this happen.'

'It's all right,' Raymond snaps. 'Jeremiah?' he addresses his brother softly.

Jeremiah turns.

'It's okay. I've got this under control. It's just a little divine punishment. Nobody's going to die. Well, as long as they do what I say.'

He takes the gun from Raymond, who lets it go with a slight tug. Jeremiah points the gun at Padma's skull. Martyn begins to undress with greater haste.

'Come on, then,' Jeremiah says, looking her up and down.

Padma stares into his eyes. And then a look comes over her face. When I see that look my heart caves in with love for her and I don't know whether I want to kiss her or yell at her for being so stupid.

'No. I'm not going to.'

'Do as I say.' Jeremiah's voice is ice. 'I am the leader here.'

'You won't shoot,' Padma says. 'I'm your hostage. You can't shoot me because then what else do you have? You'll all just go to jail.'

'You think we care about that at this stage? God isn't letting any of us go to jail. You were due to die anyway – nine hours ago.'

'Well, I won't undress. It's too cold.' She shrugs.

The gun fires.

We all jump.

Padma clutches her head, shaking.

The bullet missed her by inches.

She gulps, then takes off her jeans.

Her knickers are frilled with sprays of folded toilet paper and I remember that she told me she had her period. She manages not to cry, but her face is crumpled with defeat.

Suddenly, I snap. I fly at Jeremiah, knocking him sideways. He turns in surprise. And then I feel arms locked around my shoulders and Raymond grabs my gun, flinging it into the snow for Chris to pick up. I lash out, thrash about, but Raymond holds me tight. Jeremiah laughs, shaking his head, then trains his gun back on Padma. I lower my eyes, refusing to look at her. I might be watching but I am not involved in this humiliation. I hear her clothes drop into the snow. Hatred burns inside me – whether good or evil I don't know and don't care. I am ready to grab the gun and kill them all. I struggle again and cry inside: Oh God, stop this, you can't let him touch her, oh God, you can't let this happen, I will read my Bible every day from now on, but I can't believe this can happen if you exist, I can't bear this evil, you can't allow this to happen –

'Okay,' says Jeremiah lightly. 'Now. You – put on her clothes. And you – put on his clothes.'

Padma looks bewildered. Martyn picks up her knickers, shaking out the blotted toilet roll and pulls them on. Their red hearts looks absurd against his hairy thighs. Padma picks up his yellow Y-fronts and pulls them on with great disdain. Jeremiah looks at them and starts to laugh. He turns to his brother and Raymond gives him a confused grin and Jeremiah hoots.

'Come on, come on,' he says. 'Put on her bra. That's it. And her sparkly top.'

Padma reaches down to pick up Martyn's grey vest. As she does so, her long hair parts, revealing her breasts. Raymond's grip softens in distraction; I hear Chris draw in his breath sharply. Without even thinking, I turn to Chris. *Wham!* I punch him across the face. Chris stumbles, blood pouring from his mouth. Jeremiah turns and stares at me, then grins.

'Hey, hey, steady.' Raymond takes hold of me again and I don't protest. I let him hold me. Suddenly I am limp and weak. My knuckles ache. I feel dirty, spent, useless.

Padma and Martyn are now fully dressed. They look ridiculous. Padma's black sparkly top stretches across Martyn's chest; Martyn's hooded top hangs over Padma's wrists in ghostly fronds and she has to hitch up his jeans around her waist.

'Well, Martyn, you look divine,' says Jeremiah. Martyn tries to grin but it ends up a snarl; he is close to losing it.

Jeremiah seems to sense this. He pauses, frowning, watching the snow for a few minutes. And then in a flash he is the old Jeremiah again, our cool, calm leader.

'Okay. We're going back. The punishments are over. We'll return to our Holy Base and Martyn and Chris will be judged before God.'

# 9 P.M.

**Collectively, we all seem to wilt.** The day is over. The coup has failed. Nobody has escaped and I can't save Padma. We just want to get back to the cottage, to fall into a black pit of forgetful sleep. But Jeremiah orders Martyn to show him where the shack is.

'I'm tired,' Jeremiah declares. 'I need a horse. Martyn, be my horse.'

Martyn has given up on fighting now. He sinks to his knees and carries Jeremiah with awkward waddles. Jeremiah picks up a twig and thwacks him from time to time.

Jeremiah suggests that Raymond should use SNAKE as a horse too but he declines, quietly muttering that she wouldn't be strong enough.

I want to use Jeremiah as a horse. I want him to bend down before me and admit he has lied. Because it is all lies, I am certain of it now. Tonight I have seen the real Jeremiah, stripped of his layers of guile and charm, his fancy words about miracles and dreams and compassion. He is power-hungry; he is – what do adults call it? – a megalomaniac. He wants us to worship the cult of Jeremiah and if we don't want to let him wrap the bit of devotion around our heads and slot it into our mouths, then we will all suffer the whip. Hatred burns in my heart. He is just like my father. He is worse than my father. He made us kidnap an innocent girl all because she came from a country he didn't like, had a tone of skin that didn't fit into his colour scheme.

I want to kill him. I want to tear him into pieces. But Padma walks ahead of me, her spine rigid with tension and anger and every ripple of her body in Martyn's clothes reminds me of the danger she is in; there is no knowing how far Jeremiah will go. One part of me feels terrified for her but another voice inside me whispers with relief that she didn't escape, that's she's here with me, helping me to survive this nightmare. And I hate myself for thinking it, but it's the truth.

We come to the clearing and wait while Jeremiah gets off his horse, kicks it and examines the shack. He inspects it with a scientific curiosity, oblivious to the cold. I step closer to Padma. She turns and scowls at me with flashing eyes.

'Okay,' says Jeremiah, 'we can now return. Horse. Come on, get up. Tired, are you?' He kicks and his horse whines. Jeremiah sighs. Padma takes a step back. 'I shall have to walk then. Pathetic.'

Raymond stares at his brother, his jaw set; Chris hovers with a tense fist. For one curious moment we sense that we would all like to pummel Jeremiah, cut ourselves free from the net of fear he has thrown over us and if only one of us would do it then all of us might stop him, but none of us do and so we keep on walking.

The journey back seems so long, so long. The night has reached its rawest point and there is no moon to give us relief. We stumble, drag ourselves in stunned misery. I walk behind Padma, staring at the dark tangle of her hair. Why did she scowl? Why so angry at *me*? Jeremiah is the monster here. Maybe she is angry with me for not protecting her better, for my pathetic punch at Chris and no more than that. Yesterday I tasted love in her kisses; what if that love has died now? Our love feels so precious, so fragile and perhaps tonight Jeremiah has thrown it to the floor, smashed it into irredeemable pieces. Suddenly I feel panicky, desperate to hold her, to feel reassured by her kisses; suddenly knowing she still loves me seems more important than anything, even escaping.

I could turn on them. I could knock Jeremiah sideways and grab my gun back. I could point the gun at him and I could shoot him. I would do it: for her. I'd happily murder him for her. But then what? Raymond shoots me. Raymond shoots Padma. We all die. It's hopeless; we're trapped; I have to come up with a better plan. We won't hang her tonight; I'm certain we won't; Jeremiah seems more intent on punishing Martyn than her. I will come up with a plan this time. Even if it takes all night. *Oh Padma*, I whisper silently to her back, *please forgive me, I won't let you down again, I promise.*

As we go back into the cottage, the smell of death hits us. We hadn't noticed it before because we'd been breathing it in until we'd become immune to it, but the freshness of the forest highlights it: the old woman, still lying in bed, is slowly decaying.

# 11 P.M.

**Jeremiah summons me to the Prayer Room.** Chris, Martyn and Padma are all cuffed and tied down in the Hostage Room. Thomas is guarding them at gunpoint. Raymond is guarding Jeremiah's door with a crowbar and a gun. He actually has the nerve to feel me for weapons. My temper flares up; my dislike of Raymond, which I tried to repress in the Brotherhood, now biles into hatred. He is not my Brother; he's not even my friend.

'Are you crazy?' I spit out. 'You know I'm on your side. Just let me in, okay?'

To my surprise, Jeremiah is lying on the floor, his cheek nestling against a Hebethean symbol, eyes lowered. I stare at him, wide-eyed, searching his face. There ought to be a wicked glint in his cool blue eyes; there ought to be a nasty scar slashing his baby skin. Just some sign, some warning of the viper in him. The innocence of his appearance suddenly seems inhuman. I can't understand him, his morals, his ethics; the cogs of his mind don't work in the usual way normal people's do; they belong to another culture, another country he has created inside himself.

I want to confront him. I want to scream and shout. I want to pull apart his faith and see if it stands up. I want to force him to admit that Padma is innocent. That he lied and made up the phone story. But will I just end up in cuffs too? And if I'm in cuffs what use am I to Padma?

And I admit it. I'm afraid of him. We all are. And so I sit down carefully and I don't say a word.

Then he glances up at me and I realise his eyes are covered with a film of tears. I look away in embarrassed surprise.

'I knew they'd betray me,' Jeremiah says softly. He sniffs. 'I had a dream – God warned me they would betray me. I didn't take the warning seriously. I trusted you all, I thought you were all my brothers.'

'They just –' I break off, confused. A moment ago I wanted to kill Jeremiah for what he did to Padma. Now my feelings have swerved towards pity. Why is it so difficult to hate him, when it's safer to hate him?

'Look,' I say, 'we all just feel –'

'We? So you're on their side?'

'No! No! I didn't know anything about the coup. It's just – things feel out of control. We were meant to stand for peace. We're in the papers, people think we're criminals. People hate us, Jeremiah.' I break off, knowing he will only tell me that that is their weakness, not ours.

But instead Jeremiah sits up, blinking.

'I'm just trying to do *good*!' he cries. 'Why can't they see that? Why can't you see that? Can't you see? I just want everyone here to be happy and find their Soul Shift. That's all I ever came here for. I never wanted to hurt anyone.'

'But you did!' I cry back, hardly able to believe my nerve. 'You did hurt –' I break off, about to say *Padma*. I glance back through the ajar door to Raymond, note the black tip of his gun and rein in my words. 'You hurt Martyn. I know he did wrong but you . . .'

'Martyn?' Jeremiah winces. 'I refuse to hear his name spoken aloud. From now on, his codename is BLACK.

And Chris's codename is DEMON. Tonight I'm going to get to the bottom of this. We need to interrogate BLACK together.'

'But I thought you said before that we use codenames for terrorists!'

'Exactly.'

'Come on, Chris and Martyn aren't terrorists!' I cry. 'They're just – I mean – they wouldn't be out here with us if they were terrorists –'

'They tried to undermine us and steal our hostage.' Jeremiah's tears are gone now and his face is stern. 'Look – I'm speaking to you in black-and-white terms. I tell you this, Jon, because there's no room in the world for grey any more. It's too dangerous for that. People are either with us or against us. They're either Brothers of the Hebetheus or they're terrorists.'

'Matthew,' I say without thinking.

'I'm sorry?'

'That's from Matthew. In the Bible.' I flush. '"He that is not with me is against me." I just – just remember from . . . before . . .'

'Well, whatever, we know Christianity is full of lies but there may be glimmers of truth in their literature. But that's not my point. I'm talking about those who stand in our way. Okay, I'm not saying they're planting bombs. But the definition of a terrorist is really much wider than that. It's becoming wider every day. It's someone who doesn't want to save the world and bring peace, and anyone who doesn't want to do that in this age of war and chaos can only be a terrorist.'

'But what if the rest of the world doesn't want to be in Hebetheus? What if ninety per cent of the population doesn't want to be in Hebetheus? What if the only people who believe are just us? What then? Does the rest of the world have to die?'

Jeremiah shrugs.

'What – you're saying that like, entire countries, millions of people should just be wiped out if they don't agree with us?' I cry.

'Look at Eden. There was only room for two people there. For God's sake, Jon, you have to see that your mind has been shaped by society. No – don't interrupt me – just listen. *Listen.* I know this idea is new to you but I want you to listen to me with an open mind and heart. Who says the world is suited to a population of millions? It clearly isn't. There's a lack of resources everywhere, so most of the world starve. And let's look at those who aren't starving – if you walked up to the average person on the street in this country, this privileged country where people think they're poor if they only have one TV set, for crying out loud – and asked if they were generally happy or unhappy with their lives, you know what they'd say? Unhappy. They'd say life doesn't feel quite right, life isn't satisfying them, giving them what they want. This world just isn't working. That's why we're driving it to destruction by killing the trees, the ozone, turning the sea levels topsy-turvy. The experts are telling us, day by day, that we're heading for disaster, but does anyone listen? No. Why? Because we all want it to end. We know the world isn't working. Deep down we want to push that self-destruct button. Maybe the world would be suited to just a few very select, spiritual people, living in harmony together.'

I have to remind myself that this can only be bullshit. And yet. For one wistful moment I want to believe him. I remember Chris, lying in the forest, whispering from the bottom of his soul, *I wanted to believe in it, I so wanted it to be true.* I feel the same pain stab my heart. I thought I'd found an ultimate truth; I thought I knew the answers that people spend their lives searching for. I thought I was the luckiest boy in the world to be saving the world. And now – I don't know anything. I don't even know if I believe in Christianity any more. I feel as though I'm floating in a womb – lost, white, shapeless.

Jeremiah watches me carefully and I try to hide my thoughts but I know he has seen into them, sensed a crack he might prise open wider.

'Come on, Jon, you know there's sense in my words. Even if you don't agree with them, even if you might not say yes to every detail, can't you feel in your heart some beat of truth?'

'Yes,' I say quietly. 'Yes.' My mind is spinning in confusion. Has he been right all along? Even though he seems mad, perhaps the words he speaks are those of God. Is his teaching just too advanced; are we just too *raptored* to understand it?

'But,' I say more firmly. 'I don't think Padma is a terrorist, I really don't, Jeremiah. I know you . . . I know you know what you're doing . . . and God talks to you . . . but I think you got that . . . maybe wrong . . . maybe you misheard that conversation . . . maybe . . .'

'Oh you do, do you?' Jeremiah pauses, eyes narrowed. 'Have you forgotten the sixth book of the Hebetheus?'

I blink at the change of subject and then quickly recite:' "Ah – God made woman first and he made her imperfect. Then he shaped man and he improved on woman and made man perfect."'

Jeremiah nods, wets his lips and looks at me slyly.

'Women are a dangerous sex, Jon. They lie. They're snakes

that weave and slither and sidle into your consciousness and just when you least expect it, they bite.'

I look down sullenly. I don't want to hear his words. My love for Padma feels like a flickering flame that I must shield with both hands from the powerful winds of his persuasion.

'Just be careful,' he says. 'SNAKE trusts you. Which could be useful for us. Just don't allow yourself to be useful to her. Remember: she has nothing here. No God, no hope, no weapons. She's desperate. Believe me, if we weren't in this cottage, Jon, she wouldn't give you a second glance. I remember the night we brought her here, when she was in the nightclub . . . but maybe I shouldn't tell you this.'

'No, what?' I cry.

'She was standing in the queue and this guy had his arm around her and he was kissing and licking her neck – it was gross.'

'What!' I tell myself to calm down; I tell myself he is only lying. But even so, jealousy squeezes my heart into pulp. 'Well, maybe,' I say quickly. 'I mean, she is SNAKE.'

'Exactly. She's a slut. All women are, at the end of the day. You see, they can't reach God as easily as men can. Women aren't as naturally spiritual as we are. They have babies, their place is in the home, at the cradle, that's their role. Whereas we . . .'

His voice fades; I won't listen any more, won't allow any more words to pollute me. I close my eyes and think of Padma, her lips like a rose, of brushing my finger along the silk of the petals. The image is broken open by an image of her in a smoky club, of her – but I smash it. *Don't let him get to you*, I whisper quietly. Oh God, protect my love for her. Keep it pure, keep the dirt away from it, keep it clean.

And then his words make my heart stop:

'From now on you are forbidden to speak to SNAKE. I am laying down this rule for your own good.'

'Okay,' I say, struggling to keep my face a smooth mask. 'Sure.'

I go to rise, when he says: 'When did you last have something to drink?'

'I – I don't know,' I say, caught off guard, my words stumbling into each other. 'Erm – before the Betrayal.'

'So about four hours ago?'

'Erm, yes.'

'Good. Then you won't drink anything for another twenty hours. Not one drop of water.'

I picture myself sneaking into the bathroom and –

'I shall inform Raymond. He'll be in the hallway so he'll be able to see if you enter the bathroom or the kitchen. When you do, you must keep the door open so he can see what you're doing. And if you do dare to take just one sip, then – well – SNAKE will suffer on your behalf.'

'But – but – why?' I cry.

'It's your punishment.'

'But I'm not on Martyn's side, I had nothing to do with the Betrayal! I told you, I'm with you!'

'Jon, you don't have to betray God with your actions. You can betray him inside, in your heart, and in many ways it's a worse betrayal. Fast without fluids, feel the pain, and purge her from your heart. Let God back in. Because I'm warning you, Jon, if you don't deal with this now, then the evil will fester. And I might not be able to save you in time from the wrath of God. He might be too angry. There may be one way you can prove yourself, however.'

'How?' With one word, I fall tumbling into his trap.

'We will now interrogate Martyn our hostage. I may need your assistance.'

'Of course,' I say quickly.

'When I give the signal, I'll need you to put Martyn's head in the water.'

What? To do what? The words don't quite sink in, and then it's too late: Jeremiah is already out in the hallway and Raymond is tugging Martyn.

'Ow, you're hurting me!' Martyn cries. His hands are cuffed behind his back and Raymond has a fistful of Padma's sparkly top. He opens the bathroom door and throws Martyn in.

Outside the door, I pause. My hands begin to tremble. I have a terrible feeling that I am about to walk into a nightmare. I don't want to go in; I want to run, I want to grab Padma and run and run into the cool freedom of the night.

Then Jeremiah looks at me and I nod dully, knowing I must play along, knowing I must do whatever it takes to keep her alive.

# MIDNIGHT

**Thomas comes into the bathroom too.** He doesn't look sick any more, but it's as though his illness has stripped away some essential spark, some essence of him; his eyes are dull, his voice is flat.

Jeremiah nods at Thomas. Thomas spins on the taps. Jeremiah kneels down next to Martyn and nods at me. I am not sure what the nod means, but I kneel too.

'So, Martyn, when did you first conspire against the Brotherhood of Hebetheus? When did you first feel you could challenge God?' Jeremiah dips his fingers into the water and splashes some on his face. Martyn recoils in terror. But Jeremiah's touch is soft; he washes away the dirt and sweat on his face.

'It was just a whim,' Martyn gabbles. I've never seen him look so scared and for a moment I feel an odd, cruel sort of pleasure that his cockiness has finally been stamped out of him.

'I mean – it was Chris,' Martyn goes on, 'it was just a dare – we just thought . . . it would be . . . a dare . . . we didn't really think it through. We just came up with it this morning'

My eyes flick uneasily to the water, slowly filling up the bath. Is Jeremiah preparing some sort of warped cleansing-baptism?

'Oh really?' Jeremiah's fingers close around Martyn's chin. 'Just this morning, you say?'

'Yeah, this morning.'

'And it was your idea to defy God?'

'No – no – it was Chris's!'

Jeremiah nods at Thomas, who turns off the taps. Martyn struggles, sensing trouble. Then Jeremiah nods at me. I sit paralysed. Jeremiah nods. I raise my hands slowly to Martyn's head. Jeremiah nods. I can't move. Martyn whispers, 'I'm sorry.' Jeremiah says to me, 'Are you with us or against us? Because if you're against us, we'll interrogate you next and find out the true colour of your mind.'

I push him down. Martyn kicks against me but his hands are cuffed and Thomas moves forward to pin down his ankles. I hold him under the water for just a few seconds – though the horror of the moment seems as though it goes on for hours – and then let him go.

'Jesus – I'm going to drown, you're going to drown me,' Martyn shrieks in panic. 'Jon – you have to help me – Jon –'

'Just tell the truth and we won't drown you and we'll let you go,' Jeremiah says. 'How long have you been plotting against me?'

'Like I said, this morning –'

'How long?'

'A day! It was after my Sacred Cleansing – all that stuff you said about my dad – I was upset –'

Jeremiah nods at me. I pause, my hands jelly. Jeremiah nods again. I can't move so Jeremiah reaches over, puts his hands on top of mine and forces Martyn back down into the water. Martyn thrashes about. Water licks into his hair and spills over the back of his neck. I feel blank. I feel strange. And then for one electric moment I feel powerful.

I almost want to shake away Jeremiah's hands, to show him I am tough, I am mighty, I can administer this judgement.

Then as I lean in against him I breathe in Padma's scent, lingering on her jumper. Suddenly I am desperate to let him go. I push against Jeremiah but Jeremiah holds my hands down tight. The white mildewed walls spin; how long has he been under the water? A surge of panic shoots through me with a sudden strength and I shove Jeremiah away violently so that he knocks back against the bath.

Martyn bursts up from the bath, vomiting water. He gasps air. Tears pour from his crimson face. He whimpers, 'Please, enough, no more, enough please.'

Jeremiah nods: enough. Martyn crashes on to the floor and lies on his side, his ribcage heaving *in out in out*. His fingers twitch like butterfly's wings. I look up at Jeremiah, who looks down at Martyn with the eyes of a scientist testing out a new and dangerous experiment.

'Don't disobey me or the God of Hebetheus ever again,' he says. He doesn't bother waiting for Martyn to reply.

I watch Jeremiah undo his cuffs and I think of Padma. I tell myself I can go to her now. I will get her alone; I will kiss her; I will feel the sweet purity of her breath entering my body, cleansing this black in my heart, bringing me back to life. But she seems too distant – like a character in a book I read long ago. I close my eyes and search my heart. It feels as though the God of our love has curled up into a foetal ball and even though I try to coax him, he is too afraid of Jeremiah.

Later that night, when I lie awake desperate for the relief of sleep, my mind keeps playing the scene over and over. I can hear a high-pitched ringing in my eyes, like a sort of tinnitus and as I feel Martyn trembling beneath me it rises to a shriek. I feel dirty. I ache to bath but the thought of going anywhere near the bathroom terrifies me. I feel as though my soul wants to shake off my body and climb out for a while, float in clouds, breathe. I realise then that it can feel worse to inflict violence than to receive it. No bruises; no pain to throb and heal; it is the nothingness that is the pain: to have become less than human. To feel a mark branded for ever on my conscience; to feel a little bit of my heart chipped away. To know too, that I might have to pay that karma back and suffer it myself. Was Jeremiah punishing me, most of all? Was he trying to kill the love in me?

Surely this is not the work of God?

That moment of power. When I nearly wanted to drown Martyn. Was that really me? Is that human nature? To feel compelled to tip the see-saw against someone so that their weakness supports our rise? Maybe this urge for power is the root of all evil; in order for one person to gain something in life someone else always has to miss out; we can't all get As or win football matches or stars; someone always has to lose and that's the way society works. Maybe in murderers, the weakest people of all, this urge for power is a hunger so acute they have to 'take a life' in order to gain a double life: their own and someone else's shadow. So when I pushed Martyn under the water, for that moment when I enjoyed his torment – does that make me evil? Does that mean I might be capable of murder?

I was close to killing Padma.

I want to pull this evil from my heart by its roots.

I cannot bear this black feeling inside. My mind scrambles desperately for images of goodness. I think of St Teresa, St Francis, Jesus. None of them ever needed to use violence. St Francis had a father who was worse than mine. He was worse than Martyn's father; when St Francis sold his clothes to give money to the poor, his father beat him, took him to court and disowned him. But St Francis loved him still. I remember how my father told me the story of the wolf who terrorised the people in the village of Gubbio by eating their animals. Every villager who tried to stop the wolf perished. Then St Francis went into Gubbio and the wolf appeared. St Francis made the sign of the cross and the wolf bowed his head and lay down at St Francis's feet, meek as a lamb. St Francis asked the wolf to make a pact and the wolf put his paw into St Francis's hand and agreed to leave the people alone. In return, whenever the wolf came into the village, the people would feed him. All these saints, these people who loved God; none of them have ever said *We must kill* in the name of the God. None of them have wanted to kill a fly in the name of God. They never tried to solve the world by stamping on evil, by bombing nations; they just shone a light into the darkness, washed away the evil with pure compassion, with love.

I try to think of good things I have done. But they seem so few. I cling to a memory of Harvest Festival. This was a few years back, before Dad left. I took five baskets to old people that week and Dad gave me the last basket to take. The address was on a dodgy housing estate, graffiti crawling in neon ivy across the walls. The old man who opened the door smiled toothlessly, spread out his arms and cried *Wontyoucomein?* I thought he was drunk. I wanted to run but I was scared he might complain to Dad so I crept in. Then he explained to me *Ivegotcancerinmythroat* and when I gave him the basket his face lit up and he danced around the room and then made me play Scrabble with him for an hour and even though he kept cheating it was the best game I'd ever played in my life. When we said goodbye, even though he was a stranger, I felt I loved the man as though he was family. As I walked home, I felt my body singing with sunshine, blazing with love for life. I promised the old man I'd visit him again, only the next week I had too much homework. Then a few weeks later Dad left and I never did go back.

I promise myself that if we get out of here alive, I'll go back and see him.

At last, I feel the relief of tears and weep quietly until dawn comes.

# Day Six

# 9 A.M.

**I am prodded awake by a gun** in my ribs. Raymond's face leers above me. He informs me it's time for prayers.

The cartoons in the Prayer Room now lie hidden beneath a fresh sea of white paint. And yet still they seem to linger, sniggering quietly. Every corner of the room has been cleaned to a pitch of desperation. The few tiny specks of dust left gleam black against the desert of white. I wonder sleepily if it's possible to ever remove every speck of dust or the moment you thought you'd achieved pure whiteness a speck would always appear somewhere.

Chris and Martyn are no longer in cuffs, but they have to sit apart from us, in a new black circle that seems to have been painted during the night. I cannot see what the symbol is beneath the fold of their knees.

I kneel down quickly, trying to ignore the whimpers of hunger in my stomach. Thomas and Jeremiah enter. I look at Jeremiah but he doesn't look at me. He gives Chris and Martyn a pained gaze, then sits down, cross-legged, eyes closed, while Thomas stands up and makes an announcement.

He unfolds a sheet of paper and declares that some new rules are being introduced for our Brotherhood.

'1. *Prayers will be set at 8 a.m., midday and 6 p.m. All shall attend.*
2. *Nobody is allowed to open a window, leave the cottage or use the bathroom without asking for Our Leader's permission.*
3. *Nobody will be allowed to speak directly to Our Leader any more. If you need to ask permission to open a window, leave the cottage, or use the bathroom, or you have any other queries, than you must ask the Second in Command, the Seer Thomas, who will then consult with Our Leader.'*

(Raymond shifts; Thomas flushes slightly.)

'4. *There will be a curfew at 9 p.m. every night.*
5. *Nobody is allowed to read anything or write anything down.*
6. *The guard shift will continue to last for twenty-four hours. Please consult Raymond every morning for your shift.'*

(Thomas pauses and coughs slightly, the piece of paper shaking in his hands.)

'7. *The penalty for breaking of these rules will be severe.*
8. *Any traitors will be punished. Martyn and Chris have apologised for their treacherous behaviour and are now pardoned in the eyes of God, provided they abide by the new rules of the Brotherhood.'*

Chris and Martyn shift and nod solemnly at Jeremiah.
Thomas folds up the sheet of paper and kneels down without looking at any of us.
Jeremiah half-opens his eyes and nods.
We all bow down to pray.

Is it because I no longer worship the god of Hebetheus that this prayer session feels different? But it's more than that; there's a sense of strain between us. Our prayers are just words; we're gripped too tightly by fear's fist to think of God. I feel sad, remembering how only a few days ago we sat in such deep prayer we no longer felt six but one. Funny how when we were brothers together, our rules were there to gently guide us; our strength lay in our love for God and for each other. It's only now that we're individuals, now that our chains are slack and weak, that we need rules.

And I realise: *It's all over.* Our God once stood strong and tall but now he has cracked and crumbled into pieces of dead stone. My heart quivers with a pang. I know that the Hebetheus religion is bullshit. But it was once real to me; it did change my life; it gave me hope, it gave me a vision; it explained the mysteries of the world to me. I feel as though I am looking through closed gates, catching glimpses of a beautiful garden I will never walk in again.

How can it be so easy for faith to slip away?

And how did it happen so quickly? Just in the space of six days. Where did it begin? With little things. The woman at the door. Martyn's doubts. Just little breezes that began to blow gently at our house of cards. Is that the danger of evil – that it poisons in the tiniest doses, a little here, a little there, until one day you wake up and something that was once beautiful has rotted and shrivelled?

Maybe the only way for faith to last is to love a God from within, so that it's just between you and Him, so that every day a prayer binds a thread between you until there are so many threads they can't be snapped. A private love that nobody from the outside can look in at, or shape, or have any say in. But how long might that take?

I've deserted my Christian God once; what if he won't take me back now? What if I have nothing?

For a moment I am full of despair, and then I remember Padma. She is all I have left.

I close my eyes and remember that moment in the forest when Padma showed me the God of Love. But too much pain has blurred the memory. I can't quite pin down exactly how I felt then; it was as though I was in an exalted state, tasting a heaven on earth. Maybe the God of Love is the answer; maybe I should pray to him even though no religion defines him, even though no prophet on earth is shouting his message, even though I feel him more than I understand him.

I start to pray once more. But I feel lost. My soul fumbling blindly between all these different versions of Him: Hebetheus, Christian, Love. In the end, I give up on prayer and simply hope, just hope that I will find a plan to help Padma and that she will help me, that everything will come good in the end.

# 10 A.M.

**We have just finished prayers** when there is a knock on the door.

'Who's that? Who's on guard?'

'Martyn was meant to be, but now he's on probation, there –'

'There wasn't e-e-enough p-people –'

'Who is it?'

'Go and look!'

'Shit, it's that woman again!'

'Wh-who i-is she?'

'The one who came the other day –'

'Who –'

'Who spoke to her then. Tell me now, who spoke to her then?'

'Jon did, it was Jon –'

'Jon, go, speak with her. Be calm. Remember. God be with you.'

'But who the hell is meant to be on guard? They should be hung, drawn and quartered –'

'What if she –'

'Quiet! Let Jon go.' Jeremiah narrows his eyes and picks up his gun. 'Jon has yet to prove himself. Careful, Jon, careful. Be very careful. All now depends on you.'

*

I open the door.

'Ned!' she cries. 'Hello, my love, is Brenda better yet?'

'Er, no. Not really.' My face burns despite the raw air. 'Can you come back another time, she's kind of busy –'

'Well, I brought her some eggs.' She proffers a box, her own stencil sketch graceful on the lid. 'I'll just come in if you don't mind. I know Brenda won't mind a jot, I expect she's sketching again, is she –'

'No – no – you can't! You can't come in! Brenda's in a very delicate state.'

She starts, staring at me. It's a fatal moment. She notices me. My features, previously an impersonal blur to her, now come into focus.

'You . . . you look . . . like . . .' she trails off. 'You look like one of those boys on the – where's Brenda? You're not Ned, are you? I thought you looked too young, I thought to myself, Ned should be at least a little older than that.'

Very slowly, she pushes her eggs back into her bag and risks a look at me again. Her shoulders seem to shrink back into her 'Barber' and she drops her eyes hastily.

'Well, now, I ought to be going . . .'

'Yes,' I say brightly. 'I think you should go.' Oh, thank God: we're going to be saved. She'll call the police. Careful now, Jon, don't give away a single clue, let Jeremiah think you played your part.

'Hey!' Martyn suddenly cries, coming up behind me. 'Hey, don't go!'

The woman swings round. My heart crumples.

'If you're looking for Brenda, she's just in here,' Martyn says cheerfully. 'She really wants to see you.' He punches me on the shoulder, so hard I whimper. 'Ned – you space-head, you should have let her in.'

The woman steps in cautiously, lost in confusion. Now

she's thinking: *Did I get it wrong?* Are these boys just boys?

'She's just in here,' Martyn says, spreading open his hand as though inviting her into a friendly hotel.

Martyn opens the door where the dead old lady lies. Martyn beams as though he can already hear Jeremiah praising him for his ingenuity, for his fucking *improvisation*. The woman enters the room, crying, 'God – the smell in here! You should have opened some windows!'

Then there is a long, long silence. And then her voice, like a little girl:

'What did you do to her?'

'It wasn't us,' Martyn giggles nervously.

'You monster!' she shrieks.

Raymond appears, tinkling cuffs. I listen to the sounds of him silencing the woman. Then he leads her into the Hostage Room to join Padma. Jeremiah sidles into the hallway, nodding. A moment later, Raymond steps out, slamming the door behind him.

Now we have two hostages.

# 11 A.M.

As Thomas and I walk down the hallway to the Hostage Room, I feel as though I am floating above myself, dancing on the cracked ceiling. Jeremiah's command echoes inside: *You won't drink anything for another twenty hours. Not one drop of water.* I can understand why Moses and Daniel and Elijah fasted; there is a strange, black euphoria to my dizziness. It acts as an anaesthetic to the horrors around me, muffling the outside world into a woozy haze.

But when we enter the Hostage Room – when my eyes fall on Padma – my body sings awake in shock.

Padma and the Woman are sitting side by side, hand-cuffed. The woman looks bedraggled and the bruise on her cheek is like a ghostly apple imprint.

Thomas turns to me. He doesn't look me in the eye – I assume because I am supposedly too inferior.

'Jeremiah has instructed you to recite the *Book of Hebetheus* in order to soothe the souls of our frightened and ignorant hostages.'

I sit down, cross-legged. Thomas stands behind me. I look at Padma, desperate for reassurance. Her eyes are soft; I am forgiven. My eyes shower her with a thousand kisses; her eyes kiss me back a thousand times in return. But then they flash with – a message? With some urgency I can't translate.

Thomas lays a hand on my shoulder.

' "Imagine for a moment that human beings are in a cave." ' *You won't drink anything for another twenty hours. Not one drop of water. And if you do dare to take just one sip, then – well. SNAKE will suffer on your behalf.* ' "From childhood, each human has their legs and necks in handcuffs so that they can only stare straight ahead of them at a light reflected on the wall – which comes from a fire burning far above and behind them." ' Each word sucks the last dregs of saliva from my mouth; each word becomes heavier and heavier, a boulder I roll up my throat and force from my lips. ' "On the wall, they see dancing patterns of life like shadow puppets –" '

'You stupid little boy!' the woman suddenly bursts out.

'Sorry?'

'I mean – honestly! What on earth are you talking about? You're sixteen years old, for God's sake! What are you doing sitting here and quoting Plato at me! If I wasn't wearing these handcuffs, I'd take you over my knee and give you a jolly good spanking!'

'I –' I look back at Thomas who suddenly looks sheepish.

'And are we to sit here without food or drink?' the woman demands.

'Well – your meal is set – is set for midday,' Thomas says firmly.

'Well, we're thirsty!' the woman booms. 'You might have guns and we might be your victims, but it's not right to abuse us. If you really believe in God, then give us something to drink.'

I feel a dizzy rush of laughter inside. But I also feel relieved. As though I've been wanting someone to tell me off for some time.

'I'd like something to drink,' Padma says loudly. She

gives me an urgent glance again. 'And I'd like some paper and a pen. I think the Rules of the Hebetheus are so interesting I'd like to write them down. Can you get them for me, Thomas?'

Thomas stares at her, looking sweaty and tense. The woman crimps her lips furiously.

'But – the new rules.' He frowns, muttering to himself, then pulls the piece of A4 paper out of his pocket. 'Rule number five – "Nobody is allowed to read or write anything down." I'm sorry. It's not allowed.'

'But these are the rules of Hebetheus,' Padma objects. 'These aren't *anything*. They're obviously the exception. As the new deputy you ought to be able to allow this instead of wasting Jeremiah's time. He might be angry.'

'Yes – well – yes.' Thomas looks uncertain. 'Well. Jon should go,' he says at last, running a trembling hand through his hair.

In the kitchen, I twist on the taps, filling the cups. I think of waterfalls, of flowing rivers that trickle clear over shiny stones. *You won't drink anything for another twenty hours. Not one drop of water. And if you do dare to take just one sip, then – well – SNAKE will suffer on your behalf.*

Back in the Hostage Room, I pass them their water and give Padma her sheet of paper. She scrawls something on the top and flashes her eyes at me again.

'I don't know what the matter is with you boys,' the woman breaks off from spilling most of her water down her front. 'You boys with your knives and guns, you take it all for granted, how good your lives are, this would never have happened in my day.'

'Um, Jon, can you just help me – I can't quite remember rule three?' Padma asks, patting the floor. A tremble flickers through the veins in her hand.

I kneel down next to her, peering over her shoulder. I give Thomas a nervous glance, and then look. Her writing zigzags across the top:

*The woman has a mobile just now when we were alone she pressed* 999

I let out a gasp. My eyes flit to the woman, who gives me a stout glance. But there is guilt in her feigned innocence. I picture her, hands struggling in her cuffs like crabs, easing her mobile out of her pocket, tapping in emergency services with one finger, bending down, whispering into the phone, *I'm in Suffolk, I've found the boys, they're here with the girl, come quickly . . .*

'What is that?' Thomas suddenly asks. 'What's she written?'

'Nothing!' My heart is screaming in shock. 'Nothing – she just wrote down a Rule and she got muddled –'

'Run,' Padma hisses. 'Before they get here – run, Jon!'

'What is it?' Thomas asks. He holds out his hand. 'Show me.' His voice turns to ice. 'Show me or I will get Jeremiah now.'

I stand up, shakily, looking round. They could be here already, creeping up to the house.

'It's nothing –' I try, but Thomas wrenches the piece of paper from me. I stand in helpless, heart-hammering pain as his eyes moon.

'Jesus,' Thomas cries. 'The police –'

'It's too late now,' the woman crows. 'I had a feeling something funny was up, I knew it in my gut – and I was right! They'll be here any minute and it won't be any good reciting more Plato.'

Plato? The word lingers in the periphery of my shocked mind. What does she mean by Plato? Something inside tells

me there is some terrible connection . . . something . . .
what I have read about Plato – but there's no time –

'Run,' Padma cries. 'Jon – just go – I'll be all right now
the police are here – go!'

I make for the door, but Thomas slams against me,
knocking me to the floor. I lie there, winded, tears burning
my eyes – oh God, oh *God*, please can they just get here,
please can this all be over with –

And then the sirens start to scream.

'Jeremiah!' Thomas yells.

# 12 P.M.

**We are standing in a line** in the front hallway: a winding snake of nerves, of bitten nails wrapped around guns, of jerky whispers and flittering eyes and desperate prayers. When we heard the sirens, the Brotherhood flew into a panic, but Jeremiah calmed them down. He announced that it was time to leave our Holy Base. He ordered Thomas to bring Padma into the hall with us, adding, 'We will leave the woman behind. Give her this.' He passed Thomas a copy of the *Book of Hebetheus*. I waited for Thomas to inform Jeremiah of my betrayal but to my confusion, he has not said a word.

*Come on, come on, come on*, I silently beg the police to hurry. The two sirens play a duet: an undercurrent, a repetitive shriek of *wee-ah-, wee-ah*, and a soprano that swells and retreats over the top. It reminds me of being back at home; sometimes I'd be in my bedroom, flicking through a book and I'd hear a siren and feel a sense of dread and wonder: *Who's it for?* A robbery? A murder? Will they come into our street? But the sirens would fade away and the mystery would pass. I'd never imagined I'd be in a situation when the sirens would be a war cry for my blood.

Then, suddenly, they stop. An eerie silence stretches out. Jeremiah peers through the front door and mutters that he can't see any police cars. We whisper in bewilderment: have they parked the cars down the road to fool us? Maybe they are slipping through the fields, creeping up behind trees, pacing towards us . . .

'Shouldn't we go out through the back?' Martyn whispers.

'No – then we have to cross two entire fields without cover. This way is risky but we can be under the shelter of trees much quicker,' Jeremiah hisses.

Oh so slowly, Jeremiah eases open the door and Raymond slips out, taking Padma with him. The sight of his meaty fingers curled around her slender brown wrist sickens me. We keep the door open a slit, a cold blast hitting our legs, watching them creep across the road, climb over a stile into the small field, dart to the clusters of trees. I feel my heart banging; I can hear Martyn's heart banging, feel the quiver of his shoulder pressed against mine. I see his lips moving in prayers like mine. Our prayers must be enemies that clash and fight in the heavens above.

Raymond and Padma make it safely to the woods. A pale sweat washes over me. What's gone wrong? Why haven't the police got the right address, why are they at the bottom of the road? Is this a game? Are they waiting for us?

Jeremiah seems to be wondering the same thing; his eyes narrow in confusion. Then he says, 'Okay, we go. We go quickly. Thomas – you keep your gun trained on Jon.'

'What!' I bluster, my cheeks flaming. 'I'm – I'm on your side – I wasn't the one who tried to –'

'There isn't time for this,' Jeremiah hisses. 'We go – now.'

How does Jeremiah know? How has he seen into my heart and detected its true colour? To my fury, Martyn nods at Thomas, whispers, 'Yeah – watch him!', then sneers at me with a smug smile. I glare back at him. Only yesterday he was a so-called traitor; now he is desperate to bind himself back to Hebetheus.

We head out into the front garden. Our sacred circle of stones lies jagged, like fallen statues of gods broken into pieces, half covered with forgetful snow. The air is bitingly cold. At the gate, Jeremiah hisses *Wait* and we cower behind the hedge. If I had a gun I could fire it into the air. Just one shot would do it. I eye up Thomas's gun but he is clutching it tight, with both hands.

Jeremiah watches the faint flash of a distant police light.

'I do believe,' Jeremiah says with a chuckle in his voice, 'that the police have cornered the wrong house. How inept. Well, God has protected us. Let's move.'

I watch my trainers rise and fall on the road, an echo of my first night here, when I tried to run. If only I had run then. If only I'd run.

At the stile, I hang back, but if for a second a door of escape opens, it closes instantly, as Jeremiah waits for me to climb. In the field, I stand up, raising one arm to wave at the police – who are too far away to see it, but who knows, they might, they just *might* – but Martyn thwacks me hard on the back and I lurch down, my spine screaming.

We go into the woods.

And then the sirens scream once more.

# 1 P.M.

'Look at them,' Jeremiah sneers in a whisper. 'This is why the world needs us. They shoot a Brazilian man on the tube thinking he's a bomber. They act as though *we're* the terrorists and *then* they get our hideaway wrong and now we've escaped. Idiots.' He shakes us. 'This is why the world needs us to fight terrorism. Only we can do it.'

We watch them from the safety of the trees.

The scene before us feels as though it can't be related to us. As though it's being shot for a movie. Cars pull up. Policemen tumble out. They have megaphones and everything – and fancy big black bulletproof jackets. They creep behind the hedge: they call out threats, they cajole, they warn through their megaphones, words ringing like metal through the cold air. I could call out to them, but they wouldn't hear; we're too far.

I look at their faces. Raymond looks stern, Martyn shocked, Chris frightened, Thomas blank. Jeremiah looks thrilled, his eyes gleaming.

So, as the police invade, as they discover the dead woman and release the living one, as they enter the room full of strange symbols, we hurry into the forest. Every so often, I slow down and feel Thomas's gun in my back. I'm terrified he will slip on a branch and set it off by accident.

Martyn is ahead of me; he keeps glancing back to check I am at his heels. He might not have a gun but his fists are sprung. Only yesterday he was against Jeremiah; only fear has persuaded him back on to our side; is he just going along with this; can I change him? But mostly I sense he just wants revenge for last night; he is scrambling to become Jeremiah's golden boy again, to be the one who inflicts rather than receives pain. I glance back at Thomas, who frowns and nudges the gun sharply: *Keep going.* I want to grab him and shake him and yell, *Can't you see? We've lost! The police will start on this forest, they will find us. Can't you see how stupid this is?* But Thomas is lost in doctrine, in fear, in devotion.

The line ahead of us slows to a halt; I see a flash of Padma's face. Where are we now? For all I know, this was part of Jeremiah's plan. He may have another house lined up. The thought of being crammed into another lost place makes me feel dizzy and claustrophobic and my prayers turn into begging.

We're at the side of a house. A big house. It looks like a country retreat for some city couple. There's a huge gravel driveway with two cars – a BMW and a Land Rover. A chicken clucks and pecks the gravel.

We kneel down for some time, shivering, our breaths creating white dragons in the cold air.

Then Jeremiah suddenly stands up and starts walking towards the house.

'What the fuck are you *doing*?' Raymond hisses.

Jeremiah turns back and smiles.

'I'm going into the house. We're all going to go in. We're hungry. We need to eat and God will provide.'

We all glance at each other. Jeremiah becomes impatient.

'We have guns. They don't. Now come on.'

Jeremiah strolls across the lawn, hands in his pockets. We crawl out of the bushes, trailing behind him. Melted snow rolls over my shoes in sweet droplets. He's screwed, I realise in stunned bewilderment. Jeremiah's finally completely lost it. They'll call the police. We'll get caught.

Padma will be safe.

I move closer to her, letting my finger whisper against the side of her palm before moving away.

Ivy crawls blackly over the house. Double-glazed windows protecting rooms filled with monuments to IKEA. On the door is a lion grinning in swirly gold. There's also a doorbell. Jeremiah pings it and it sing-songs down the hallway. Behind the warped glass, blurry dots join together to form a shape. Jeremiah turns to Raymond and asks for a gun; Raymond passes it over.

A man opens the door. He's wearing black trousers and a white pullover and his fingers, raking through his greying hair, pause in horror.

'If you call out, I'll shoot,' Jeremiah says.

The man stares at us, open-mouthed. Jeremiah's eyes flit across the hallway, up the stairs, computing rooms, phones, dangers. The man must be in his forties but suddenly he looks like a little boy. 'Oh God,' he says. His life has been on a steady and safe path for so long and maybe he was just looking forward to retiring and getting a nice villa in Spain and suddenly life throws this at him; suddenly, in the space of a minute, we've spun his wheel of fortune with a savage wrench. 'Oh God.'

I want to say to him: 'I'm sorry.'

'Daddddy,' a voice calls out. 'Daddy.' A little boy with yellow hair comes down the hallway. 'Daddy – they've got guns!' he calls out in excitement.

'Ian, could you just pop out and get me a lemon –' the

294

woman calls as she pads down the stairs, holding a recipe book. Seeing us, she freezes. The recipe book slips from her fingers and bangs, stair by stair, to the bottom, where it sprawls with a broken spine. She stares at us with rabbit eyes, then turns and flees back up the stairs –

'STOP HER!' Jeremiah cries. He fires his gun. His body shudders with the kickback and a small painting shatters across the stairs. Raymond leaps up the stairs. There's a scream. The man yells, 'Leave her alone!' and takes a step forward – but Jeremiah threatens his gun at him. The man shakes his head, tears in his eyes. He looks at each of us in turn with a pleading, desperate gaze. When he looks at me, I quickly drop my gaze. My stomach is churning so hard I think I might spew and I just want to grab Padma and run –

– but they'll pepper me with bullets –

– I can't do anything –

Raymond comes back down the stairs, his paw locked around the woman's wrist. I let out a shaky breath of relief; the woman isn't harmed, though her face is stone with terror. Her mobile hangs between Raymond's teeth; he lets it fall to the floor and stamps on it.

'I pulled out the connection on the upstairs phone,' Raymond adds. 'But I don't know about downstairs. And he might have a mobile too.'

Jeremiah points his gun.

'There's a downstairs phone,' the man says. 'And in my study – on my desk – there's my mobile. Look, whatever you want, we'll give it to you – please just don't hurt me or my wife or my little boy.'

His son, registering that our guns are not toys, is now behind his legs, peering out with wide eyes, his chin trembling dangerously.

'Look – I've got money – I've got hundreds here.' The man pulls out his wallet and shows off a sheaf of shaking notes. Jeremiah puts his head to one side like an intrigued pet being offered a game by his master.

'We'll take it,' Martyn says eagerly.

'No,' Jeremiah says sharply. 'We don't need that. We're from the Religion of Hebetheus. You may have seen us on the news. We come in peace; all we ask is that you give us some food. We don't wish to harm you or cause any hurt. We'll just need to use your house for a few hours, that's all.'

The man pauses, digesting this incredulously, the notes wilting in his hand. I realise just how insane we sound to the outside world. How big the gap is between us and them. Can Jeremiah see it? Or does he just choose not to see it? I feel my skin crawling with shame; I want to tell the man; look, I'm not one of them, can you see that, I'm not really one of them . . .

The man's eyes fall on Padma. He clicks.

'You're the boys who are saving the world,' he says blankly.

'Yes,' says Jeremiah proudly. 'Now, Martyn – go to the study, kill the mobile, kill the phone. The rest of us will proceed to the kitchen. Do you have a telephone connection in your kitchen?'

'No.'

'You're sure?'

'Yes. Yes, I swear.' The man looks up at his wife and Jeremiah nods. Raymond lets her go. She stumbles down the stairs and collapses against her husband, clutching him tightly. He clenches her face and kisses her hair. Then she reaches down and picks up her son, though he's too heavy. He wails to be put down, but she won't let go;

he begins to cry.

Jeremiah sighs.

'Can we just go into the kitchen? We're all really very hungry.'

# 1.15 P.M.

**As we enter the kitchen,** delicious smells uncurl and seduce us.

Suddenly I'm back home, on a Sunday afternoon, playing outside the kitchen door, Mum cooking in the kitchen, Dad in his study preparing his sermon, the anticipation of food tasting better than the food itself. I wonder if my mum is cooking right now and if she still lays a place for Dad. I wonder if she is laying a place for me.

'Help yourself to anything you like,' gabbles the man. 'We have crisps, snacks, biscuits –'

'There's chocolate, some Green & Blacks in the cupboard,' cries the woman.

'We've got Coke, we've got beer – anything you want – please just take it.'

'Can I have some Coke?' the little boy wails and his mother scoops him again.

'Give him some,' Jeremiah says, waving his hand.

As the woman gets a Coke from the fridge, her eyes fall on Padma's streaked face.

'You poor girl,' she whispers. 'Oh, you poor girl. What have they done to you?' And suddenly she reaches out and holds Padma to her, hugging her tightly, her eyes filling up.

'Let her go,' Jeremiah says quickly, but he looks startled.

The woman draws back with a stony face, giving us glances as though we are animals. Once more, I want to protest *I'm not one of them, I love her, I'd never hurt her.*

The woman gives her son his Coke, patting his head and drawing him close. Jeremiah eyes up the chopping board, the spray of carrots and potatoes and cauliflower. 'You're about to cook?'

She freezes, then nods quickly.

'Then let us cook. We will all eat together.'

The arrangement is very surreal. Jeremiah won't let the woman use the carving knife, so Chris and I have to chop up the vegetables following her instructions. The man sits at the kitchen table, his son slathering over his lap, persistently asking, 'Dad, can I go and play, Dad can I go and play?' Every so often, the man looks up, gives us a nervous glance and holds his son more tightly. In the oven, the chicken and vegetables bubble merrily in their roasting tins. Raymond trains his gun on the woman while she lays the table in the dining room. She tells him, with a tender fear, that he can put down his gun; she'll feed us like her sons, her boys, and he frowns, but still holds the gun at her. They don't have enough chairs for all of us, so we carry in stools from the kitchen. Then Jeremiah orders the woman to serve. She heaps each plate with meat and gravy and vegetables. We lay out our guns on the striped tablecloth; they nudge salt and pepper cellars. Even Padma is given a place, next to the little boy, and her gag is removed. She remains silent.

The man and the woman sit at opposite ends of the table. They exchange a look of tender desperation.

Jeremiah stands up and says, 'Before we eat, I'd like to begin by telling you all a message I've just received from God. The world is coming to an end. And it is coming to an end soon.'

I see a quiver of hysterical laughter brush the woman's lips and she quickly contains it, her eyes bulging. I bow my head as Jeremiah's words flow over us. Have we always been like this? I wonder. Were we always this crazy?

'A man who has not experienced a Soul Shift is, from God's point of view, a worm. Worse, he is a worm trapped inside a golden palace – and that palace is the mind of a human. He fails to use his divine nature. Instead he is trapped in a small, petty wriggle of thoughts, fears and worries.

'Our world is full of worms and they offend God! Increasingly over the next few years, unless more Soul Shifts take place, God will show his anger with punishments! People foolishly believe that the ice caps are melting and holes are forming in the sky from the use of aerosols, believing with typical egotism that their trivial actions dictate the shifts of weather. No! That is not the case! They fail to understand that the weather is a representation of God's mood. The sun is his happy smile. The wind is his frustration. The rain is the tears he weeps. As God waits for more Soul Shifts and people fail to respond, to turn to the message of the Hebetheus, disasters will begin to become more frequent: hurricanes that eat up millions of homes, typhoons that eat up races in one easy gulp. And God, breathing warm breaths of anger, is slowly destroying the world – slowly because he is giving us a chance to Soul Shift in time – breathing on the ice caps and melting them, sending tidal waves flowing to drown entire countries. England will soon sink beneath the waves and become a forgotten land, a myth people speak of in one thousand years' time.

'God has had enough. I can feel his rage! I can feel it in my heart. We have only twenty-four hours left before a terrible disaster will strike us all down and change life on earth for ever. We must eat this food in absolute love for God, and then we must spend every hour praying, praying, praying, because time is short, my friends, time is too, too short.'

Jeremiah sits down. There is a shocked silence. Chris looks close to tears; Martyn looks red with anger.

Padma and I bite back smiles and look away.

'Now,' Jeremiah announces. 'We shall eat God's food.'

I haven't eaten for nearly twenty-four hours. As I look down at my plate, I am gripped by a ravenous urge to just plunge in, push aside this madness for a few minutes in the pleasure of food. But just as I am about to take my first mouthful, Jeremiah says,

'No, Jon.'

I look up at him.

'You're fasting, remember?'

Slowly, I put my fork down.

Across the table, Padma stares at me with soft eyes. She's only taken one mouthful of food and a crispy piece of potato still hangs on her fork. But she puts down her knife and fork on her plate and gently pushes it away.

And I feel in that moment that I've never loved anyone as much as I love Padma.

Jeremiah watches us with narrowed eyes. Martyn frowns. But I don't care.

Except: if they know I love her, can I still help her? How can I trick them and release her if they stop trusting me?

'I need the toilet!' the little boy cries. His mother tries to shush him, but he keeps on singing, 'I need the toilet need the toilet need to wee need to wee.'

'I can take him,' the woman begs.

'Jon will take him,' Jeremiah says.

'Don't worry,' I assure the woman, who looks frantic. 'I'll be very gentle with him – I won't hurt him, I swear!'

'Be quick,' Jeremiah instructs. 'Or SNAKE will be in trouble. Okay?'

The little boy tells me that his name is Peter and grabs my thumb, locking it into his small, fleshy hand. He drags me up the stairs, across a plush hallway and into a bathroom. The sight of the bath, the sheen of light falling on its white curves, unleashes too many images: Martyn's face plunging into water, the weight of his neck pulsing through my arm as I yanked him back up. I turn away, muttering that I'll stand outside and wait.

The little boy keeps calling that his wee-wee is stuck. I ignore him and hurry into the couple's bedroom. Everything glimmers and glitters with ivory silk and opulence. In the midst of it all, a Bible sits sternly on a bedside cabinet as though frowning at its lavishly sinful surroundings. Next to the Bible is a half-empty bottle of Snapple. I yank open the top drawer, searching desperately for a hidden mobile – maybe one last spare – but I find nothing but socks and ties. I think of Padma below and quickly slam the drawer shut. Then the Snapple drink catches my eye. Jeremiah would never know. I feel saliva ooze into my leathery mouth; my parched throat screams for the relief. I pick it up slowly, swallowing. I hold it up in the air in front of me, blinking. I bring the plastic edge to my lips.

I stop.

I cannot help thinking that he is behind me. The God of Hebetheus. That if I take one sip he will strike me down or punish me by killing Padma. *Drink*, I try to fight back, *you're just paranoid from hunger, just drink, you don't believe in Him any more, just drink*.

I try to tip the bottle but once more a terrible fear grips me.

'Hey!'

I jump violently and turn to see the little boy in the doorway. Quickly, I put the Snapple back down. I wipe sweat off my brow and smile at him.

'Come and see my room,' he insists. I tell him we have to go back down, but he yanks me insistently so I agree that I can take a look for one minute. He shows me his paintings, primary colours smudged in crayon. A picture of Jesus, of angels, of Moses and his burning bush and finally, one of God.

'He looks just like your father,' I say, laughing weakly.

The boy imitates my laugh though he doesn't really understand it. Then he looks sober.

'Are we really all going to die?' he asks unhappily, his lip trembling.

'No.' I kneel down before him. I think of how this day might impact his life, of the fear we may strike into his soul, of the nightmares he may suffer in the weeks to come. And I feel determined to preserve his innocence, to keep it shining inside him; to do one good thing in the midst of this darkness. 'No,' I say, smiling. 'You mustn't worry. God loves you. Everything is fine. We're very happy that you let us use your house –'

From below, Jeremiah suddenly roars up: 'JON, WE'RE GOING. NOW!'

Down in the hallway, Jeremiah shakes the woman's hand and the man's hand and thanks them for the beautiful meal and their kind hospitality.

'We're leaving now,' he adds. 'And don't think of calling the police or we'll track you down and shoot you, okay?' But his words sound like a line from a film and though the man smiles with wild relief, I can tell he'll pick up the phone the moment we leave.

Jeremiah knows it too, and the moment we get out, he screams, 'RUN!'

Raymond begins to head for the forest, but Jeremiah cries, 'This way!' To my confusion, he sends us heading down the road, in the direction of the town.

As soon as the house is out of sight, he orders a left turn across the fields. And I realise he was just fooling the couple. In despair, I picture the police shooting in the wrong direction, searching houses, shops, pubs, while we get further and further away from them.

We streak across the field and into the forest, zigzagging through the trees. We slither and slip on the snow, branches and bushes tearing our hair and faces. I fall back in line with Padma but Raymond comes up behind us, pointing his gun and yelling, 'Keep going, you guys, keep going!' and my heart sinks because I know that once more I have failed her, that I haven't found a way to escape, that we are trapped still in the net of the Brotherhood.

# 8 P.M.

**It's dark in the shack.** There's a lawnmower propped up against the wall, with a birdshit-splattered handle and rusty teeth. A hole in the corrugated roof above, framing the darkening sky, and wooden walls filled with holes like gaping eyes. It feels both hot and cold; our warm breaths mingling to form a collective fog against the cold blasts that the wind blows in.

There's only just enough room to pack us in. Padma is sitting between Chris and Martyn; Martyn's gun nudges her thigh. Raymond guards the door. Thomas is by my side and Jeremiah is standing in the centre, looking up through the hole, as though he can see some frigging comet or some other sign of his stupid apocalypse.

We've been told to pray. To pray that when the disaster strikes tomorrow we'll all reach Manu. I keep trying to focus on escape plans but my body is weak, my mind exhausted from lack of food and drink. I find myself half-sinking into sleep, my neck dropping forwards, then snapping back. I blink and risk a look at Padma. She is staring at the floor. Her tired eyes look as though they are filled with sand and her expression is doleful.

She makes me feel so wonderful. Even here, in the midst of all this darkness, all this pain, knowing that my life is ruined, she makes me feel wonderful. And you know, Dad, you know how she makes me feel? She makes me feel divine. As though the God of Love is beating brightly in my heart.

She reminds me of that day when I was thirteen years old. I remember it was a difficult time for me. People kept telling me about God; I'd drawn sticky crayon pictures of Noah and Jesus at Sunday School; I'd heard my father expound a thousand sermons, but their words were just words: none of them ignited a spark and I was worried there was something deeply wrong with me.

Then I woke up one morning and went into the garden. I wanted to check on the treehouse we were building; you'd said, Dad, that you'd carry on with it after I'd gone to bed. It was dawn and the sky was a vague mass of clouds with moments of pure golden clarity. The light lit up green streaks in the grass stalks, glittered dew-diamonds on a spider's web, surfed off a bird's wing as it soared overhead. There was a stillness in the light, a calmness in the trees, in the soft breath of the wind, as though the landscape was alive, alert but at peace. I thought: this is what Eden must have been like. My heart filled up with beauty until I was drunk on it. Just watching the light travel up a leaf, or shimmer on a glossy line of ants. I thought: *This is God.*

The feeling lingered with me all day. I noticed things I'd never noticed before; and that evening, when I sung hymns in church, my new faith breathed life into the words and they flew from my lips like birds that circled up to the heavens. Later, I tried to explain it to you, but you frowned and said, 'Don't go turning into a pantheist, Jon.' And I realised I had been mistaken.

Was I mistaken, Dad? Was this in some way a taste of God as Love? Or maybe you just never understood me.

Maybe that's why you never wanted to know. D'you know how it felt to me, that day I came to see you? I guess it was ironic because at first after you'd left I didn't want to see you. But then Mum promised you'd come on that Sunday and I sullenly agreed.

Only you never came. You never turned up because you were 'busy with Harvest Festival'. And the following Sunday you had to visit some elderly Christians. And then you were at a conference.

I kept on waiting. Every Sunday. Whenever anyone asked me to meet them on a Sunday, I said no, I was busy. Just in case you were going to come over. I'd wake up early, full of excitement and the morning would yawn past, tingling, and every minute would stretch out with longing until at 4 p.m. I'd be stuck in front of the TV watching boring *Songs of Praise*, jumping every time a car came driving past, and then somehow I'd know you weren't coming and the disappointment would ping back at me and I'd feel too sick to eat my tea. I thought that maybe Mum was lying, keeping you away from me and I started to hate her.

Then one day I decided to surprise you.

I left school an hour early that day and caught the train back to my old home. All through the journey, I kept getting paranoid that someone was going to spot me and call up the school, so I pulled my tracksuit hood down over my face and fixed my eyes on the window, watching the carriage's ghostly reflection mirrored on the houses rushing past.

When I got off at the station, I got lost a few times. I ended up in a scary housing estate with graffiti everywhere. There was a little girl sitting on the grass, playing, and her mum appeared and told me where to go.

As I turned into my old road, I slowed down. I reached into my rucksack to check they were still there. I realised that I needed to make you remember that I was special, that I was a gift from God. So for the last few weeks I'd worked harder than I'd ever worked before. I'd stayed up all night some times. I'd got five grade As for my last five essays in geography, maths, biology, physics and English. I had them all here to show you.

But when I rang the bell, then what? Your stupid piece of scum-fluff opened the door and said you weren't around. She told me to go back home. Though as I walked away I happened to glance up at the window and I saw your face in the shadows as you quickly moved away.

The next day, I sat in the playground. I had bought chips from the canteen and a greasy nest sat perched in my lap. I wanted to eat to take away the pain in my stomach but every time I looked down at them they looked like yellow worms. I kept trying to think of ways I might make you remember I was special. Maybe I could save up and buy an amazing chess set and take that. Or maybe I could offer to build a new treehouse, or maybe I could organise a new church group. And then I ran out of ideas. I stared into my chips and a quiet voice said: *He doesn't want to see you because he never really did think you were special. Really, you're just stupid and useless. If your own dad doesn't want to see you, you can't be special, you can't be worth anything.*

I suddenly became aware that someone was staring at me. I looked up and saw Jeremiah, standing across the playground, and that was the day he came and spoke to me.

I got sucked in, Dad. I've made a mess of everything and I guess you're not surprised that I'm sitting here in a stupid shack full of loonies waiting to be arrested. I guess you were right: I'm not special. Just stupid.

I feel tears in my eyes and I look over at Padma. She raises her tired eyes and risks a smile. A sad smile. A resigned smile. One that whispers that she's given up, it's too late now, it's all beyond hope. And I say to her silently, fiercely: *It's not too late. I'm going to think of something, Padma, it's not too late. I'm going to show you and Dad that I can do something, I can do something good, I can save the day.*

# MIDNIGHT

Is that a *raptor*? There: that little dark shape, as though cut from the night itself, creeping from behind a bush?

I shake myself. I tell myself it's nothing, *raptors* don't exist. I have to get a grip. For Padma's sake.

Thomas and I are crouched outside the shack. Thomas is meant to be on guard duty; Jeremiah told me to sit with him. I suspect it was just a sadistic urge to separate me and Padma. Thomas has been given a gun to hold. It lies slack in one hand. His eyes flit nervously between me, his hostage, and the outer world, as though not sure which holds the greater threat.

The snow has eased off now but the air is still frosty and our teeth chatter in time with each other. The police must have finished going through the cottage by now, they must have taken a statement from Brenda. I can hear her voice in my head, declaring, *And I wanted to give those naughty boys a spanking!* I repress a hysterical giggle. Surely they will be here soon, God, surely? My mind reels, drunk with hunger; my body keeps convulsing into shivers.

If I could just get Thomas on my side. And if Thomas could persuade Martyn, Chris will follow . . . Raymond is hopeless, he'll always be on Jeremiah's side, but it will be four against two. I wish I could determine the colour of

Thomas's mind; how much has been stained by Jeremiah; how much of his own pigment still remains. If only I had the gift of the gab. I need to be like Jeremiah; to pull my words out of hats like coloured scarves; to make them whizz and bang like fireworks.

I look back at the shack. Can they hear us? I whisper:

'Thomas?' Go in gently, I decide, go in gently. 'Do you really think the world is about to end?'

'Well, Jeremiah says so,' Thomas whispers back.

I nod firmly.

Silence. The snow is settling now, glimmering crystal in the moonlight.

'Maybe it's the Apocalypse coming – maybe it's a sign,' Thomas whispers.

Did I just catch a note of sarcasm? Or is it feigned sarcasm? Is he testing me? Can I trust him, God? It feels as though there is nobody here I can trust except for Padma, my rose in this junkyard of pain and misery. I would trust her with my life and she has trusted me with her life and time is running out running out.

'But d'you really believe it?' I whisper.

'I suppose,' Thomas whispers, 'that we have to think the Apocalypse is coming.'

'Do we?' I whisper uncertainly.

'Well . . .' Thomas looks back at the shack, then drops his voice so it is a whisper of a whisper and I can only just catch the words. 'Don't you think that every religion has to have a story? And that story has to end somehow, doesn't it?' His words gabble as though he's been holding them in for some time, churning with them. 'I mean, why is the end of the world so appealing? Maybe because it gives our lives a richer meaning. You know – we were the last ones on earth – God saved us for the end, we were the ones who saw it out. Because if life does on go for ever, millions of years unrolling from millions of years, then our lives seem pointless, meaningless. Our lives which stretch out minute by minute, each minute weighted with so much importance in our minds, are really just tiny blinks in time. We're all nothing in the end . . .' He trails off, swallowing, staring into the distance. Waiting to see if I run to the shack.

'We can do something about this,' I whisper breathlessly and Thomas's eyes moon. 'We could –' A faint noise creaks from the shack and I break off nervously.

Then comes the sound of Hebethean chanting. The sounds float across the forest: strangely beautiful, almost eerie.

I turn back to Thomas.

'You know, Jon, I've got to say this, I've been meaning to . . . it's just . . . you're stupid if you believe that she loves you, Jon,' he whispers. He scoops his fingers through the rubble of winter earth, a fruitcake of dead leaves and writhing insects and rotting twigs.

I blink in bewilderment at the swerve of subject.

Then I realise: *He's talking about Padma.* I laugh quickly.

'Yeah – only – I don't love her, she's a terrorist, right?' I whisper brightly. I swallow, a weak saliva washing down my parched throat.

Has Jeremiah told him to grill me? Is this all a trick?

'The thing is,' Thomas whispers.

'What?' I watch his fingers pull away, now rimmed with dirt.

'Oh nothing . . .' he looks back at the shack quickly, then looks away. 'Nothing.'

We sit for some time. My heartbeat begins to quicken. He doesn't seem interested in interrogating me. Something tells me that the shadow of Jeremiah is absent. I sense that

I'm on the edge of a dark abyss. Though I'm screaming at myself not to ask, I do. I do.

'So what information do you have about SNAKE? I should know. I mean, I'm the one who's going to kill her. I need to be prepared.'

Thomas glances back at the shack; the chanting is rising in pitch, coming to an end.

'She . . . when she first got here – when some of us went in to interrogate her, she'd ask us to kiss her. Jeremiah says it's because she's a vixen but I think she's just desperate. She doesn't have our strength, so all she can use is her female charm.'

'Some?' I pounce on the word, snarling. 'Who? What d'you mean by some?'

'Ssh!' Thomas hisses. 'Keep your voice down.'

'Okay okay, I'm sorry,' I whisper.

Thomas glances at me sharply.

'Well, I don't know about Martyn or Chris, but she certainly did with me.'

'Yeah? And did you?'

'What?'

'Kiss her? Did you kiss her?'

'Of course I didn't.'

A long pause.

'The thing is –' I force the emotions rising in my chest, push them back into my stomach where they swirl and howl, '– the thing is, she was desperate, I guess.'

'Did she try that with you?'

'No! No, she didn't.'

Thomas frowns.

'Well, maybe it was just me then.'

'But – but – did she ever ask you to kiss her again – ever?'

'No – but sometimes . . . there was a vibe. But she's just

desperate. That's why I'm warning you – if she had a chance to wind any of us round her little finger she would.' A pause. 'So you're not in love with her then?'

'No, don't be stupid!'

'Look, I'm sorry . . .'

'She trusts me, that's all and I guess –' my voice cracks and I swallow and mend it. 'I guess it just goes to show that we need to be on our guard.'

We sit in silence for some time. Thomas takes a bottle of his pills from his jacket pocket. He takes one out and spins it up in the air, catching it, then throwing it, catching it, then throwing it, until he drops it and it lands somewhere in the earth.

'I'm so sick of being here,' Thomas whispers dully. 'I'm so sick of everything here.'

Silence.

'Did you hear that?' I whisper.

'What?'

'A noise – I heard a noise.'

'It's just Martyn,' Thomas points, 'he's just come out, he's gathering sticks. Jon, Jeremiah told me you have to stay by my side –'

'I'm on your side. No – I think it was something else. Over there. I'll just go and check.'

As I rise, I am amazed that my legs can carry me and hold me up; my body feels like a machine where a cog has snapped and all the parts are about to fly apart. I wait for Thomas to tell me to sit down, to point his gun at me. But he just looks at me with sad eyes and lets me go.

# 1 A.M.

**I walk away until Thomas** can no longer see my face and then I let his words sink into me, very slowly, their poison travelling softly through my body.

The wind blows and then falls silent.

I feel as though a hand is clenched around my heart, squeezing it into a tighter and tighter ball. My stomach feels empty, as though filled with smoke. So: I was nothing to her. Her puppet: nothing more. *Nothing.* I hate her. Oh God, I hate her. I am ready to go now, to take the gun and hold it to her temple. Then I picture her eyes made soft with tears and my heart whimpers with love. Surely Thomas must be lying? How can I feel like this, how can my heart be so swollen with love for her and her heart so empty for me? How can that be, how can God let it be? Is this what love really is? Pointless?

I am aware of the cold wind driving at me. It plucks my skin into goosepimples, batters my cheeks with harsh fists, pinches my ears into purple shells. I want to curl up into a ball and howl like a baby; I want her to come and cradle me in her arms. I want to die, to slash open my wrists, and her to find me, see the last blood ebbing away. I want to run and run until my body is in so much pain I can't distinguish this pain inside any more, run so far away she spends the rest of her life waiting for me to come back. But I don't move. I just stand in the wind as it freezes the tears in my eyes and nose. I stand there as the wind turns my tears into dribbles of melting ice down my cheeks.

She has killed the God in me.

I turn back to the shack.

Now I believe in nothing.

# 1.15 A.M.

**I pause. The shack is a hump** in the distance; Thomas cannot see me.

I realise that I can run. That can be my revenge; I can leave her in the hands of jackals.

I step away, when –

'Jon?'

Martyn's eyes gleam in the moonlight. His face looks haggard, as though he is middle aged, not a schoolboy.

'Jeremiah wants to talk to you. Now. For a private discussion. In his Sacred Space.' He pauses, frowning. 'You're not meant to be on your own. Thomas shouldn't have let you walk out here.'

I open my mouth. I search my mind for the arguments I spent hours building. Ways to bring Martyn on to our side. But they lie in my mind in a chaos of scattered blocks. And what is *our* side, anyway? I don't belong with her any more. I don't know who I belong to.

'Come on,' Martyn says impatiently. 'He's waiting.'

I think about running again, but I am too tired to even try.

# 2 A.M.

**So tired. Tired of everything.** My armour crushed and ruined. I stagger into Jeremiah's 'Sacred Space' – a small patch in the woods by the shack, warmed by a freshly burning fire – and collapse down beside it. Martyn stands by with a rifle; Jeremiah nods at him to take a brief walk.

I stare into the fire. I am vaguely aware of Jeremiah's gaze on mine. Flames blur into a red haze of anger. I want to spring up, run back, ask Thomas to repeat the whole story again. What if he was mistaken? What if he misheard her words? Or what if he was just joking . . . ?

I tremble, ready to rise. Then I notice Jeremiah and slump back down again. His eyes are full of tender compassion.

*Did you know?* I want to yell. *Did you know all about it all along? Were you laughing at me, telling me to fast, telling me not to speak to her?* I look up at the sky through the knives of branches. I feel God laughing at me from behind the stars; I can feel his mockery in the moving clouds; hear his chuckles in the play of the wind, the giggles of the rustling leaves.

At first when Jeremiah starts to talk, I feel like screaming at him to shut up. He drones about how the Hebetheus is a special religion, about how I am special, about how even

318

special people make mistakes, can wander from the path and find themselves pricked by thorns, thorns that in fact are blessings from God, reminders of how we have strayed. I carry on staring into the fire, shoulders hunched, brooding. My mind keeps spinning back through the past, remembering phrases, kisses, looks, rewriting phrases, kisses, looks. Did she ever really want to kiss me? Was she wincing in disgust when my lips touched hers? Did she ever mean what she said about me being different from the others?

'You're very special, Jon,' Jeremiah's voice comes into focus, 'but I fear you are suffocating with doubts. And I don't want to force you into a faith you don't believe in. The Hebetheus doesn't work like that. I mean, go into any shopping centre on a Saturday and the Christians are out, banging their drum, speaking through their megaphones, trying to armlock people into believing. Well, that's not our way. The Hebetheus religion is only for the chosen ones who have reached a high enough spiritual level to drink the nectar of our knowledge in. I realise times have been tough over the last few days. I've had to inflict certain punishments that I've had no desire to do. But I had to do so, Jon, you must understand, to fight with the *raptors* in our group and keep us together.'

'How do I know that you didn't just get Thomas to say it?' I burst out. 'To lie to me?'

'Say what?' Jeremiah asks.

I shake my head, dangerously close to tears.

'Is she a terrorist? Is she really a terrorist?'

Jeremiah stares at me until I look at him. He doesn't even need to speak.

'But the conversation you overheard about her bomb plot – she says you made it up. She says it never happened.'

'And you believe *her*? You believe the girl who has just used you and played you like a puppet? Who has come between you and God by *pretending* she loves you!'

'I – so – it's true then . . . So . . . she's a terrorist. My God.'

'Of course, it will always be my word against hers. I didn't tape her conversation. There is no proof but my word. But my word was, in the beginning, good enough for all of you. Because – why would I lie? *Why?* To lie is a sin. And I would never commit a sin.'

I frown.

'If I misunderstood her, if I – then God will judge me in heaven, but I know this cannot be so. But I heard her. I heard her every word. I must be right. I *know* that I am right. And now you have seen the real SNAKE, you have seen who she is – now who do you believe?'

'But she said –'

I gulp.

'Tell me.' Jeremiah's voice is steel. 'Tell me. Let me know your every doubt.'

'She said you were being racist.' I lower my eyes. 'That you just picked on her because of the colour of her skin.'

Jeremiah gives me a cold glance.

'That,' he hisses, 'is ridiculous. This is about terrorism, not about race. Look: the IRA were terrorists and they weren't black. There are terrorist groups operating all over the world, evil *raptors* of every creed and colour. And her to play the race card, to play the PC argument – *Oh, you're just picking on me because of the colour of my skin*,' he imitates her voice perfectly. 'It's just another one of her manipulative games. It's very clever, because none of us want to be accused of such a terrible crime. But it's not my motivation.'

'God. She's such a liar. She's such a *liar*. And – and – she seems so . . .' I swallow, my voice catching. I still can't digest it. How can I have been so stupid, such an *idiot*, to allow myself to be so *used* . . .

'Seems so innocent, so beautiful?' Jeremiah's voice sharpens and he leans in closer. 'Didn't I tell you from the start? I know it's hard to accept, Jon. For God's sake – nobody *wants* to believe it, and it's human nature to only believe what we want. That's why we ended up with her mother up on the screen, sobbing her eyes out over her baby girl. Can the mother of a murderer ever believe her beloved, the girl or boy she loved and gave toys to and read bedtime stories to at night, ever really accept that they've grown into a monster? No. And Mr Abdilla too – did you see his face in that last TV broadcast? You could see the exhaustion, the pain in his eyes – God, he could see it! He knows she's a terrorist, he knows deep down, but then what does that say about St Sebastian's School? Imagine how the parents, the teachers feel, having to explain that they have a terrorist in their midst? And so they have to keep on pretending. They're all fakes,' Jeremiah's voice thickens with disgust. 'It's just typical of the adult world. They lie to us and they lie to themselves. But you're not like that, Jon. You're ready to face the truth about SNAKE. You're finally facing reality.'

I think of Mr Abdilla's broadcast. My heart frowns. How could I have been so deluded? To paint over the truth; to pretend to myself that I saw pity in those eyes?

'And you – Jon – I can understand why you questioned, why you fell into that same trap. We're told all the time that we should always question, question, question. But sometimes doubt can be a worse tyranny than faith. Sometimes you just have to trust, Jon. Trust me. Trust God. She planted seeds of doubt in your mind. She manipulated you, she turned you against me.'

'I'm sorry, I'm sorry. I should never have believed her – I'm sorry.'

'I understand, Jon, but can we forgive her for this? She nearly succeeded in tearing apart our group, in turning you from God, of condemning your soul to hell! All for her own selfish aims! All while she was using *you* to escape. And why did she use you? She used you so she could go out into the world and kill more innocent people.'

I clench my jaw and say, 'We should hang her now. Right now!' My heart revolts at the thought but I push it aside. 'We should hang SNAKE!'

Jeremiah pauses, the firelight flickering over his face. For a moment I see doubt. Is he chickening out? But then he says:

'But are you really ready, Jon? I remember the day I first saw you . . . I remember gazing across the playground and you didn't know this at the time, but the clouds just behind you had merged into the shape of a *zapor*. It was extraordinary. *You* seemed extraordinary.'

What is he saying? That I'm not special any more? That I was one of God's Somebodies and now I'm a Nobody? I thought Jeremiah was trying to persuade me over to his side; I don't understand, I don't understand –

'You seem to be suffering from doubts. Severe doubts. If you were to hang SNAKE as a true believer of Hebetheus, then it will release her soul from her body. If you were to hang SNAKE as a false doubter – then any doubt – no matter how small – would make it an act of murder.'

'But . . . I do believe . . . I . . . I want to . . . I did doubt – but I was wrong – I was stupid . . .' Suddenly I feel frantic. 'Is it too late?'

'You should have come to me about your doubts.' His voice hardens. 'You should have confided in me. Haven't I always said that you can tell me anything?'

'I'm sorry, I'm sorry. From now on, I'm going to become a true monk,' I stutter thickly. 'I'm – I'm never going to speak to a woman again. I'm going to be a true monk, I'm going to give all my love to the God of Hebetheus . . .' I stare at him, trembling. If he says no . . . if he says no . . . oh God forgive me he won't say no, will he?

Jeremiah pauses for an agonising length of time.

Finally, he says: 'You have turned your back on the God of Hebetheus. You need to ask his forgiveness. As for your Initiation – normally in this situation there is no way I would allow it to continue. But your faith is so fragile that you must make it firm before the world breaks it apart. But I am warning you, Jon, that God will only open this door to you one last time. If you do not follow his wishes now, then your soul will be lost. For ever.'

'Yes!' I cry. 'Yes! I'll do it! I'll do it now.'

It's strange: the moment he lets me back in, the moment I have to stop knocking on the door, my inner fists droop. *Do I really want this?* a small voice asks. Is this really the truth? But then I think of her. My father loved me and then decided he didn't; Padma loved me and then it turned out to be false. I thought they were both perfect but they both turned out to be *raptors*. For a moment I feel plunged into a deep despair . . . but then I look into his eyes and realise I am back, back with my Brothers again, and sweet relief washes away my pain. Tears slip on to my cheeks and I find myself reaching out. We hug each other tightly. Guilt pinches me; I have doubted him; I have denied my God; I have been lured into a terrorist trap, and yet still Jeremiah is giving me a new chance. I am gripped by the urge to tell him everything: the whole story of Padma, from start to finish. But when I open my mouth to speak, I find tears choke my words back down. Jeremiah clenches me so tight it feels as though our ribcages interlock, our breaths interlace. Love overwhelms me; the urge to hold him becomes a ravenous hunger, an urge to eat him, become purely one with him.

And then he takes a knife and cuts away the tiny wisps of my hair that have regrown so that it is completely shorn again, throwing the fuzz into the fire. And then Jeremiah asks Martyn to bring me some water and though there is a flicker of jealousy in Martyn's eyes he also pats my back and says, *Welcome back, my Brother.* And I say sorry to him and he says sorry to me and Jeremiah sighs and says he is sorry too that at times he had to be harsh with us but he did it all out of love. And then we chant together and pray together and recite the rules of Hebetheus and I feel as if I've been sitting in a dark room for a long time, hunched into a tight ball and someone has suddenly lit a candle. As though a *zapor* is standing by the door, flickering with beauty and hope and light, and is offering me a chance, a way out. Familiar feelings begin to creep and unwind inside, the feelings I had when I first joined Hebetheus: a feeling of excitement and thrill combined with a sense of security, of knowing I would always be safe and protected and I am grateful, God, oh so thankful that you did this, even if you tricked me, even if you mocked me with her false love in order to test me and bring me back to you, oh thank God, I believe, I believe that the world is on the brink of ruin and I know, yes I know, that I will be ready to save SNAKE's soul.

Jeremiah asks me back into the shack to join my Brothers. The police may find us soon, he says urgently, but we have just enough time to say final prayers; God will God will protect us for just a little longer. I tell him I want to stay outside for a while. His face shines with admiration and he draws Martyn away.

I pray. I pray and pray and pray and pray. I keep waiting for the relief to come, as though every minute of my new devotion might cancel out every minute of my past doubting. But the more I pray, the more frantic I feel that it's not enough. The fire dies into embers and the cold of the night begins to sidle up on me. First, it shivers and caresses my skin; then it seeps through into my blood and finally sits in my bones. I relish the pain; I relish its punishment. It chills my heart until it is too numb to ache for her any more. But God, dear God, will you ever forgive my doubting? I look back at the shack, but resist temptation; I sit and recite the Rules of the Hebetheus and the Books of Hebetheus from beginning to end. Then I begin again. On the fifth rule, a *raptor* sneaks up on me: *Every man is both good and evil. But man is inherently lousy* . . . no, that doesn't sound right. *By doing evil actions* – no, it's good actions, Jon, good – *by doing good actions* – but that's the tenth rule, stupid, stupid! My mind spins and words fly up like snow and settle in chaos and for a moment I find myself unable to remember any rule or any chant. A lightning-bolt of cold shudders through me and I find myself pitching forward into the dirty snow.

I yank myself up as though by a noose. I let out a shaky breath, pleading for God to forgive me. And then I return to the first rule and decide to begin again.

# Day Seven

# 4 A.M.

**Our eyes lock.**

I've been avoiding her gaze since going back into the shack. After the cold of the night, it felt lurid: a wooden fug of collective breaths and sweat. Everyone silent, heads bowed, lips moving. Everyone knowing what we were about to do. The air felt thick with prayers, molecules clotted with their frantic intensity.

As I entered, Jeremiah beckoned me. I sat down by him, crossed my legs. I tried to whisper my final prayers, but inside my heart was shaking. Her presence undid me. I tried to focus, but they kept hitting me. Thomas's revelations. Again and again, like a punch in the heart, in the same place, creating a bruise on top of a bruise. For a moment I was undone: a jelly of longing and weakness and pain and I just wanted to reach over, to whisper in her ear *Did you, did you* and then, even if she said *Yes, I only wanted Thomas, I just used you*, even then I would still kiss her, hold her, let her use me.

But: I recovered. I quietly recited the Hebetheus rules until my heart hardened against the evil terrorist.

SNAKE hunched into the corner, watching us as, one by one, we gathered ourselves. Stood up, stretched, put down our prayer books. Nobody spoke, our silence becoming self-conscious in its solemnity, amplifying the clatter of guns and zips. Everyone aware of the last grains slipping through SNAKE's hour glass.

Then everyone looked at me. Martyn came up and gave me a hug, whispering, 'This is your time, Jon, this is your moment.' Even Raymond shook my hand. Chris smiled and Jeremiah nodded, his eyes vivid with pride. I felt as though I'd just scored a winning goal and the group were lifting me up high like a god, crying out my glory. My heart swelled. We swelled; we became aware that we were One again, that this was how we felt at the beginning. I was close to tears.

I felt her eyes on me, enjoyed the hunger of her pleading, but I refused to fling her a crumb of a glance. I felt a pleasure in knowing I was hurting her, only a little, only little to compared to the pain I felt, but still a little.

I felt her horror as Jeremiah wound a length of rope into a noose; I relished it. He instructed Thomas and I to find a tree and set up the backdrop for SNAKE's redemption. He looked weary, his face pale, his eyes pockets of black. He warned us to hurry, we had little time left. I reached out and hugged him once more and he clasped me so tightly our ribs fused.

I turned to go and without thinking I looked in her direction.

Our eyes lock.

A few seconds later, Thomas and I leave the shack. Her look keeps singing in my retinas. The love, the unexpected love. I pass the noose to Thomas without thinking. He tries to pass it back, then shrugs.

'I guess we should find a tree.'

We walk in silence. The forest is beautiful, the darkness fading, waiting for the first streaks of light to break. Melting snow is fragile on the branches and rain falls, but so light it feels more like breath than mist. I feel strange; as though the cold that seeped into my body is still lingering, causing my body to ache all over like flu.

'Here,' says Thomas. 'This tree will do.' He pats the trunk.

A grand, ancient oak. Thomas begins to climb. He has chosen the tree well: there are two branches running parallel; Thomas paces along the lower one, tying the rope to the upper. He ties it very tightly, winding the rope over and over, tying knot after knot, testing for strength. I look out into the forest. Through the pillars of trees, a tiny glitter of dawn shimmers like a distant torchlight. I notice for the first time that the branches look as though they are reaching towards the light, aspiring Manuwards. Guilt keeps scratching at me. It hisses that I haven't prayed enough; I can still feel darkness lurking inside me, rot in my soul. I wonder if I could ask Jeremiah to delay the hanging so that I have time to pray for another hour; perhaps even until tomorrow so that I can pray all day today.

But that *look* in her eyes, that look of love –

'Do you believe in the God of Hebetheus?' Thomas asks, pulling the noose over his head, testing it.

'Yes.'

'I don't.'

He tightens the noose and steps off the branch.

# 5 A.M.

**We are happy that Thomas** has chosen to release his soul from the cage of its body. As Jeremiah explained, Jeremiah our Great Leader, our Voice of the God of Hebetheus, Thomas knew that Apocalypse was nearly upon us, he had visions of ruined stars, burning bodies, the sky an ocean of smoke, and he chose to pass to Manu early where he will wait for us all to join him. Now as we stand in a circle, Thomas's body laid out on the floor, we rejoice in bliss and joy that we, his Chosen Brothers, his dearest, his Beloved Brothers, can aid and witness the passage of his Soul. We have removed his school shirt, a symbol of the ignorant world he chose to leave behind, and painted the symbol of Hebetheus on his chest and look! – the paint is still wet, gleaming beautifully, blackly, against his white skin. We do not stare at the purple bruises on his neck or the strange slant of his head which seems propped up against his broken body because after all it is just a body. We have opened his eyes, for in order to pass to Manu his soul needs to hover beneath his forehead and look up though them towards Manu, and so we have placed him directly beneath the hole in the shack roof which, as Jeremiah says, is a kind of divine blessing, not so much a hole made by chance but a portal which Fate carved out long ago knowing this moment would come.

A little rain falls through the hole and on to Thomas's face, the soft pitter-patter of God's tears as though weeping in love for Thomas. Chris weeps a little too, tears of joy that his Brother has reached Manu, and tears also trickle from the eyes of the wicked traitor even though his death must be her fault . . . it is the evil of people like her that drove Thomas to despair. They must be crocodile tears, or else she is just jealous that Thomas will reach Manu and I do not feel any tears in my eyes, I am just happy that Thomas's soul has been saved – I squeeze my eyes tightly shut, trying to scratch away the images: the twitch of his fingers, the purple of rope pressing against his throat, veins pulsing in dying wails up his arms – and we chant and recite the Hebetheus texts for the departure of his soul – *if only I had saved him, I tried, I tried, I climbed the tree I still have the bark in my palms but it was too late, too late* – and we RECITE and we CHANT the Hebetheus blessings – *and I lay down in the forest by his body wailing I want my mum, oh God why did he do it, why did he do it? I want my mum but there was a terrible heaviness inside, a black smoke blown through my soul, a sense of a door that has just slammed shut; as though the outside world, beyond this forest, is a mother who might have forgiven us before if we had said sorry but now will never take us back* – AND WE CHANT AND RECITE THE HEBETHEUS BLESSINGS – *I won't tell Jeremiah about Thomas's last words I won't tell him* – AND NOW THOMAS'S SOUL IS LEAVING HIS BODY – *God forgive Thomas for his last words I know he didn't mean them he wants to be with you he does* – AND JEREMIAH SAYS HIS SOUL IS STRUGGLING, IT IS TWISTING IN CONFUSION –

*

This is when it happens.

She is standing beside me, weeping, and I feel her reach out. Her little finger brushes mine.

Her skin, warm against mine.

I feel in that moment as though I've been plunged underwater in dark murkiness and suddenly I come bursting up into the light and I *breathe* –

AND WE *MUST* PRAY, THOMAS'S SOUL IS SEARCHING, SEARCHING FOR THE LIGHT –

Tears begin to spool from my eyes. My heart cleaves open. I want Thomas to be alive. Oh God, what will we say to his mum and dad? Why did he do it; I know why he did it; we did it to him. Oh, Mum, I want you here, Dad, I want you here, I want you to take me home, I want to say sorry, oh God, what am I doing here?

THOMAS, OH THOMAS, FIND MANU, FIND THE LIGHT! FIND THE LIGHT

Padma reaches out and her fingers flutter against mine. I pause. I want to pull back; I want to slap her and scream at her and yell at her that she's a terrorist –

But I know that's not true. I know it isn't true.

I watch Jeremiah's lips moving. Past words echo and spin: *It will always be my word against hers. And now you have seen the real SNAKE, you have seen who she is – now who do you believe?*

I reach out. I let her fingers slip into mine and we hold hands, tightly, painfully.

The warmth of her skin cracks me open, tears down my Brotherhood shield like paper. She binds me back to the

334

world, to everything I've left behind: school, home, my teachers, my mum. I want it all back, all of it. I want to be the Jon I was.

I feel forgiveness flow. Tears spill down my cheeks; my emotions blur like water streaming over colours. I cry for Thomas; I cry for her; I cry for all of us, for what we have done. I hear Padma's mother, my mother, Mr Abdilla. I feel my heart howl.

AND THOMAS'S SOUL IS FINALLY REACHING MANU – OH YES, HE HAS FOUND THE LIGHT!

I re-taste that moment, in the forest, when I looked at her and saw the God of Love. And I know that even if she never loved me, I love her now despite everything.

AND WE ARE ALL GREATLY BLESSED FOR NOW IT IS TIME FOR JON'S INITIATION.

Jeremiah turns to me.

'Now, Jon, it's time.'

'Jeremiah,' Raymond says. 'I think I just heard someone outside.'

Martyn breaks off and kneels down, peering through a wooden eye.

'I can't see anything,' he says. 'D'you want me to go and search?'

Padma starts. I pull my hand away. She tries to take it back, but I recoil, shaking myself, the bubble burst. I wipe away my tears, my heart stunned, my mind reeling. I look around at the faces of my Brothers. I remind myself that I belong to them.

Jeremiah shakes his head.

'No. We will continue honouring God, though if our enemies are near we must hurry.' He turns to Padma and gently strokes her hair. 'I'm afraid it's time.'

# 6 A.M.

**The rope swings gently** above her head. We – the Brotherhood of the Religion of Hebetheus – surround the terrorist.
Raymond discovered an old hook, driven deep into the
ceiling of the shack, perfect for tying a noose to. Our gal-
lows is makeshift, her platform a few blocks of wood
which Martyn assembled. She bows her head, weeping
quietly, shoulders slumped, resigned. I gaze around at my
Brothers' faces. They are hollow-eyed, shadowed with
exhaustion, hunger, dirt. Our guns sit on the floor like
extra spectators.

'This is your moment of greatness, Jon,' Jeremiah says.
'This is your moment to save the doomed soul of a terrorist, and in doing so, to take a crucial step to saving the
world. This is the moment that you pass from being human
to being divine, from being an ordinary boy, to being special. To being truly one of us.'

Was it weakness? That love that I felt just now, the love
that flowed from her hand into mine and mine into hers?

Or was it just fragility? Jon being too *nice*? My throat
feels dry; my mind weak and watery with exhaustion. The
dawn twilight surrounds the shack thickly; I want the sun
to hurry up and rise, to pour light through the jagged hole,
to bathe me in energy and conviction. I want the light to

shine on the rope, to glint on her face, to surround her hair with a halo. To make this deed feel clean. There is something dirty, furtive about this lingering darkness. I feel myself sway. Jeremiah steadies my shoulders.

'This is a deed of great compassion. Her soul is poisoned – you have tasted its poison when she betrayed you. Now is the time to intervene. It is a humane act to intervene. This is not murder, Jon, this is an act of compassion. You are giving her soul true freedom! God is looking down on you now. I can feel his energy in this room. At this moment in time, God has taken his eyes off the world and is looking at you – just at you. Nobody else. He is astonished by you, by this great gift you are about to offer him. He has marked you out as a chosen one, as someone special, as one of his most precious sons. Now he looks down on you like a father, knowing in return you are about to make a great sacrifice, an act of true love.'

Jeremiah passes me the noose. I stare down at the weave of the rope. I look up at the group. Chris looks wide-eyed, a little fearful. Jeremiah looks firm. The expression on Martyn's face shocks me. There is a kind of savage hunger in his eyes. Raymond, too, looks hungry. As though relishing the moment that her neck will break.

For this is how she will die. We tighten the noose, kick away the wood, and then –

*Crack!*

My knees shudder; Jeremiah steadies me again.

'Now, Jon, *now*. This is your moment. Release the soul of the terrorist!'

Unless it fails. If the noose isn't tight enough, her neck won't break. Her death will be drawn out, minutes of gasps and clawed air.

'Remember, Jon, that you do not do this duty alone! You

will act for all of us. You join us as a Brother! And you will always be protected, we'll always be here for you – *I'll* always be here for you. I'm never going to let you down. No matter what happens, from now until the end of your life, until we're together in Manu, I'll always be your friend. I love you, Jon! Be my Brother! Join me, Jon! Do it now!'

'Come on, Jon,' Martyn calls out. 'God is with you!'

'God is with you!' Raymond echoes.

'God is with you,' Jeremiah cries, 'and we are with you! Jon, hurry! Do it now! Kill her! Don't delay, do it! This is the girl who used you and betrayed you!'

Yes. This is the girl who used me. I look into her eyes and their innocence claws me. Did she pick me out at the beginning because she thought I was too *nice*? Because she thought I was the easy target? The weakest link, the rotten apple, a cliché? Jeremiah's words flow through me, pumping through my blood like drugs: *Jon, this is your duty, to save the world, to be sacred, to be great.* Yes, I feel God. The God of Hebetheus is real; I can taste him. He wants me to kill her. This is right. Come on, Jon, Martyn cries, kill her, kill her. Come on, Jon, Chris stammers. My hands are shaking as I raise the noose. The spirit of the Brotherhood balloons and swells. We are more than five boys; we are God; we are great. We are a roaring, spitting beast and I am its heart. I feel my arms rise up as though lifted by divine hands. I place the noose around her neck. I pull it tight. She will die now, my heart cries with savage glee, she will die.

I look into her eyes and she reaches out and gently touches my cheek.

I slap her hand away as though burnt.

'Come on, Jon!'

'Jon,' she whispers, 'I love you. I love you. *Please.*'

I swallow. I reach out, fiddling with the noose, even though it is tight enough. Suddenly my resolve has gone. I try to pump it up, to feel that furious anger. I close my eyes, clawing desperately for God, wanting him to bloom and fill my body. But I am empty. Fantasy slides away and I find myself standing, here and now, in reality. In a dirty wooden shack, with four angry boys, and an innocent girl. About to commit murder. Despair saps me.

In the distance, I hear the faintest cry, like a siren, or the call of a bird.

The sunrise breaks. A shaft of light falls through the hole and illuminates her stained cheeks. I look into her eyes and my heartbeat slows. I suddenly feel heavy with exhaustion. This is not God. I want the police to come, to lock us all up, to take her away. This hate is not God.

I have seen God, and I know what God is.

I reach out and tear off the noose and pull her into my arms. She bursts into violent tears of relief. I find my eyes welling up too. I hold her tightly, closing my eyes, shutting them all out. She whispers, *I love you, I love you, I'm so sorry*. My heart cleaves open with forgiveness. I love her. Even if she is lying now, even if she betrayed me. I kiss her hair and squeeze her tight.

'Jon, what the fuck are you doing!' Martyn pulls at my arm. 'Kill her! Kill the terrorist!'

I open my eyes and face the ring of startled faces.

'She's innocent,' I say, her hair muffling my voice. I try to pull away but she clings to me tightly. I hold her and say, 'She's innocent. I don't think she did it. I think – I think Jeremiah was just lying. I don't think there was ever a plot.'

'It's true, I'm innocent,' Padma twists away, crying. 'He's lying!'

Jeremiah's face turns to stone.

'For God's sake, Jon, don't go over to her side, stay with us!' Martyn yells.

'She's a terrorist, Jon, she's playing with your mind!' Raymond calls.

I look at Jeremiah. He stares back at me with an expression of such betrayal that I drop my eyes.

'Even if she's a terrorist, we should forgive her!' I cry, my voice shaking. 'That's what God is, this is the God of Love. I mean, I've been confused – but everything is clear – the God of Love is the answer.'

'The God of *what*?' Jeremiah's voice is like a whip.

'I think that's what God is.' My voice sounds small and pathetic and I swallow, trying to explain, trying to search for fancy words, to inspire them as Jeremiah does. 'I – just think – God is . . . love.' I break off helplessly.

'That's so simplistic!' Jeremiah cries. 'The world is too dark for that! What, we love the terrorists and let them carry on bombing us! For God's sake, Jon – *this* is love! To kill is love! If you really love her, then release her soul! Set her free! Join her in Manu! We have to do this now and if you're not ready then we will do it! We have to kill the terrorist!'

Martyn takes up his cry,

'Kill the terrorist! Kill the terrorist!'

'Kill the terrorist! Kill the terrorist!' Chris and Raymond join in.

Their shouts fill the shack like choking smoke. Padma wails and I hold her tight. They try to pull her from me but I cling on to her. We lock together into one foetal ball, sinking to the floor as they hammer us with fists and cries. I feel a punch into my shoulder and I curl in tightly. *I love you*, I say into the darkness, not knowing if she can hear, *I love you so much*.

They tear me away from her. Raymond and Chris hold me down. I try to punch them away but Raymond thwacks his gun against the back of my head. I collapse to the floor, ears singing with high-pitched pain. A wet warmth gushes through my head and blackness spins . . .

I open my eyes and see them. *Animals*, I whisper, *you're animals*. I'm aware of a presence beside me and I turn. Thomas, staring upwards with glazed eyes. I sit up, tears falling into my mouth as I beg them to stop, stop, this isn't God. But they have her. Martyn pins down her arms as Raymond pulls the noose over her head. Jeremiah smiles into her face, kisses her and then kicks away the wood.

I duck my head, my hands over my ears, my heart screaming.

I curl into a ball and in the darkness I pray for her soul, I pray that she finds heaven, the God of Love – but *oh God* –

I try to stand up but find myself falling and then I feel warm hands around me, Jeremiah's hands, holding me up and my head is in his chest and he is stroking me gently and whispering, 'It's all right, it's all right, her soul is taken care of now, we've saved her, Jon, we've saved her.' He grips my head in his hands but I bury it deep in his chest, my nose in his cotton and sweat, but he clutches it and forces it up, thumbs fierce beneath my chin. His eyes are inches from mine. His breath cools my face and he whispers, 'We have done the right thing, Jon, we have saved her soul and though we acted for you you are still one of us –'

'MURDERER!' I yell.

I push him away and turn. I dare to look at her face. My heart gasps. She's still alive.

The rest of the group stares at her, stunned. The beast of anger lies flat; their eyes are glazed and frightened.

She's gasping. Swinging. Her eyes bulge. Her hands claw desperately at the rope. I can hear Martyn whimpering, '. . . the rope . . . we didn't do it right . . . I told you if we don't do it right her neck wouldn't break and then – now *look* – what we've done –' and Chris's voice cuts through his crying, 'I need some air, I'm going to be sick!' and Raymond yells, 'You can't be sick, you pussy, we haven't finished yet!' and she is still alive still alive.

I leap up and tear the rope from the hook and her body falls to the ground.

Jeremiah gets up but he doesn't say anything. I look round at the others. They stare at me with big eyes. Nobody stops me; but nobody helps me. Even Raymond is still.

'We have to help her,' I scream at them. 'What are you – animals! Help her!'

Chris suddenly darts forward; Martyn tries to grab him but Chris shakes him off. He kneels down by my side.

I clutch her face; my hands are shaking so violently her cheeks shudder against my fingertips. I tear at the rope; Chris passes over his knife, crying, 'Cut it cut it' and I can't cut it because my hand is shaking too much so I pass it to Chris and then I cry, 'Be careful don't cut her! DON'T CUT HER!' and he yells, 'I WON'T, MARTYN! HELP ME' but Martyn stares down at us with blank eyes. The rope falls away, revealing a purple bracelet branded across her neck.

Outside, a voice, filtered with a megaphone, magnified and metallic-sounding, orders 'COME OUT NOW AND LAY DOWN YOUR WEAPONS, PLEASE COME OUT SLOWLY AND LAY DOWN YOUR WEAPONS.'

'Shit!' Martyn curses. 'The police!'

'Nobody panic,' Jeremiah orders. 'Nobody goes outside.

We all stay here, until we reach Manu. We're all Brothers together.' He holds out his lighter at arm's length. 'The world is about to end – let us die first.'

A flame roars across the door of the shack and Martyn screams 'NO!'

'Padma, can you hear me, can you hear me?' I stare into the brown shell of her ear. Chris puts his fingers against her throat but I push him away and bend over her mouth, listening. Nothing – oh God – nothing – but –

*Something!*

A whisper, a hiss of breath, faint as the shudder of butterfly's wings. I lean in to listen again –

'COME OUT NOW AND LAY DOWN YOUR WEAPONS.'

'SHUT UP!' I hear myself screaming, 'I CAN'T HEAR HER! OH GOD!' I yell up at the ceiling, through the hole in the roof. 'LET HER LIVE! LET HER LIVE!'

'YOU ARE SURROUNDED. COME OUT NOW AND LAY DOWN YOUR WEAPONS OR WE WILL BE FORCED TO SHOOT.'

'It's all right, nobody panic.' Jeremiah lays his hand on my shoulder and I half-rise, crying, 'You murderer, you murderer!' He looks stunned and I raise my fist; then wilt, turn back; my love is more important than my hate. I drop back down by her side, hearing Jeremiah repeat firmly, 'It's all right, it's all right, nobody panic.'

Padma; oh Padma. Chris tells me, 'Do mouth to mouth', and I lean down and blow into her mouth but no that's wrong, oh God help me help me. I try again, then cough, choking on smoke. Fans of flame erupt across the floor, competing to spread the fastest.

'No!' Martyn yells, his face ashen, waving his gun. 'We have to get out of here!'

'We have to stay, we have to die – don't you want to go to Manu?' Jeremiah screams back. He flares his lighter against another wall, and a fresh volley of flames shoot up.

Raymond runs up to the door and kicks it open, yelling as his trouser leg catches fire. Jeremiah gapes at his brother in betrayed shock. Chris gets up, grabbing Martyn and they flee. Jeremiah glances at the flames with nervous eyes.

'Jon! Come on – just leave her – leave her!' Jeremiah cries. 'We should live, God is telling me we should live, we should run!'

He grabs my shoulder and I punch him away. Flames fan and thicken; smoke steals the air. The door has been kicked flat into the snow, the frame a burning arch of flames, as though a portal to hell. Bits of the frame lick and fall and in one blurry moment it feels as though the shack is no longer made of wood but a shifting red lava, a volcano about to collapse in on itself. Jeremiah yanks me but I pull back. I reach down and scoop Padma up in my arms. Jeremiah yells at me to HURRY and I run forwards through the door and hear myself scream as we tumble out into the snow.

White flashes explode on all sides, catching the moment: a boy, holding a ruined girl in his arms, his leg on fire.

Jeremiah thwacks my leg violently, throwing snow against my trousers. I nearly lose hold of Padma; her arm and head swing dangerously and I quickly put her down on a bed of snow.

I lean over her, my tears falling on her indifferent face, whispering desperately, *Oh God, please be alive, Padma, please, I love you, please –*

I reach down to kiss life into her when I'm aware of a figure behind me groaning – Martyn. He's been shot.

Jeremiah holds out his gun, spinning about in bewilderment. Smoke fills the trees with black veils of confusion.

'Raymond?'

Chris. He runs towards us, followed by a figure who suddenly lunges forward through the smoke like some strange beast, wearing a black helmet and black padded jacket – a policeman? A *raptor*?

'Jon, we have to get out of here, NOW, COME ON!'

I yank him away. Then: the shot. I lean down to breathe my life force into her mouth but at the sound of the bullet my mouth freezes and the breath floats away, lost. For there is blood. Chris's eyes bulge; he crashes to the ground, his gun spinning into the snow.

The *raptor* turns his gun on us, yelling, 'PUT DOWN YOUR WEAPONS, PUT DOWN YOUR WEAPONS OR WE WILL BE FORCED TO SHOOT.'

'They'll kill us, come on, come on!' Jeremiah screams, waving his gun.

I stumble up, reeling; he catches me. A man in neon yellow darts forward and kneels down by Padma.

'Come on, he'll take care of her, they're going to kill us –'

Fear screams through me. Jeremiah grabs my hand and we run, nearly tripping on Chris's body, we run, skid and spin through snow and ice, trees grabbing out to meet us, and I turn.

I turn. I turn to run back to run back and risk their bullets, to tell them I am not with the Brotherhood, I am not with Jeremiah, I turn to be with her, to tell her I love once more, to kiss her before it might be too late for kisses, and it's my fatal mistake, that moment like Lot's wife who turned and got transformed into a pillar of salt, for another black-helmeted figure yells and runs towards us –

There is a cracking noise. A shot.

The policeman lets out a bellow, clutching his stained stomach. His face contorts: his veins become red snakes writing beneath the skin. He falls forward, crashing across a bush, its spiky arms coming up to hold him, impaling him several feet from the ground. He groans, a foamy white-red river flowing from his mouth across the leaves.

I turn. Jeremiah is holding his gun with shaking hands. His face is green but he is smiling.

'I – look out!' he cries.

I spin. Another *raptor*, running towards us. We both scramble to flee, and then –

Then:

the bullet splices through my skin, splitting open my stomach in a hot soup of pain. Then somehow somewhere the bullet hits muscle, bone and comes to a halt, like a giant lead splinter, reverberating poker-hot. Pain: too much pain. I hear the cry from my lips like the *yeowl* of an animal. Sky and ground tip like a see-saw. Cold snow on the ground. Pain: like a giant black dog, taking huge bites out of me.

Above me, a voice:

'Please don't shoot me. Oh my God, oh my God, please don't. I've thrown down my gun. Look. I've thrown it down. Please don't shoot me . . .'

The voice fades away. Everything is going black. I feel myself sinking into that blackness and suddenly the life instinct kicks sharply and I push the clouds aside, gasping for air, for life . . .

'Oh Jon, are you okay, Jon, are you okay?'

Above me, a face: Jeremiah. His fingers stroke my cheek; quiver-paths of pain crack and splinter beneath my face. I try to speak to him, I need to speak to him, but all I can taste is a thick blood that soaks my teeth and drowns my tongue. I need to tell him to say goodbye to Padma for me, even though it might be too late. I feel a wetness soaking my cheeks and realise that I am crying.

Jeremiah's tears mingle with mine. He grabs my hand, sobbing, 'Oh Jon, please don't die, please don't die, Jon, I love you, God loves you, please stay with me, please don't leave me.' I want to spit in his face, I want to say to him *You may have killed her you may have killed her and it wasn't what God wanted and I die now hating you can't you see Jeremiah this wasn't what he wanted* but I can't speak, no words will come out, too much pain. Here's his wrist: I press my fingers tight against the throb of vein. Pain draws me under again; sobs fall from my lips in shudders. Fast breaths. I flicker my fingers against his wrist, my desperate Morse code of death: *You were wrong, you were wrong.* I squint into his eyes: what's he saying, his mouth is moving, what's he saying oh God I can't stand this – pain –

And then suddenly, his voice, like poison honey dripping through my wounds . . . *Focus on Manu, Jon, focus just look up look up to Manu.* I want to scream, put my hands over my ears, spit his words back out. I want Padma, I want her dying kisses, I want her by my side, whispering that we will be together in heaven. Blackness flowing over me. Where is my body now, where is this pain? It feels as though I am everywhere, like Padma says, I am a Brahmin, my body is a shattered mirror lying in pieces, and thoughts fly like dirt in a wind and *Look up to Manu, Jon, know that you did what God wanted you to do, die knowing that you are a saint, that you helped to save this world, just a little, just a little* I'm sixteen and I'm Jon and I'm dying and this is what it feels like to be dying. The whizz of bullets; more bullets; shouts and sirens screaming. Yes, I want the light; I crave it; not the light of Manu, not Jeremiah's false light, but a light, any light, to be with God; give it to me now, God, give it to me now. *Find the way, Jon, find your peace.* My resistance dies; I am desperate now. I want his words, his lies. I cling to the sound of his voice, I push away all the other noise and concentrate, very hard, using every last drop of sweat and blood in my leaking body, to focus my eyes open until the pupils burn –

Beyond the curve of Jeremiah's head, beyond the policeman, past the leaves reaching up from the trees. Up to the dawn sky. A watercolour of pink and blue cloud. I want to drink that blue like a nectar to wash away the pain –

*Find the light, Jon, find the tunnel of Manu's light*

– Oh God I can't take any more of this pain take me God take it away. The sky is blue and I am Jon and this is what it's like to be dying and where is the light I need to grab it and let it pull me up

> . . . where is the light God where is the light –
> *suddenly*
> – a *flash!* – so bright – so bright!
> But fading,
> fading softly . . .

As my eyes sink shut, one last vision: the white bulb of a reporter's camera, capturing me for ever in her light.